EDIT

RICK CHESLER

SEVERED PRESS

HOBART TASMANIA

EDIT

Copyright © 2020 Rick Chesler
Copyright © 2020 by Severed Press

WWW.SEVEREDPRESS.COM

ISBN: 978-1-922323-29-3

CHAPTER 1

Coral Gables, Florida

Detective Rene Bravia of the Coral Gables Police Department pulled up into a flagstone driveway lined on both sides with coconut palms. He stopped his patrol car in a turnabout area fronting the entrance to a house that was nice by most standards, but nothing particularly special for the tony neighborhood. Single-story stucco with a red-tile roof, carport on the left side with an SUV parked beneath. Two large bay windows, curtained off, flanked the front door.

"What do we have here?" Officer Francisco Alvarado, Bravia's partner, mumbled from between bites of his breakfast burrito. It was his first day back to work from a family vacation, and he'd showed up a little late that morning, sunburned and full of amusing anecdotes from his time on the beaches of Aruba. Alvarado had been shuffled directly into the patrol car that morning with little by way of briefing. He knew they were not responding to an emergency, but not much else.

Bravia shut off the engine and picked up the radio transmitter, answering Alvarado's question while checking with Dispatch at the same time.

"At the address for that Wellness Check. Any updates?"

An older-sounding female voice with a slight southern accent came back over the radio speaker almost immediately. "No update yet."

"Copy that. Looks like his SUV is in the carport. We'll check it out."

"Roger."

Bravia put down the transmitter and looked around at the neighboring houses. No sign of activity, it being early morning with most people at work. "Let's see if anybody answers."

The pair of cops walked to the front door. Bravia pressed a doorbell which produced a pleasant chime from within the house. They waited for a moment, listening for footsteps inside, but heard nothing. At length, Alvarado put his hand up to the mouth of a brass lion affixed to the door, grabbed the ring held between its teeth and used it to knock loudly a few times in succession.

Still no answer. Bravia sighed heavily as he turned away from the house and looked around the neighborhood. "Let's try the immediate neighbors. I'll knock on this one to the left, you do the one to the right. If no one there can tell us anything, then we bust it in." Bravia glanced back at the lion, and banged the knocker down one more time. After more silence, he shrugged, and the two cops separated to the two neighboring houses.

A few minutes later they reconvened on the same doorstep. "Nothing," Alvarado said.

"Same here." Bravia knocked one more time with the lion while Alvarado rang the bell. The same silence greeted them. Bravia nodded to Alvarado. "I'm going to walk around the back, see if I can find an open door there. Doubt it's open though, so you get the ram while I'm doing that." Alvarado promptly jogged over to the patrol car and opened the trunk while Bravia made his way around the house.

In the back of the residence, in addition to a small semi-manicured yard that looked as though it was tended by a professional landscaper, Bravia found a rear entrance. Sliding glass door with a screen on the outside. Curtains prevented any view to the inside. He tried the screen door and found that it slid freely open. The glass door, however, was locked. Bravia informed his partner via radio that he was coming back around to the front.

Alvarado had the battering ram and was hefting it up onto one shoulder. Per protocol, Bravia knocked one last time, and yelled into the door, "Police, we're coming in. Stand back!" He drew his service pistol and stepped back to the right, in case the house had been taken over by drug squatters who intended on some sort of warped defense of their ill-gotten territory. It was Miami, after all, and with things like bath salts and flaka going around, one never knew.

But when Alvarado bashed the front door open with the ram, they were greeted with an empty, silent house.

"Police, anyone here?" Bravia called out. No answer came.

Well aware that just because no one answered did not mean that no one was inside, Bravia issued Alvarado hand signals that indicated they should split up. With no upper floor, it would be a relatively simple search. Bravia moved into the kitchen while Alvarado took a hallway to their right.

"Clear," Bravia said into his radio.

"First bedroom clear," Alvarado returned.

Bravia swept carefully through the house, moving down the same hall his partner had taken earlier. He joined him in the second bedroom, which had been converted into a home office, hardwood floor with built-in bookcases lining the walls. A large desk occupied most of the floor space.

A deceased man sat on the edge of the leather desk chair, slumped forward such that the desk supported his upper body. His head of silverish, wispy hair lay flat on the desk, a large pool of congealed blood spread out onto the flat surface, with some on the floor directly below.

Alvarado pointed to a piece of paper on the desk, not far from the right hand of the deceased; a white male who looked to be in his early sixties.

"I'm sorry."

"What's that?" Bravia asked.

"That's all it says," Alvarado said. "The note. 'I'm sorry'. And there's a signature under it, and the date. Four days ago."

Bravia held his shirt over his nose, a rebellion against the odorous revulsion characterizing the room. "So you think this guy offed himself?"

Alvarado shrugged with an accompanying doubtful look. "If he did, he could have at least left the A/C on. Stench is killin' *me,* never mind him." His partner shot him a disapproving stare and he continued while staring at the corpse, slumped over onto the desk, the pool of congealed blood spread across its surface from his open neck.

"Okay, most people who do that, they use a gun. Or maybe pills. How many people you see choose a knife?" He paused while leaning in to examine the implement of death now laying under the dead man's ruined neck. "Or, a *claw* or whatever this thing is."

Bravia turned his attention to the implement on the desk that apparently led to the demise of the deceased. He spoke into a voice recorder as he described the scene.

"White male, late fifties or early sixties, found deceased, seated at desk in home office after apparent severing of jugular vein with a...a detached *claw* or maybe tooth of some sort. It's browning, roughly triangular but curved, very sharp, and approximately nine inches long."

He paused while moving around the desk to observe from a different angle. "Large pool of dried blood covering most of the desk area and part of the hardwood floor. Lack of A/C inside accelerated the decay process." He looked around for a moment as if about to add something more, but then abruptly turned off the recorder and instead addressed his partner.

"So this guy...*Dr. Archie Landis,* is what I remember in the initial dispatch report—do you have any notes on that? He was some kind of hotshot scientist, is that right?"

"Yeah, a 'computational biologist', whatever the hell that is, with University of Florida," Alvarado said.

"Family?"

Alvarado flipped through his notes. "He lived here alone. Divorced eleven years ago, hasn't remarried. One kid, an adult now living in Washington State."

"Moved about as far away from pops as he could get, eh?"

Bravia shrugged. "Don't know too much about his personal life. Guy was a workaholic, from everything I can gather. Last ten years or so, his work was his life. He's a bigshot in the genetics field, lots of papers published in the leading science journals. That's all I know, pending interviews with next of kin—the kid in Washington, the ex-wife—as well as his colleagues at the university."

Alvarado glanced stoically at the handwritten note, the edge of which was stained with blood.

"What? You got something to say, say it," Bravia prompted.

"If it's a suicide note, 'I'm sorry' can mean a lot of things. Like is he sorry he killed himself, or did he do something else, like kill somebody else beforehand that we don't know about yet?"

Bravia shrugged. "Not that we know of yet, but yeah, could be." He nodded toward the claw. "I think the next thing to do is to bag up that claw and call somebody from...I dunno...Animal Control? Or maybe Fish & Wildlife to come look at it and see if they can ID what kind of animal it came from?"

"I've never seen anything quite like it, that's for sure. Who knows, it might not even be real."

"Looks pretty damn real to me. Sliced his neck clean open, that's for sure."

"No I mean, it could just be some plastic thing from the Internet, not from a real animal."

Bravia looked amused. "Plastic thing from the Internet?"

"I dunno. It does look real, I'll admit that, but I can't say for sure."

"Right, well that's why we need an animal expert. Maybe someone from the Zoology Department at this guy's same university."

"Kill two birds with one stone—ID this thing and ask what was going on for him at work?"

Bravia nodded. "Exactly."

The pair took a lingering look at the corpse on the desk. After a couple of shakes of the head, they left the house.

#

Florida University, Department of Zoology

Dr. Rebecca Trout looked up from a microscope at the knock on her open laboratory door to see two uniformed police officers. She had long, straight, brown hair tied back in a ponytail, and wore a white lab coat over slacks and a casual shirt. She took off her slim reading glasses to address the visitors.

"Sorry to bother you, Dr. Trout," one of them said. "My name is Detective Bravia from the Coral Gables Police Department, and this is my partner, Officer Alvarado." Both of them nodded. Try as she might to appear nonchalant, as though two cops at her lab door was something to which she was accustomed, she could not hide her surprise. She was a zoologist, not a forensics lab technician, or even a medical doctor. Law enforcement visits to specialists like her were few and far between. Once, she'd been called into court to testify for the defense as to whether a particular species of wasp favored a certain kind of flower, the point being to assign fault to the defendant in a lawsuit, the neighbor of an old woman who had been stung in her yard and suffered serious injury. She claimed he'd deliberately planted the flowers close to her yard so as to attract wasps. Rebecca had been a little sad to have to break it to the woman that the flowers in question, did not, in fact, attract wasps more than any other flower, nor did they repel them. The defendant was found not to be at fault and the woman was denied compensation for damages. That had been seven years ago.

"We were wondering if you could help us identify an animal part," Bravia said.

"What we think is an animal part," Alvarado added.

"You have it with you?" Her eyes went to the manila envelope clutched in Bravia's hand. He held up the package.

"Yes. Some kind of claw, we think, but an expert opinion is needed."

"Sure, come on in. I have to leave in about ten minutes to teach a class, but that should be enough time." She stepped aside and waved them into the lab, which was a roughly rectangular room with black lab benches in the middle, cabinets and shelf space on the sides, and a closed door to an office at the far end.

"Have a seat over here, please, and let's take a look." Dr. Trout led them to a clear space in the middle of one of the lab benches fronted by stools. She took a seat and when the two cops had done the same, she watched as Bravia unwrapped his parcel. He removed the brownish, wedge-shaped claw from the Ziploc bag and placed it on the lab bench. The academic's eyebrows furrowed even before she touched the piece of evidence.

She suddenly looked up at Bravia. "So you said you thought this was a claw, right?"

"That's right," he said while Alvarado nodded.

"Well it's a claw, all right," she said, reaching out to pick it up. "At least a really good reproduction of one."

"Reproduction? How do you mean?" Bravia asked.

She chuckled lightly before answering, genuine humor, not condescension. "It can't be real, because if it was, that would make it a *Tyrannosaurus rex* claw. It looks good though, it really does!"

"I told you, plastic stuff from the Internet!" Alvarado blurted.

Bravia held up a hand while he stared down at the item, still untouched on the table. "So it's from a kid's toy dinosaur or something?"

Dr. Trout shook her head. "Oh no. Or at least if it is, it's a very sophisticated one, maybe from a science kit." She glanced again at the claw but this time her gaze stuck, and she slowly reached out a hand toward it while she talked. "The shape of the claw is instantly recognizable to anyone who has even cursory knowledge of Tyrannosaur morphology. It's quite distinctive, but the real giveaway," she said, picking up the claw, "is that…"

She brought it up close to her face, examining it from behind her spectacles. Her expression took on a more puzzled look.

"Is that…*what*?" Bravia prompted.

She turned the claw over in her hands slowly while answering. "Is that it's not fossilized, of course."

Both men looked alternately at her and the claw, but said nothing.

"This is an actual *claw*, with the protein keratin, as if this just came off a recently dead animal. It's cracking, and it flakes apart if you pull on it. It's like a lizard claw. You've seen an iguana or maybe an alligator claw before, right?"

Both men shrugged. "Never paid much attention," Alvarado admitted.

She sighed before continuing. "Okay, well you see how this material here is…well, sort of like finger-*nails*?"

"Yeah," Bravia said.

"That's because this claw is not fossilized," Dr. Trout said. "Here look….come over here, I'll show you a real one." The two police officers followed the scientist to the rear of the lab where she stopped in front of some long drawers built into a wall cabinet and pulled one of them open. "Here we go. This is a genuine *T. rex* fossilized claw."

"Lot smaller than the other one," Bravia commented.

"Right, that one might be from an adult female, which are thought to be larger than their male counterparts, but the sample size that's based on is very low, I'm afraid, so that's said with low confidence. This one, however, is definitely from a juvenile, so it's smaller but you can see it has the same shape." Both cops leaned in to look at it as she held it up in her hand. "But more importantly," she continued, "you see how it's basically been turned to stone by the fossilization process. Take it, see for yourself."

She handed it over to Bravia, who hefted the stony claw in an appreciative manner. "Yeah, I see, it's like a rock, nothing like the one we have." He handed the fossil over to Alvarado while the professor walked back over to the suicide implement on the lab bench.

"So what's weird about the one you have," she said, picking it up, "is that it seems real but it's not fossilized. No petrification has occurred."

"But it's not plastic?" Alvarado asked, approaching the scientist and setting the fossilized claw on the bench.

"Definitely not. That's the weird thing. It's biological tissue of a type consistent with what would be found in a reptilian claw. Almost as if someone took real claw material from contemporary lizards, like crocodiles or alligators, maybe, and used them to construct a claw in the shape of what a *T. rex* would have had. But it's strikingly accurate…" she said, once again turning the unfossilized claw over in her hands.

Abruptly, she looked up from the claw and addressed the two policemen. "May I ask where you got this?"

Bravia and Alvarado exchanged glances until Bravia indicated with a hand gesture that he would answer this. "Dr. Trout, please have a seat."

CHAPTER 2

Everglades
Later that night

The pickup truck's headlights cut a swath through the near pitch black, moonless night beneath the tangle of overgrown vegetation. A stack of wire cages occupied the vehicle's bed. In the cab, Todd Spaulding sat behind the wheel while his common-law wife, Linda Belle, rode shotgun. She swatted a mosquito from her face while glancing over at him with irritation.

"Damn, Todd. Tell me again why we have to do this now? My shift starts at eight."

Her partner spat out his open window onto the state road. "I told you, Tommy says he saw some here a few days ago. Pass me a tall-boy, would you?"

"Okay, but why at night? Can't we come back tomorrow in the day?" She passed him a domestic beer, and he timed the crack of the tab opening with his sigh of exasperation.

"Like I told you, chameleons are much easier to spot at night. They're a brighter shade of green, for one thing. For another, they hide more behind branches and stuff during the day. Everybody says they're just easier to find at night, trust me on this."

Linda cracked her own beer as Todd slowed their truck. "Up here looks good." Ahead, the road was nearly tunneled over by thick tree growth that blotted out the night sky. Even in daylight, it would not be very bright here, but now it was almost black without the vehicle's headlights. Todd picked up a Q-beam spotlight powered from the truck and held it outside the window as he leaned out. He aimed the halogen beam up into the canopy, searching for the telltale splotches of lime green that signified a probable chameleon.

"This looks like a pretty good area. Let's get out here." He stopped the truck and killed the engine, leaving the headlights on to light the road in front of them. He strapped on a headlamp and flipped it on while Linda did the same. Taking their beverages with them, contained in neoprene koozie holders emblazoned with the logo of a local bait and tackle shop, they exited the truck.

On this muggy late May night in South Florida with 100% humidity, the air temperature hovered around 83 degrees Fahrenheit. Even so, both wore jeans and long-sleeved flannel shirts to ward off the mosquitos and no-see-ums. A hat protected against the occasional falling spider or who-knows-what-else, while work boots took the place of the usual flip-flops in order to keep their feet safe from various ground-biters including the occasional rattlesnake or even water moccasin.

"You take that side, I'll take this side," Todd told his partner. Besides the headlamp, he also carried a handheld flashlight, which he now directed up into the foliage as he walked slowly along. Linda did the same, and the pair slowly ambled along in the path of their truck's headlights. Around them, the buzzing of cicadas could be heard above the patter of rain on the leaves.

To a casual observer, it might seem like an impossible task: wander around in a jungle-like setting at night looking for a particular kind of small lizard. But Todd knew that there were a lot of chameleons out here. Originating from places like Madagascar, they were shipped worldwide as part of the pet trade. In much of America, if Little Johnny's chameleon managed to slip away from its cage into the backyard, it meant certain death, either from pet predation, lack of suitable diet, or freezing temperatures. But here in South Florida, an escaped chameleon found itself in a wonderland of nature not all that much different from its natural environs. Suitable climate, food to eat. Natural predators did exist, but in enough balance that chameleons were able to make a go of it, to find one another, mate, breed and survive across generations. They lived here now, enough so that there was a small cottage industry comprised of people like Todd who profited from their presence.

Another thing in the chameleons' favor was that they had not been deemed an "invasive" species by the state Fish and Wildlife Commission, meaning that they were not harmful to the local ecology. Nor were they declared an endangered species. This meant that Todd and others like him were not doing anything illegal; they were not poachers, and no license was required to capture chameleons, since they were not supposed to exist here in the first place.

And yet they did.

It was the eyeshine that gave it away.

Todd hadn't expected to get lucky so soon, but there it was. Not three feet above his head, perhaps ten feet off the road, in a tiny clearing.

A Panther Chameleon.

After spotting the reflective eyes, it was easy to make out the body itself, which was a tropical shade of lime green against the more olive drab leafy background. Todd steadied his footing in the wet, spongy ground and smiled to himself while aiming his light at the creature. In the daytime, this thing would be nearly indistinguishable from its surroundings. Venturing out at night had paid off.

"Linda. Hey, Linda!" he hissed, without taking his eyes off his prize.

"Yeah?" came her voice form the other side of the road.

"Found one. Bring the net!"

Todd approached a little closer to his target but knew better than to move too close, too fast. Until he had the net, there was no reason to get much closer, anyway. He heard the sound of the net's long-handled wooden pole being slid from the truck bed, and then the soft crunch of Linda's boots as she jogged over to him.

"I see it!" her voice came from behind his right shoulder. He reached back and took the net without moving the light beam from their target.

"Yep, that's our guy. Take my light, will you, and just keep it steady on him while I handle the net. Just take the light from me without letting the beam move off of him, he might move if the light changes too much."

He exchanged the flashlight for the net while Linda kept the light beam trained on the chameleon. "That's it. Now just stay here and hold it steady while I move up…" Todd crept toward the lizard with the net, moving slowly, testing each footfall before placing his full weight to avoid loudly snapping a twig.

When he was within the net's reach of his quarry, Todd stopped and began to slowly raise the net; very slowly, so as not to startle the lizard and cause it to jump away, where it would be lost in the foliage. He extended his arms painstakingly until the white netting was only a foot below the creature. *Almost, almost…*

And then, inexplicably, the chameleon leapt away, out to the side from the net.

"Damn it!" he cursed.

"What happened?" Linda's voice came from behind.

"Sucker jumped before I could make a move with the net!"

"Did you move too quick?"

He turned around to look at her in irritation, even knowing he'd be staring into the flashlight beam, he wanted her to see the irritation on his face. "No, I did not move too fast with the net. I did what I always do when I catch them. I know what I'm doing. I tell you—"

"Todd, what's that?" She had to repeat herself two more times before she got his attention, and by then she had begun to back away.

"What's what?" He turned back around toward where the chameleon had been. "I don't see anything. I guess I could walk over here a little farther and see if I can find it."

And then he heard it.

A bird-like clucking that signified a chicken or a rooster. Agriculture was common in the rural towns on the outskirts of the Everglades, and so while it would be mildly surprising to see one out here in "the sticks," as he thought of the wilderness, it couldn't be all that unusual. The sound was strange, though, not quite like poultry fowl he'd ever heard before. It had the percussive clucking sounds, but also a certain nasally wheeze to it that he found unsettling.

"I think it's off to the left," Linda said, shifting the light beam in that direction. Todd stared that way. He still heard the sound but couldn't see anything special.

A heavy crumple of leaves a couple of feet away caused him to jump. *What was that?* His wife's piercing scream echoed a millisecond after he felt the pain. Sharp, piercing agony that signaled something very bad was happening to him physically. Worse, he jerked his leg away—everything around the knee was red-hot—but the pain stayed with him.

"It's on you, Todd, it's on you!" His wife's yells seemed faint, far away, but the words registered in his consciousness. Then he felt the same kind of pain in his abdomen and felt the impact as something struck him there and pushed him back. Losing his balance, Todd, who had forgotten all about the chameleon by now, fell backwards until his back struck the mercifully flat ground, hard.

And yet the pain in his abdomen and his leg persisted.

"They're still on you, Todd!"

"Help!" was his response. He lay there on the damp earth, thrashing about as he looked up, his headlamp—now slightly askew and pointed at an angle—illuminating an otherworldly creature poised over his belly. His first impression, stressed out as he was, was that he was under attack by some sort of birds. At least two of them, the one on his belly and the other still ripping away at his right leg. The head of the animal was moving too fast as it moved rapidly up, then down again to hammer at his belly like a piston. But the body, Todd thought, looked like…His mind couldn't dwell on it since he was preoccupied with the pain and how to stop it, but the only impression he had time for was that it looked like a chicken. A somewhat larger, heftier version of a chicken, but not all that much. Perhaps a turkey.

Linda ran over and he saw the big black flashlight held in her hand bash into the head of the creature gnawing away at his gut. And that's exactly what it was doing, he understood, as a crashing ball of fright erupted inside his brain. *These things are eating me alive!*

Out of his peripheral vision he saw his wife's boot slam into the gizzard-like neck of the other animal. He heard something snap and saw the thing drop lifeless a couple of feet away.

"Get up, Todd. Come on, I think more are coming!"

When he bent to sit up he felt something slosh weirdly in his gut, a second before a gush of hot liquid ran down the lower portion of his belly and his thighs. Before he could assess what was wrong, he heard Linda's voice saying, "We've got to get you to a hospital, come on…" He saw her hand reach down and then her eyes widen in horror as her gaze shifted to his belly. It must be bad.

It must be really bad!

CHAPTER 3

Everglades
Next morning

Park Ranger Sara Cliff could hardly contain her sense of excitement as she drove away from the visitor center and onto the two-lane blacktop that threaded its way into the actual park, into the Everglades. Her first day on the job! She had done it, had become a federal park ranger, fresh out of college, having earned her bachelor's degree in ecology. The gun holstered on her hip reminded her that this was all too real, and a job that came with real dangers. While most people commented on the alligators, snakes, and various critters she'd be working around, her parents had fretted over the law enforcement aspects of the job.

"You'll be miles away from civilization! What if you come across a band of criminals by yourself, and they're armed, too?"

Telling them that she was not truly alone, that she could call for backup anytime and had an entire law enforcement system behind her did little to assuage their concerns. Still, her father, especially, was all too glad that she'd secured solid employment for herself, and so they wished her well along with endless reminders to be careful.

Sara smiled to herself while she followed the road as it curved into a hardwood hammock—a patch of dry land with actual woody trees on it as opposed to the more ubiquitous river of sawgrass that so characterized the 'glades. Here she was, day one on her dream job, using her degree and working outdoors in a pristine natural environment. Well, as pristine as the outdoors can get these days, anyway. She knew it was only kept this way due to its protected status as a national park. Were it not for that, she had no doubt that all of the Everglades would by now have been paved over and developed as was much of the rest of Florida, including the famous Keys to the south. And even with its protected designation, she knew it still faced dangers. Oil drilling allowed by more business-minded and short-term oriented politicians, development on the fringes, traffic from tourists, legal hunters and fishers, and the illegal variety, too—those who took game without a license, out of season, kept fish that were undersized, poached game, took specimens to sell on the black market, those who tried to grow marijuana on public lands, who camped without a permit....it was all here, and it was now her job to stop it, to keep this place as natural as it could be while still allowing public use for those who obeyed the law and respected the land.

She was on patrol, with no particular assignment today. Just get used to being out there, her supervisor had said. He'd given her a sedate route that should take her most of the morning to complete, was not known for major issues requiring ranger intervention and would have her back to the station for lunch, something that was not a given for the more experienced rangers. Many of them were in the field all day, or even multiple days. Rangers worked alone, without a partner, even those who patrolled by boat.

Sara heard her field radio crackle with the dispatcher's voice. What was his name? Kevin Hardison, he seemed nice....She smiled and shook her head as she eyed the road ahead. It was clear and straight for now, with a thick cover of mixed trees—Australian pines, gumbo limbos, fan palms and more—on either side. She knew that further up would be the turnoff onto an overgrown, dirt road. For now she snatched up the receiver and held the transmit button.

"Unit 33 responding. Hi Kevin!"

"Hey Sara. How's going? Seems quiet out there, is that the case?"

"That's how it's supposed to be, right? And yes, that's the case. Over."

She felt silly saying 'Over', like she was on some TV cop show or something, but she wanted to show that she could follow protocol, especially her first day on patrol. She'd been on the job for a month already and this was the first time she'd been allowed on patrol alone, and she didn't want to blow it.

Don't blow it. You got this! Some part of her still couldn't believe she was a ranger, like wow, am I really doing this? And yet another part felt relaxed out here in the natural environment. This and other places like it had always been her favorite means of recreation, after all. Every summer as a kid, family vacations had revolved around backpacking, river rafting, hot air ballooning, snorkeling, fly fishing and the like. Meanwhile, in school, biology had always been her favorite subject and she sought out its related electives whenever possible—marine biology, geology, environmental science--classes that usually had some kind of field trip—whale watching, tide pooling, collecting specimens of various types. When it came to college, majoring in ecology was a no-brainer. Her parents had fretted over the job security, but when she had showed them about all the park ranger jobs, at all levels from county to state to federal, they had relaxed.

And here she was! Gainfully employed right out of university, her first day on patrol in the famous Everglades. And this place was deserving of that fame, she knew well by now. The most expansive mangrove forest in the entire Western Hemisphere. The biggest subtropical wetland in North America, and the drinking water source for millions of people. Although often stereotyped as one giant swamp, it was more accurately described as a very massive, extremely slow-moving river, comprised of millions of deltas, bays, tributaries, and creeks, with sections and patches of land between them. Some of these land areas were truly swamp land, with an inch or two of fresh water covering spongy, "useless" ground, while others were dry forest land that supported populations of large land animals including the Florida panther, the gopher tortoise, the Eastern cottontail bobcat, and the whitetail deer.

Kevin's reassuring voice came back over the radio. "Copy that, Unit 33, glad everything's going smoothly out there for you on your first day. Just holler if you need anything. Over and out."

She smiled at the radio. "Over and out." Sara put down the transmitter and slowed her patrol vehicle, a 4x4 SUV prominently bearing the green and brown national park logo. She glanced at the GPS display which featured her route outlined in blue. She was only supposed to drive the route, monitor what was happening, which wasn't expected to be much. It was designed to be easily done before lunch. But here she was at the intersection with a dirt road, one she'd taken before during her training explorations, free-hiking, driving around the park in her own time to familiarize herself with it. She knew it led to the edge of the old state road, which marked the end of the national park jurisdiction and beginning of the neighboring state preserve. Both agencies, the national and state, attempted to work together on their bordering lands to report wrongdoings or environmental issues.

She pursed her lips as she considered an optional action. *I could shoot out along the dirt road here for just a couple of miles until it intersects with the state road. Then I can say I checked that out in addition to my standard route. Fit in a little extra patrol, show them I'm not wasting time and that I can take some initiative.* She checked the time and reconfirmed that the side trip would fit into her schedule. Why not zip out to the end of the road and have a look-see, maintain a presence for the park service?

She put her service vehicle back in gear and turned onto the dirt road. Took it slow, as it had some twists and turns, and there were muddy spots here and there. But overall it wasn't bad and a little while later she was pulling up to the intersection with the paved, two-lane state road. No traffic on that one, either. She was going to love this job, she was sure of it. The dirt road she was on was narrow enough that turning around would be difficult, so she drove out onto the state road and made a left. She had just swung into her U-turn when she spotted a pickup truck parked up ahead on the shoulder. Her eyes immediately went to the cages stacked up in the bed.

Sara pulled her vehicle back onto the shoulder on the park side of the road and got out.

CHAPTER 4

Coral Gables

Rebecca Trout went through the motions of getting out of bed for work, getting showered and dressed and driving to her university lab, but she knew she would be useless today as far as getting any real work done. She still reeled from the news delivered yesterday by those cops.

Dr. Landis gone, *and not only gone, but apparently by his own hand...and with one of those oddball T-rex claws.* She had thought about it all night and it still made no sense to her. Why would he do such a thing? As far as she knew, he was happy; successful at work, pleasant to be around. She knew he was once married and been divorced, but that was a long time ago. So what could have led to this? The two cops who had broken the news to her seemed more concerned with simply crossing the Ts and dotting the i's on their case than in actually finding out what happened—not just that he died, but why he died. But she supposed that wasn't their job.

She felt a deep sense of loss as she forced herself to go about her day, making coffee and booting up her computer. One of the first people to get to work as she usually was, Rebecca was glad she didn't have any classes today. No lecture halls, no walking across campus and stopping to chat. She could just hole up in her lab's office and enjoy the solitude while catching up on drafting that research paper, the one she hoped would be accepted by the prestigious journal that was the current darling of the academic and scientific community.

She sat down at her computer and had just opened the file that contained her paper, when her desk phone rang. She stared at it like it was an alien. The display told her it was an outside line, so she picked it up, thinking maybe it was the police following up with more questions about Dr. Landis.

"Dr. Rebecca Trout here," she said in a no-nonsense tone.

"Good morning, Dr. Trout. My name is Ben Offstead, I'm a park ranger with the US Park Service, stationed in the Everglades."

"Good morning, Ben. How may I be of service?"

The man sounded peppy, like he was on at least his second cup of coffee. Rebecca took a sip from her own mug as he spoke, trying to catch up.

"There has been an unfortunate incident in the park involving an animal that we've been unable to conclusively identify. We'd like to get your help in telling us what it is."

"Sure, I'd be happy to help. You want to send me some tissue samples, or what do you have?" She'd dealt with the federal park service before. These were professionals who managed wildlife for a living, and simple species identification was not something they required her assistance for. But occasionally they'd find a piece of meat—usually something killed by a hunter and cleaned prior to law enforcement contact to avoid having game identified that was either out of season or undersize. Which was why she was surprised when next he asked her to come out to the field. And the unfortunate incident?

"Dr. Trout, we'd like for you to come out to State Road 249. Right now, if at all possible, so you can see the scene *in situ*. It's messy, two people were killed, and we're not sure what the animal was that did it."

Now this *was* different. Still, she didn't understand why they didn't know what they were dealing with. Her own time was valuable, of course. As a busy academician trying to juggle course loads, lab work and publishing, she had to be careful with how she spent her days. She occasionally got calls from Bigfoot hunter types asking her to confirm or deny sightings, which she always politely but firmly turned down.

"Is the animal no longer intact, is that why you can't identify it? Because if it's roadkill or shotgun splatter, you can have tissue samples delivered to my lab and—"

"No, the animals are fully intact as far as we can tell."

"Well then, what—" She was speechless. Here was an experienced national park ranger telling her that he had animals inside his own park that he could not identify.

"You're telling me that you have full carcasses and you still can't ID the species? Are we talking about sub-species of water moccasins? Because if that's the case---"

"No, they're not snakes at all." In the background she heard urgent voices apparently directed toward the ranger. "Dr. Trout, I've got to get going. But I'd really appreciate it if you could get over here now. You'll probably find it quite interesting, that's all I can say."

His line clicked off and she was left staring at her desk phone, eyebrows furrowed. *What could it be?* She spent some time checking her email, but found her attention wandering as her mind kept revisiting that odd phone call. Before long she pushed her chair back, stood and grabbed her umbrella before heading out of the lab.

#

Everglades National Park

When Dr. Trout arrived at the site, she found Ranger Offstead there along with another ranger, a young woman she did not recognize. Rebecca parked her car next to the two park service trucks and got out. While Offstead managed a smile, the woman's mouth remained fixed in a tight line.

"Thanks for coming out on such short notice, Doctor Trout, we really appreciate it!" Offstead extended a hand as she approached, and she shook it. Offstead turned and gestured to his fellow ranger. "Allow me to introduce you to Sara Cliff, a new Ranger with us. Unfortunately, Ranger Cliff has made a rather gruesome discovery her first day on patrol."

Rebecca eyed the young ranger but her expression remained unchanged. Offstead continued. "We probably only have a few more minutes until County Sheriffs get here. That's because the vehicle of the deceased was found parked on the State side of the road. Normally, we do our own investigations when crimes are committed, or if someone dies on federal park land," he finished with a sad look.

"So these deaths involve an animal of some kind?" Rebecca asked. Offstead nodded and she went on. "I guess I should see what happened."

He gave her a serious look and then waved an arm toward where Sara's truck was parked. "This way, please." The three of them walked past the truck and to the edge of the dense forest that crept up to the road. Rebecca eyed the cages stacked in the back of the pickup on the other side of the road.

"What were they collecting?"

"Chameleons."

"Uh-huh." This was no surprise to Rebecca, who knew all about the chameleon trade in South Florida. She followed him a little deeper into the dense foliage lining the road. Offstead paused in front of her and then turned around. "I apologize, Dr. Trout, but this is a rather bloody scene, and the bodies of the deceased have been left in place until the Sheriffs get here."

The zoologist had to admit she now questioned what she had gotten herself into, but she was all the way out here already. She'd heard of zoologists being asked to confirm deceased victims of animals attacks-- whether it was a particular kind of bear, or big cat, but she'd never been called upon to do anything like that herself. Until now. *But how strange that the offending animals were still here, and yet they don't know what they are?* That fired up her curiosity once again, and so she took the few remaining steps toward Offstead, who parted some branches and stepped aside as she approached.

A slaughter.

That was the first thing her mind registered. Two bodies, or what remained of them, lay about ten feet apart on the leafy ground, still damp from the previous night's rain. If it weren't for the heads, she probably wouldn't have been able to say for sure that it was two bodies, such was the extent of mangled flesh. Blood was everywhere—on the corpses, on the ground in what must have been large pools only a few hours ago, and splatter as high as eight feet up into the tree leaves.

Offstead must have recognized that it would take her a few seconds to process the carnage, and for that she was grateful. It took her a bit to discern the animal carcasses in the midst of the mutilation. She had been expecting something larger, given the scale of the injuries. Instead her eyes lit on first one, then two, then three chicken or turkey-sized creatures—all dead—scattered about the macabre scene.

Her first thought was that they were birds, but as a professional zoologist, she knew better than to listen to her first thought. Take a close look, she told herself. *Be sure.* She forced herself to put one foot in front of the other until she was standing over the nearest of the bird-like creatures. In spite of the gruesome sight, her face took on that expression of surprised curiosity she sometimes got as a scientist, the one that said, *Now wait a minute, what's this, what do we have here?* She knelt next to the dead beast.

It had a bird body at first glance. Feathers. Two legs, and the one foot remaining was webbed. The head was intact, which should have made identification that much easier, but instead it was causing her to make sure she was thinking straight, to ask if she had gotten enough sleep, to question everything she knew about animals.

What is this?

Behind her, the pair of rangers remained silent as they watched her go through what they had already experienced before deciding to call upon her expertise. "Give me a minute," she called back to them, lest they think she was too freaked out by the gore to do her job.

"Take all the time you need," Offstead came back. *Right. I'll just hang out here with these bloody corpses….*

Yet Dr. Trout did find herself getting even closer to the dead animal that had presumably wreaked such vicious havoc. Is this animal capable of slaughtering these two people like this? She forced herself to think rationally in the face of the messy carnage. She leaned down and pulled her reading glasses from her shirt pocket and put them on. She took a close look at the head of the creature.

This was where all resemblance to a bird—chicken, turkey or otherwise—ended, she could now see. The neck was strangely elongated, for one thing, and featherless. Not only featherless, she realized, subconsciously reaching a hand out to touch it, but composed of a different cell type altogether. Its surface was hard, and comprised of small overlapping plates…*scales!!*

What on Earth? That was not even the weirdest part about it. The dead eye she could see staring up at her, open and now forever unblinking, was not a bird eye at all. A yellow-greenish iris surrounding a black and narrow, vertically oriented pupil, this particular eye was far more reptilian than avian, Dr. Trout thought. Avian body characteristics with reptilian head and neck traits? She racked her brain for any precedents. Nothing came to mind. Until that is, she thought back, way back, in time.

Her zoological training told her that birds were evolutionarily close to dinosaurs; dinosaurs were very birdlike, and some exhibited feathers as well as scales. She tried to mentally envision the dinosaur images she'd seen in textbooks—artist renderings based on the best guesses of biologists and paleontologists. The feathers should be part of the skin across the entire body, neck and head, but this creature had no feathers whatsoever on the neck or head, only the strange reptilian scales. Everything about the head was different from a bird, not only the skin type (scales instead of feathers), but the shape of the head, the teeth instead of beak, the eyes….It was almost as if someone stuck a lizard neck and head onto a bird body. She turned her attention to the feet. To her they looked like the feet of a bird, perhaps somewhat stouter than a normal bird of this size.

Rebecca stood and removed her smartphone from a pocket. She held it out to Offstead. "You mind if I get a few photos of the animal?"

"Sure, but not the bodies, please. The human bodies, I mean. They still treat it as a crime scene until their investigation is complete."

"No problem." She bent down and took a few closeups of the animal's head and body, as well as a couple of shots of the entire creature. She took the time to look at the photos to make sure they were good; no doubt the carcasses would be quickly disposed of by the park service once the police visited the scene. But that gave her an idea. First, she needed to make sure the other specimens were the same species—whatever it was—as the one she had just got up close and personal with. So she walked around the bloody site and took a look at the other two dead beasties. All of them were the same type of animal.

"So what are they, Doc?" Offstead called over. There it was, Dr. Trout thought, the million dollar question. The reason she was here. Time to show off her expertise in front of these two professional wildlife stewards.

But all that would come out of her mouth was, "No idea."

CHAPTER 5

Coral Gables

Detective Rene Bravia drained the last of his Cuban coffee and tossed the little plastic cup into the trash can in the corner of the room. He brushed some crumbs from breakfast off his shirt and rolled his desk chair closer to the computer monitor. It was time to get down to business. Earlier he'd noticed an email regarding the Landis case and he was eager to have a look at it while the case was still fresh.

Bravia nodded as he opened the mail. Its simple message was something that would move the case along. It was from Computer Forensics, the detective's tech division, saying that the computer hard drive from Landis' desktop machine had been examined for contents. Nowadays a technician had to go through it first; detectives weren't allowed to start rummaging on their own—too many destructive viruses and accidental deletions, overlooking hidden partitions, things like that. So Bravia had dutifully sent it off and awaited the results, expecting they would be dry and routine but looking forward to ticking off another box on his investigative list. He wasn't required to do that. The case appeared to be a suicide, after all, but the note, he supposed, made him want to take an extra step. No one else lived with the guy, so whatever was on his computer should still be there.

Bravia wasn't fooling himself as he logged into the departmental secure system, wherein he would find a mirror image of the drive taken for evidence that any authorized detective could peruse remotely, in this case from Bravia's office desktop. He'd read the recent emails, maybe poke around for photographs that were personally compromising or worse. Over the years he'd seen everything from homemade sex tapes to child pornography to sophisticated template images used in conjunction with other equipment to produce counterfeit bills. So what would he find today?

Bravia clicked through the waiver and acknowledgement buttons that ensured he was who he said he was, this resource is for authorized officers only, and then clicked on the hard drive icon with the name LandisArchie_0983736. The screen flickered for a moment as he accessed a remote machine and then he was looking at an exact duplicate of Dr.

Landis' computer as it had been found the day Bravia had discovered his body.

He quickly checked the desktop and 'My Documents' folder for files that looked like they might contain a suicide note that would elaborate on the ultra-short one he'd left. *I'm Sorry.* Finding nothing other than routine business documents—scans of receipts for things like occasional plumbing and electrical work, he then turned his attention to email. He found mostly spam, ads for printer toner and penis enlargement and credit monitoring services. No messages of a personal nature that he could see.

But there were a few—at least one thread—that appeared to be work related. Bravia's mouth turned down at the corners. Odd, though, since clearly this free consumer email address was not his university work email, and there were clearly not enough work emails for this to be all of them. With a glance at his wall clock, Bravia clicked open the most recent of the mails, dated about two weeks ago. The subject read "Re: re: re: latest results."

Bravia read with detached interest upon seeing technical jargon and numbers. Not very exciting stuff. But then he caught snatches of heated verbiage here and there—emotive writing expressing dissatisfaction, or at least conflict of some sort. He read closer. The recipient of Landis' emails was a company, and Bravia caught his breath a little when he realized it was one he had heard of. A corporation, actually, one of the leading drug-makers. Big Pharma. Apparently they were doing some sort of business with Dr. Landis. Some of the email thread content was technical enough to be over Bravia's head, but there was also business talk that was easy enough to grasp:

...intellectual property... genetic lab work with animal DNA markers...out of your hands now...contractually bound....per the terms of our arrangement...you were paid handsomely according to said terms for ....concludes our business....

The detective looked away from the screen for a moment to focus his thoughts. *Dr. Landis was doing business with Big Pharma?* It seemed at odds for an academic. Didn't they usually just publish journal articles no one actually read except for a handful of other nerds? Perhaps he was being funded by the corporation as part of a specific grant or research project? Yet why was this exchange on his personal email account and not his university *.edu* account? Not only that, most principal investigators, as Dr. Landis was, had grant administrators whose job it was to handle the details of securing grants. No, Bravia decided as he read further, this was a direct agreement of some kind between Landis and BioGen.

More phrases caught his eye:

…you have done your part.…by way of thanks…performance bonus.…ticked all the boxes.…This concludes our business.

That was the last reply from the corporation. Dr. Landis continued to reply, however, without receiving a further response.

I have a right to be informed of the results.… full disclosure clause…non-transparent methodology…

This kind of "whining" as Bravia thought of it, stopping short of direct threats, went on for a while, but was ultimately unanswered. The detective pulled back from the computer but remained sitting, lost in thought. *Dr. Landis working with BioGen.…some sort of minor work disagreement.* Bravia knew, though, that any kind of disagreement immediately prior to an untimely death could not automatically be dismissed as minor. Of course he may have taken it up over the phone or in person at that point and resolved it that way. But picturing the slumped-over form of the geneticist at his desk, neck sliced with that strange animal part that even Landis' own expert colleague was unable to identify, Bravia doubted very much that additional dialogue was fruitful, if it had even taken place.

He was considering a subpoena for phone records, thinking how it was likely overkill for a suicide, and how he should probably talk to his colleague again, Dr. Trout, when his desk phone rang. He snatched it up and said his own name.

"Detective Bravia, this is Dr. Rebecca Trout from the university, I spoke to you earlier about my colleague—former colleague—Dr. Landis. I'm calling to give you what may be some new information regarding the case."

Bravia took a deep breath before replying. "At this point we're calling it a suicide, Dr. Trout. Foul play is not suspected."

"I understand that. But I think I'm beginning to see why he may have done what he did, and to be honest, it scares the living daylights out of me. I was called out to Everglades National Park this morning by the rangers there, who asked me to identify an animal that killed two reptile collectors early this morning."

Bravia leaned forward in his chair. "Oh? I haven't heard about that. And?"

"And even I couldn't identify it."

An awkward pause ensued before Bravia asked, "Well what was it? What did it look like?"

"It looked like a cross between a large bird, like a turkey, and a small dinosaur like maybe a velociraptor or a compythesaurus."

Bravia shrugged at his desk. "Well I do hear about a lot of invasive species being let loose around the 'glades, and they can make a go of it out there you know, because it's similar enough to whatever tropical place they came from—"

"That's correct, Detective, however, we're not talking about a python or a parrot. I'm telling you that as a professional zoologist, I have never seen this species—if it even is a species—of animal before."

"What do you think it is, then? You say it killed these people?"

"Yes, a pack of them literally ripped a couple apart into little pieces. I'm sure I'll have some form of PTSD as a result of seeing it."

"We have licensed professionals who can help with that sort of thing. I can recommend one if you—"

"I appreciate it, Detective, but I think I can deal with it for now."

"All right, so let me ask you this: what does this have to do with Dr. Landis?"

He heard her take a deep breath. "This is speculation on my part, of course, but…." She hesitated as if trying to figure out how to proceed. "But I know he was doing a lot of work with CRISPR, a gene editing program that has been used to do things like modify food crops to be more pest-resistant, or even to produce bulls that have no horns, things like that. I think—I fear—he may have taken it a few steps further than that."

Bravia shivered in his seat as he flashed on the emails to Dr. Landis he'd just read. "Dr. Trout, are you familiar with a company called BioGen?"

Her reply was immediate. "Of course, they're a leading biotech corporation, a publicly traded company on the stock exchange that does pioneering gene therapy work."

"Do you think that company also works with CRISPR?"

"Oh certainly. Of course. Pretty much everybody does nowadays. They were probably one of the very first to utilize it. I have no doubt it's one of the technological weapons in their arsenal."

"And Dr. Trout, are you aware of any working collaboration Dr. Landis had with BioGen?"

After a slight pause, she came back on the line. "No, I'm not. I suppose he could have had a small grant with them that escaped my notice, but believe me, we academics are pretty competitive and we all love to toot our own horns when it comes to getting a grant, even a small one, and

I never heard of anything with Archie and BioGen. The Department itself would have put that on the website."

"Is it common practice for professors to do private research, say outside of the university's purview?"

A laugh emanated from the speaker. "Good Lord, no. Who has time for that? Private companies do sometimes fund research, but it's still done through the university, with grant administrators and Departmental Heads aware of every major step. Researchers may occasionally do consulting with private parties, if you're talking about moonlighting type of work."

"Yes, Dr. Trout, in light of what you've told me, I do have reason to believe that Dr. Landis was involved in so-called moonlighting activities with BioGen, and that that work involved gene manipulation."

"I—I was not aware of that at all. How did you find out about it?"

"We briefly looked at his email records. There was an exchange on Landis' personal email account, not his university account, with a representative from the company, verified to be a legitimate BioGen email address."

"I had no idea!" Rebecca said.

"I will need you to keep this information confidential for the time being, Dr. Landis."

"Of course. Is there anything I can do to help?"

Bravia's gaze flicked back to the computer screen where the mirror of Landis' hard drive stared back at him. He thought about all the files he'd seen in there that he didn't understand. Files that might well have to do with Landis' BioGen consulting work.

"Would you be willing to take a look at some of Dr. Landis' files that have technical or scientific content and give me a layperson's explanation of what they have to do with?"

CHAPTER 6

Everglades National Park

"Dispatch to Unit 33, do you copy?"

Ranger Sara Cliff eyeballed her patrol vehicle's radio as she heard Kevin Hardison's now familiar voice. After spending the rest of the morning and early afternoon at the ranger station, talking about her horrific discovery with the other rangers and park personnel, she had ventured back out on patrol again. Ben Offstead had told her everyone would understand if she opted to spend the rest of the day doing office work rather than resume field patrol, but she insisted on "getting back out there." She'd already encountered what her fellow rangers were calling the worst fatalities the park had seen in the last decade, perhaps since a crocodile mauled a toddler and then dragged the father underwater when he tried to rescue his child, drowning in the process. She'd gotten the worst of it out of the way for the rest of her career, her co-workers had told her by way of consolation. She only hoped they were right.

Sara eyed the road ahead and picked up the radio transmitter with a smile. "Loud and clear, Kevin, I mean Dispatch. I'm heading down Cypress. All is well, over."

"Copy that. Just holler if you need anything."

She put down the transmitter and put both hands on the wheel as she negotiated a curve while another car rounded it in the opposite direction on the narrow two-lane road. She subconsciously slowed a little as she made the turn. She was a competent driver, but she was extra-cautious now after being shaken earlier. She thought of the university zoologist, also a woman, yet she had seemed so sure of herself in the face of the gory scene, so confident. And still she couldn't identify the creature, at least not yet, Sara thought.

As the road transitioned back into a straightaway, Sara looked out her window at the dense trees on that side of the road. So much amazing life in there, she couldn't help but think. Such incredible biodiversity. And the only reason it was still here, allowed to exist, was because of its national park status and the management of the organization she was now an integral part of. Without that protection, she had little doubt that all of this would long ago have been drained and paved over by faceless international developers, to make way for more strip malls, tract housing, motels and parking lots. She was proud to be here maintaining one of the last truly wild places on Earth and was determined to do her best to keep it that way.

After a time she reached a lonely intersection and came to rest at the stop sign. A left would take her deeper into the park, while a right would lead out to the state road that borders the park, where she had been that morning. Face your fears, she told herself. *Don't create a no-go-zone of fear in the park that you'll always be known for avoiding. Drive through now and you'll be over it that much quicker.*

Taking a deep breath, Sara turned the wheel to the right and stomped on the accelerator.

#

Dr. Rebecca Trout glanced at her rearview mirror as she approached the edge of Everglades National on the state road. There were any number of other things she could, and probably should, be doing right now, including preparing lectures, grading student papers, working on her own research paper, or checking out Archie's computer files for the detective. And yet she had been compelled to return to the animal attack site, she supposed out of a sense of professional redemption. It bothered her to no end that she had been unable to identify the strange animals, and that lack of ability needling at her inner perfectionist hurt all the more when Ranger Offstead had politely but firmly refused her request to take a tissue sample of the animal to her lab for genetic analysis. She had explained to him that that was the only surefire way to know what they were dealing with, but he had dismissed the idea, blathering on about protocols, approved vendors, extra-departmental procedures, yadayadayada. In other words, screw you, lady, if you can't tell us what it is right now, we'll get someone else to run the meat through machines and tell us what it is.

She supposed she would find out at some point, when and if those results were ever made public. But how long would that take? Six months? A year? Maybe never? She couldn't stand the not knowing. And so here she found herself, slowing her Prius as she approached the same spot at which she had pulled over that morning. She knew that the mess had no doubt been cleaned up by now, that the strange animal bodies were no doubt stored in some ranger station freezer behind locked doors. Yet she also knew that the attack had been forceful and savage, that the likelihood of every single scrap of flesh having been scoured clean—by park personnel and scavengers alike—this early on after the incident—was slim to none. There would be small pieces of those creatures tucked away back into the thickets of foliage that were inconvenient for a person to reach. But she would do it. Oh yes, she would!

Rebecca parked her car at the side of the road and shut the engine off. Windows down, she listened and looked intently for signs of people nearby. Hearing or seeing no one, she grabbed her small field sample kit from the seat next to her and stepped out of her car.

\#

Ranger Sara Cliff shook her head as her radio crackled again. *Really checking up on me.* She snatched up the transmitter. "Unit 33 here."

"Everything okay?"

"Everything's great, Dispatch. How's life at the ranch?" She cringed, unsure if perhaps she was becoming informal a little too soon. But Kevin's reply made her feel at ease.

"All's well on the Western Front. Where you at?"

Sara glanced ahead at the road before her. The state road was coming up ahead. "Still patrolling on Cypress, over." Curt, professional, quick response. Hopefully it would keep him from asking exactly where on Cypress, which extended for many miles through the park, all the way out to the intersection with the state road.

"Well you just holler if you need anything. Hey, I saved you one of those sandwiches from the lunch today if you want one later. 'Cuz you know how they take everything and somehow it never gets seen again?"

"You're the best, Kevin. Over and out."

She continued toward the state road, unsure of what she would have said had he pressed her for a more precise location. *Almost back to the spot where all the shit went down this morning!* Not that she wouldn't say later that she'd driven by there. But somehow it seemed more acceptable that way, because it's already done, she guessed, rather than, *I'm going to do it,* like she was asking permission or something.

Sara slowed her truck to a leisurely halt at the stop sign. She was about to make the left that would take her along the state road past the attack site when she noticed a vehicle parked across the road from the site. A green Prius. She didn't see any people. Still, the area was not a designated pull-over zone, and in light of what had happened here earlier, she decided it was safest to back her truck up and pull off to the shoulder in reverse. She shut off the engine and listened out the window. Heard nothing but the sounds of the Everglades—the drone of insects, the call birds, a rustle of trees in the wind.

She exited her vehicle, her service pistol catching ever so slightly on the seat as she slid out. She knew it wouldn't be a bad thing to radio Dispatch *(er, Kevin)* to let him know that she was leaving her truck. But she just wanted to do a quick foot patrol of what was now essentially an area of recent incident, and then get back to her truck and resume patrolling the greater park. *I'll just take a quick look-see and then get right back to it....*

#

Dr. Trout stopped walking when she reached the small clearing where the hellish attacks had taken place. The two human corpses—what was left of them—had been removed, as expected. Also as expected, the animal carcasses were no longer there. She frowned as she eyed the wet ground. Unfortunately, it had rained today after the incident, which meant that most of the blood splatter left on the ground—human and animal—had been washed away or extremely diluted. Looking ahead into the thick wall of foliage fronting the clearing, she hoped that some of the splatter had found its way inside, where it would have been protected both from the rain and the cleanup crew.

The zoologist glanced around, making sure she was alone. Then she hefted her field kit, a slim plastic case about the size of a laptop bag, and walked right up to the edge of the wall of plants. She eyeballed the front of it, hoping to find scraps of meat hanging from the leaves, but so far she saw nothing. Resigning herself to the fact that she was going to have to crawl into the undergrowth, Rebecca crouched low and parted a couple of branches. She was glad she'd changed into long pants instead of shorts in spite of the South Florida heat.

She spied what looked like a small pocket of space perhaps five feet into the bush, and duck-walked toward that, one hand holding her field kit while the other fended off branches and riotous thickets of brambles. It was far from easy-going, but she made slow progress, six inches at a time, cursing softly under her breath. With each step, she glanced around, above and below at the foliage, looking for dangling scraps of meat that may have ended up here during the intense fracas that ensued just a few feet away. She found what she was looking for at the edge of the pocket of space: a couple of flecks of skin and connective tissue hung up on a plant branch. She crawled the rest of the way into the tiny clearing, ducking beneath what she hoped would become her tissue samples so as not to dislodge and possibly lose them.

Once in the tiny open space, Rebecca looked around 360 degrees and found that the few scraps closest to the open clearing from which she entered were the only ones. Eyeing them closely, she was glad to see a bit of feather and scale, which meant that they were not human, but from the mystery beasts. She opened her field kit and from it donned a pair of latex gloves. Then she removed a small plastic vial and uncapped it, along with a pair of forceps. Carefully, she tweezed one of her tissue samples that dangled from the plant and dropped it into the vial. She had just capped it when she heard the unmistakable sound of boots crunching on the ground in the direction of the state road.

She tensed inside the vegetation, eyes toward the road but unable to see anything but the barest snatches of ground beyond. This was both good and bad; good because it meant she couldn't easily be seen by whomever was approaching, but bad because it almost meant that she had no line of sight to whoever approached. She silently and swiftly collected one more tissue sample, capped it, and closed up her kit box with the sample vials securely inside.

Now what? Hopefully, whoever this was would leave soon. She didn't hear a vehicle approaching, though, so she wasn't sure how she would know when they were gone, other than listening to footsteps leading away from the immediate area. She hunkered down amidst the plants, wincing as a cramp flared up in her left calf, forcing her to change her position. She lost her balance while doing so and had to put her right hand out on the ground to keep from falling over, which would have been very loud, but it still made an audible noise.

She froze.

#

Sara Cliff stopped walking at the edge of the clearing she had visited this morning and eyed the scene of the attack with trepidation. Even though it had been cleaned by now, sanitized, it still held a potent sense of foreboding for her. Something that spoke to her, *This place has secrets that even the people who know it best don't know. They didn't know what those animals were.*

Adding to this unease was the vehicle parked on the side of the road. When she had first driven up, her mind registered it simply as a car. But now, after walking past it, she had noticed that it was a green Prius, and didn't it look familiar? Yes, because that's what that zoologist from the university drove out in this morning, wasn't it? She had always had a knack for remembering details, and this wasn't even a difficult one for her. She didn't exactly see a plethora of green Priuses every day, did she? So it must be Dr. Trout, although she didn't recall any mention of her returning to the site. Not that Sara was important enough for anyone to tell her what was going on, she chided herself. Who was she but a fresh-out-of-school rookie?

But then, as she looked around the site some more, where was she? This was a small clearing, with no hiking trails—marked or otherwise—leading away from it. Only dense vegetation no one in their right mind would attempt to venture into. Which left only the state road…As she turned around to look back in that direction, she heard a noise coming from the foliage that caused her to snap her head back around.

What's that?!

It dawned on her that she was in a fairly remote area alone, and that if there were more of those strange bird-lizard creatures, that they could make short work of her…She banished the thought with a shiver. Then again, she told herself, her mind refusing to give up the taunting, it wouldn't even take a gaggle of exotic chicken-raptors to do her in, would it? A big alligator could come charging out of the brush and that could be the end, too. Or a Florida Panther? And even if she survived such an encounter, her subconscious went on, she'd be in embarrassingly hot water at work. Returning to a dangerous wildlife attack zone alone when she had not been asked to do that.…*You're too much trouble, rookie, we don't have time to babysit, we need a Ranger*….

There it was again, the noise! But it wasn't loud, not persistent. Not like an animal moving. Sara whirled back around to look into the vegetation, and there, just for a second, she registered a swatch of color. Blue. Not a color one normally saw in nature around here, not like that. Automatically, her right hand dropped to her service pistol, sheathed on her right hip. She undid the catch.

"Hello? Is there someone back there? Are you okay?"

\#

Crouched on the damp ground, Rebecca Trout exhaled sharply in the dense brush. She recognized the voice of the same ranger from this morning. *Now what? She knows someone is*

back here, and oh, geez, she probably recognized my car from this morning….Resigning herself to the fact that she'd been outed, she crawled out of the underbrush, field kit in hand.

"Hi there! Sorry, didn't mean to scare you, I'm coming out.…" Rebecca waved and pushed up from the ground to a standing position.

"Dr. Trout?"

"Yes, it's me…Ranger?"

"Sara. Sara Cliff."

"Right, we met this morning. Sorry, I'm terrible with names."

"Are you…" Rebecca saw her eyes drop to her disheveled and leaf-littered clothing, to the field kit in her right hand. "Are you okay?"

"Uh, yeah, I'm fine. Thanks for asking."

Sara walked over to Rebecca and extended a hand. Rebecca took it and pumped it up and down before looking at her case and adding, "I collected a couple of tissue samples from the animals involved in this morning's attack, so that I can do a DNA analysis on them back at my university lab."

Sara nodded enthusiastically. "Oh, great! It's really a mystery, isn't it? I mean, everybody at the station's been talking about it all day, so I'm glad Ben asked you to follow through like that."

"Well actually," Rebecca began, looking down at the field kit in her hand, but then stopped herself. *If you tell her Offstead didn't authorize you to collect the samples, that you just snuck onto federal park land on your own, you could get into trouble!*

"Actually what?" Sara prompted, also now looking at the kit.

Don't lie. "Actually I didn't come out here again because Ben asked me to. I just felt bad that I wasn't able to provide an ID of the species, and so I thought I would come back out of my own accord and collect samples for lab analysis. Those results will tell us unequivocally what we're dealing with."

From Sara's rapidly changing expression it was clear to Rebecca that she wasn't entirely comfortable with this. "Um, okay. Listen, I'm sorry but you're going to need to come with me and—"

She was interrupted by the sound of the walkie-talkie clipped to her belt squawking loudly. "…Ranger Cliff, urgent, do you copy?"

She snatched up the radio and hit the push-to-talk button. "Sara here, say again, please?"

"Sara, it's Kevin. I've been trying to reach you in your vehicle, are you okay?"

"I'm fine, yeah, just on a quick foot patrol. What's going on?"

Rebecca stood mute, observing the conversation, praying that the ranger wouldn't mention who she had just found.

"Good. We've got camper reports of an animal incident over at the Campground in Little Flamingo. I need you to respond. Where are you now?"

Sara looked over at Rebecca and they locked eyes. Rebecca hoped the young Ranger could read her silent plea. Sara spoke into her radio.

"I'm close to that location. I'll be right there, over and out."

CHAPTER 7

Everglades National Park

Ranger Cliff put down the walkie-talkie and held Dr. Trout's gaze. The zoologist had heard what Kevin said about there being a new animal incident. Before she could say anything, Rebecca said, "If you want, I'll go with you and see if I can help. If it is another one of the same attacks, maybe I could give you more insight into determining what these creatures are and how to deal with them."

Sara waved her arm toward the road. "Okay, ride with me. Let's go." The two ran back to Sara's ranger truck and hopped in. While they did, Rebecca surreptitiously slipped the sample containing the killer animal tissue samples into the small student-style backpack she carried.

"It's not far from here," Sara said as the engine thundered to life. She put the truck in reverse and turned around on the state road, heading back into the national park. She navigated smoothly through the park's winding, heavily forested roads. "This is Cypress up here on the left." She turned onto a new road, narrower than the last, that snaked into a thickly wooded area. As usual, she drove with the windows down so that she could hear the sounds of the park rather than the auditory isolation of rolled-up windows and an air conditioned cab. She was out here to monitor and respond to what was going on, not to cruise around in manufactured comfort. It wasn't long before a large RV came into view, parked off to one side of the road, barely fitting on the shoulder.

"I hear something," Dr. Trout said. And it was true. Right away, Sara could discern the voices of children yelling. Not in fear or pain, but excitement. Perhaps a kids' birthday party? She'd seen a couple of those in the park already, and usually the biggest issue was getting them to clean up their mess, to reduce the use of materials like balloons and plastic that was bad for the environment because it eventually ended up in the water where it took a deadly toll on aquatic life.

"Let's check it out." She pulled up behind the RV on the shoulder of a heavily overgrown road. Inwardly she groaned because RVs had designated camping spots and this was not one of them, and so now she was dealing with at least that, plus whatever the kids were screaming about, and then there was the reported animal incident she still had to get to the bottom of. It was shaping up to be a busy first day indeed.

A boy ran out from the backside of the RV screaming, "Dad, Dad, we can't find him, and now another one is here. Dad!" The boy ran around to the RV's door, facing the road, and then froze in his tracks upon seeing the two women. His gaze stopped on Sara's park ranger uniform.

"Ranger! I—Over here!"

Sara and Rebecca followed the boy around the rear of the RV. At least five kids were gathered on the side of the RV facing a swampy bog— waterlogged, loose mucky ground supporting thick vegetation, including Cypress trees. The only adult to be found was a woman lying unmoving on her back in the wet mulch some thirty feet from the RV.

"Whoa, kids—what happened to her?" Sara asked. Rebecca was already treading out to the woman, her progress necessarily slow and cautious due to the quicksand-like earth. Her shoes made a wet sucking sound when she pulled them out after each step.

A pudgy, red-faced boy Sara guessed to be of about ten years of age turned his face up to hers. "She's my friend Ryan's Mom, from another family we were camping by last night."

"What happened to her?"

"The thing got her."

Sara scrutinized his expression for signs of playfulness but saw only sincerity. Suddenly Rebecca called out from the inert woman.

"She's alive, but I'll need help dragging her out of here."

"Coming!" Sara walked toward the bog while unclipping her field radio from her belt. She spoke into it, hoping it would reach the station, knowing the mobile unit in her vehicle was more powerful.

"Unit 33 to Dispatch, if you can read me, I require assistance." She indicated her location using GPS coordinates displayed on the radio's screen. She returned the radio to her belt to keep her hands free and then started to walk out to Dr. Trout and the fallen woman.

"Watch out for the big bug!" a little girl with ponytails said.

Sara turned around but kept walking. It was hard to take little kids seriously sometimes. "What big bug, sweetheart?"

"It's not a bug, it's a millipede," Ryan answered.

"I told you, dumbass, it's a centipede," a girl said.

And then Rebecca's voice again from out on the bog: "She's been bitten, or...or stung by something, and something big by the looks of it. I can't move her any farther without help."

The victim's voice caterwauled across the swamp. "Help, get me out of here!"

"Coming!" Sara felt her boots squish into the muck as she long-strided out into the swampy bog. Then she mentally chided herself for not placing a radio call to Dispatch first. She should have let them know she was performing a rescue. But it was too late now, as the tricky bog walk required her full attention—where to step next, using her arms to keep her balance.

While she made her way out to where Rebecca was trying to aid the fallen victim, out of the corner of her eye she noticed an odd bubbling of the thin layer of water over the soil. She looked again in that direction but saw nothing, so took a few more careful steps toward the two women. But there it was again, and this time she heard splashing, the sluicing of water through the vegetation and mud. Stopping suddenly to take another look, she chose her footing less than carefully and the next thing she knew she was lying on her side in the mud.

Then she heard, from the solid ground over by the RV, one of the kids' voices screaming, "Look out, there it is!" No sooner did her mind register the words than her eyes caught a rapidly moving, large form. It was sizable, but close to the wet ground, partially concealed by it. But she could still see it pass close by her, its scaly body rippling as it sort of undulated along. A snake, her brain suggested, but even in the shock of the moment she knew that wasn't what it could be. Something about the movement was just...wrong. It didn't really undulate so much as...*scuttle* along the bog bottom. And it had scales, or not even scales so much as armored plates. *Segmented*, her training told her. Snakes were not segmented animals. So what was it? Once again, even though she was in the presence of a working zoologist, she was not getting any answers from her, since she was currently attempting to single-handedly extract a park visitor from the watery muck.

Sara told herself that it wasn't the professor's fault they had undergone this role reversal, and to focus on her own task at hand. The creature writhed around in the muck before wriggling back in her direction. Sort of a sinuous movement, but without the fluidity of a serpentine creature. More insect-like, the segmented body pieces opening and closing back together as the animal moved. And then, removing all doubt, she got a fleeting glimpse of the head.

The antennae. This was no reptile, that was certain now. Insect...or...? She suddenly cared much less about what exactly it was, and a whole lot more about what it might do to her and everybody else. This thing was *huge*—it was difficult to estimate its length while rapidly moving around partially hidden in the muck, but she could see several feet of the body at a time. The fact that she didn't know exactly what it was only made it all the more disconcerting.

Deciding the best thing to do was to make forward progress to Rebecca and the victim while ignoring the creature, Sara pushed herself to an upright position. By the time she regained her footing the elongated creature was hidden from sight. She trudged on through the bog, pausing to lift her foot out of a submerged root here and there. When she reached Rebeca and the downed woman, Sara made eye contact with the zoology professor.

"That animal in here has segments. Did you see it?"

"Glimpses of it. I think it's a centipede, judging by her bite wounds, since millipedes don't bite, but…"

"But it's freaking huge!" Sara exclaimed.

"Right. I don't know what's up with that, but listen. Right now we've got to help her." She nodded to the woman who lay prone in the mud, head turned to one side and being propped up by Rebecca's hands so that she could breathe. "She has two very large puncture wounds high on her chest."

"Bleeding?"

"Very little for how big they are."

"It stings, though, it fucking stings!" The voice of the stricken woman.

"Ma'am do you think you can get to your feet if we help you?" Sara asked. As a ranger, it was definitely part of her job to assist hikers, campers and backpackers in distress, and this was that type of situation, never mind the giant centipede or whatever it was.

"The suction is making it hard to pull her out," Rebecca said.

"Let's try one leg at a time," Sara suggested. She moved back to the fallen woman's right foot.

"What's your name, ma'am?"

"Tamera. Get Me The Hell Outta Here Now!"

Sara did her best to keep her tone of voice pleasant and upbeat. "We're working on that, Tamera. I'm going to try to pull your right leg out of the mud, okay?"

"Yes, just hurry!"

Sara reached down and grabbed Tamera's leg by the ankle. She pulled it up, bending the leg at the knee until the foot and calf came free of the mud with a slurping noise. She had just repeated the process with the other leg when Rebecca said, "It's coming back again."

Sara looked up to see the zoologist pointing further into the bog. "Tamera, I'm going to grab you by your right arm and roll you over onto your back. Are you ready?"

"Yes! Hurry, hurry, it's coming back. It's going to kill me this time, I just know it. Please hurry!"

Sara grabbed Tamera's arm while Rebecca took a step toward the approaching centipede. Sara grabbed Tamera and was able to get her up onto her side. By that time Rebecca was yelling, "It's here, it's here!" Then she kicked the creature in the side with her booted foot. The centipede continued to circle around them, seemingly uninfluenced by the human attack.

"Move!" Rebecca came to Tamera's side and grabbed hold of the arm Sara didn't have. "Upsy-daisy, one, two, three…"

She and Sara heaved, their boots finding purchase deep in the thick ooze as they hauled the hapless woman to her feet. The three of them began to stagger toward the RV, where the children had gathered and were yelling, "It's still there! Hurry, look out!"

It was all so chaotic that Sara found it easier to ignore the larger scene and simply focus on dragging Tamera one laborious step at a time toward solid ground. But that did nothing to change the fact that the gigantic centipede was not minding its own business. Instead it circled the beleaguered group, rapidly slicing the surface of the bog water as it circled past them again and again. As they neared the solid shoreline where the RV was parked, it became apparent that the creature's circles around the group were getting tighter and tighter, like a shark circling its prey.

Soon it became impossible to take a step without kicking the animal. Rebecca tripped over it and went down, the sudden shift in balance also throwing off Sara's concentration. Not ten feet from the RV, all three of them fell back into the muddy bog. From her one eye that was above the muck, Sara was glad to see the gaggle of kids perched on top of the RV, safely away from the mega-pede's writhing fury.

No fewer than four creatures—three human and one centipede—rolled up onto the hard-packed grass that marked the edge of solid ground. A tangling mass of movement, limbs, legs and scales collided off one another as the bodies struggled for advantage—either to escape or to win the fight. A kaleidoscope of aural chaos rent the air as adults and kids screamed, limbs thudded into the earth and the massive arthropod clicked and clacked as it wriggled around.

Sara kicked the 'pede but the ill-timed blow landed her booted foot in between two of the trashcan lid--sized segments while they were open. And the creature completed its movement, the body trundling along into a turn. The segments closed again while her foot was still in between them. The pain became acute as her ankle was crushed like a vice between two hard plates.

"Rebecca, pull me out!"

But the megapede had other ideas. It uncoiled and trundled its impossibly long body straight up out of the bog toward the RV. The resulting forward motion closed the arthropod's segments on Sara's foot and dragged her body along next to the creature. She lay on her back, head next to the animal's rippling side, watching its pairs of legs trundle along as it unknowingly carried her along with it. She wailed sharply as her ankle bent at an unnatural angle.

Rebecca ran alongside the centipede after making sure that Tamera was temporarily okay while seated on the edge of solid ground. She barreled into the side of the trundling 'pede, causing the segments to open just enough to allow Sara's foot to slip free. The park ranger came to rest on her back on the grass just as the centipede changed direction. The creature's new course took it directly over the fallen ranger. Sara closed her eyes as the underside of the segmented monstrosity passed over her entire body. A musty, earthy odor offended her nostrils as the animal's many legs stamped over her torso, neck and head. She tried to raise her arms to push it off of her face, but they were pinned strongly to the ground by other parts of the creature. She clenched her teeth and pursed her lips as she felt a footpad of some type come down on her mouth.

Suddenly the pressure on most of her body lifted and she was able to roll to the right enough to get out from under the strange beast. After a mad scrambling and tangle of legs and limbs later, she was being pulled to her feet with a wince and a cry of pain as the injured ankle bore too much weight all at once. Down she went again, dropping elbow first back into the soggy muck. But at least as she lay there on the ground, this time she was watching the primitive creature locomote itself away from her.

But then the kids began to scream. From the roof of the RV they stood and watched the centipede approaching. It moved surprisingly fast now, rippling up the contour of smooth ground on which the RV was parked, a few feet from the bog. Sara watched as the 'pede slithered up to the edge of the structure, and then, without a pause, crept right up the side, its head wagging back and forth as it sought the top edge. Wild screams from the kids ensued now as they realized that what they had thought was a safe perch was no such thing.

Two of the kids moved to the far side of the roof, hung down by their hands and dropped off.

"Get inside the RV!" Rebecca shouted while moving to Sara's aid. "All of you get inside and shut the door! All of you, go now!" As she said the words "all of you," she realized that Tamera was no longer here. She looked around and spotted the rescued woman running away from the RV toward the access road. She had taken the opportunity to flee while Rebecca and Sara grappled with the centipede. Not that she could really blame her, Rebecca thought. She was on her own, though, while the rest of them would stay here and fight together.

As the third kid started to move, Rebecca reached Sara and once again pulled her to her feet. "Let's go, Ranger, before that thing comes back to us."

"Thanks," Sara grunted as she staggered to her feet.

"Hopefully it's only a sprain," Rebecca said. "We need to get inside that RV and then call for help. Too far to go back to your truck."

"No arguments here," Sara said. They started to move, Sara hopping along with one arm over Rebecca's shoulder for support. They heard a shout of, "Hurry, go!" from one of the kids on the other side of the RV, and then a thud as the third child hit the ground. They heard the creaking of the RV door opening as they rounded the end of the camper.

Looking up to her right, Sara saw the six-foot antennae that protruded from the centipede's head flicking back and forth down the end of the RV. Then they disappeared from sight as it patrolled the RV's hood some more.

They rounded the corner. "Hurry, come on, before it comes back down," Rebecca pleaded. Sara yelped as she started to hop along even faster. They saw another child, a girl, look at them just before she entered the RV. Then the 'pede slinked off the roof onto the ground, a few feet on the other side of the door. Sensing prey, it turned its head toward them while twitching its antennae. The two women continued to hop-skip-run the remaining distance to the entrance. The creature sprung at them, hopping with the power of however many legs were in contact with the ground.

They reached the door and Rebecca had no choice but to shove Sara inside, pitching her headlong into the safety of the enclosed structure. Then she flung the door out so that it was between her and the arthropod, just as its mouth shot out toward her head. She heard the impact of the centi-head smacking against the RV door. The door smashed into Rebecca's body, knocking her inside the RV.

"Close it, close it!" she yelled to the kids, since they were the only ones still on their feet.

The pudgy boy, after a stunned second, reached out, grabbed the door handle and pulled the door all the way until it clicked shut.

They heard rasping sounds as the creature slid off the door.

CHAPTER 8

With the commotion outside that they had escaped, it took a minute to process the fact that inside the trailer was a bad smell. Sara had managed to pull herself up onto a couch and was still breathing heavily from her ordeal, looking around. The three kids, two girls and a boy, were seated on the opposite side couch, watching the adults while sharing a bag of potato chips.

Rebecca glanced around the RV. To her right was the cab, cluttered with abundant evidence of road and camp life—empty water and juice containers, fast food wrappers, sunglasses, a jacket, a Florida guidebook. To her left was a closed door that no doubt led to the bunk area and bathroom. She addressed the children.

"Where are your parents?"

All three kids suddenly became silent save for the munching of chips as they stared back at Rebecca.

"Your parents? Where are they?" she repeated.

The boy pointed to the left. "In there, sleeping."

Rebecca and Sara exchanged concerned looks. Rebecca turned back to the boy. "They didn't hear all this commotion?"

Blank stares in return. Rebecca stood and walked slowly toward the closed interior door. "Do you mind if I have a look? This is a dangerous situation and I don't want to leave you unattended."

The kids just shrugged noncommittally.

"Check it out," Sara said. Rebecca nodded and walked the rest of the way to the door. She rapped on it forcefully a few times in succession, but heard nothing in response. She turned the doorknob but found it locked from the inside. She turned back to the kids.

"It's locked. Do you know where the key is?"

Before anyone could answer, a strong impact jolted the side of the RV, causing it to sway side-to-side before coming to rest again.

"I think our friend's back," Sara said from the sofa. She unclipped the radio from her belt. "I better call for assistance."

"The key's on a hook in the front, behind the driver seat," the boy said timidly.

"Thank you." Rebecca strode over to the cab and found a row of four hooks, each with a key or set of keys on them. "Which one is it?"

"The one with only one key," the boy said. Rebecca snatched it off the hook and as she turned around to walk back into the RV, she saw the head of the centipede loom large in the windshield. Stunned as she was, as a professor of zoology she couldn't help but drink in the details of its anatomy—the antennae, the compound eyes, the segmented legs, the way it moved....

...and then its head was tilting forward and the windshield glass cracking, shattering, pelting Rebecca's face and hair with forcefully ejected shards. She turned and ran just as the scaly tip of an antennae brushed against her blood-spotted cheek.

"Door, close the cab door! Slide it across!" one of the girls shouted. Rebecca stopped, turned around and saw there was a sliding door tucked into a frame just behind the cab entrance. She slid her finger into the latch and pulled the door across, severing a section of antennae as it met the opposite wall.

"Ewwwww!" one of the girls screamed as the chunky piece of centipede landed on the floor. The sound of rasping appendages searching for purchase along the smooth door surface assailed their ears.

"I've got the key. Everybody to the back," Rebecca said, running down the bowling alley-like space toward the locked rear door. The kids mobilized immediately but Sara was slow to start running, her ankle still in pain.

"Ranger, you need help?" Rebecca asked as she reached her. She extended a hand without waiting for an answer and Sara took it. As soon as the ranger had gained her footing, the first crack appeared in the cab door. Through it was visible the black, compound eye of the 'pede.

"Come on, we've got to move!" Rebecca didn't wait for an answer, but instead bolted down the rest of the RV to the door at the end, where the trio of children waited, looking at her expectantly. She put the key into the door and turned it, felt it give. She pushed the door open at the same time as the cab door splintered apart with a loud crack.

All of them looked to see the gargantuan millipede head protruding into the main body of the RV, its antennae—one now much shorter than the other—waving frantically as it sought information about its new environs. It swung its head back and forth at the same time as it crept forward on innumerable legs.

"Inside, come on!" Rebecca was facing the kids and gawking at the ridiculously oversized centipede as she said it, so when she turned around after taking a couple of steps into the room, she was wholly unprepared for what she saw, not to mention smelled.

The stench of vomit pervaded the bedroom. On the bed, a man was sprawled out on his back, and snoring loudly. Empty beer cans and liquor bottles occupied the shelf above the bed, along with a couple of ashtrays filled with cigarette butts. A woman lay on the floor, tangled in bedsheets. Her face was stained from a bloody nose. Her eyes watched Rebecca as she entered but she said nothing.

Behind them, the kids screamed and then Rebecca felt the bustling of little bodies against hers as they sought to move away from the thrashing centipede making its way down the RV. Sara pulled a curtain rod off the window and used it to throw like a spear at the centipede's head just before she herded the children into the bedroom and closed the door.

"This door is not going to keep us safe for long," Sara announced before falling silent after comprehending the domestic squalor they had run into. She looked to Rebecca, who shook her head and said in a low voice. "We don't need to get in the middle of this now. Did you have any luck with the radio?"

Sara stared down at the radio in her hand and shook her head. "Not getting a response. Probably doesn't help being inside here."

"We're going to need to get outside now, anyway." No sooner did she complete her sentence than a large impact shook the RV from the wall opposite the door. Then, seconds later, the door to the bedroom buckled inward, a slight crack appearing down its full length.

"What's doing that from the outside?" one of the kids asked.

Before anyone could answer, the unconscious man made a choking noise and then started to vomit. Still lying on his back, a dark green bile bubble erupted out of his mouth and oozed out of his face. He started to choke and gasp, but still remained on his back. Sara jumped onto the bed and flipped him over onto his side so that he would not choke on his own vomit.

"What's been going on in here?" she asked the kids.

"Never mind what's been going on in here for now," Rebecca said. "It's what's going on out there that we need to worry about." As if to underscore her words, the entire bedroom shook again from an unseen external impact. A framed photo of the Grand Canyon fell from the wall. The hungover man moaned. The kids screamed. The woman sat up on the floor. Meanwhile, the door to the bedroom continued to disintegrate. Various centipede appendages poked briefly into the edge of the room before retreating.

Sara pointed up to the ceiling, where there was a skylight, currently closed. "Does that open?" she asked the battered couple.

"Yeah," the woman croaked in return without attempting to move from her sitting position on the floor, despite the RV threatening to shake apart. She didn't even ask what was causing the damage.

Noting the skylight was positioned directly over the bed, Sara said to Rebecca, "Can you help me move him out of the way?" The sick man still dry-heaved, now laying on his side.

"What's his name?" Sara asked the woman, who at least appeared to be following the conversation.

"Lonnie. I'm Luanne."

Sara nodded. "Thanks, Luanne. We need to move Lonnie over so that we can get to the skylight."

Another tremendous impact shook the bedroom, and this time, the rear wall bowed inward and stayed that way.

"Lonnie, get your dumb ass up!" Luanne bellowed with surprising volume.

"Shut up, bitch! When you goin' to the store?"

Luanne responded with open bitterness and frustration in her voice. "Lonnie, ain't none of us are gonna live long enough to need to go to the store if we don't do something about whatever the hell it is that's bustin' up our RV! Do you hear me? Now these nice people, including a park ranger, here, are trying to help us out, so do what they say and roll your dumb ass over so we can get to the skylight!"

With a grunt that transitioned into a prolonged belch, Lonnie rolled over once, and then once more before coming to rest on his belly on the edge of the bed. Immediately, Luanne stood, climbed onto the bed, stepped over the reclining man and moved to the middle of the bed beneath the skylight.

"I told you Lonnie, we needed to grease this summbitch, did you ever do it?"

A belch in response

"That's what I thought."

"Suck it!"

They were the first words any of them had heard out of his mouth since they'd been in the bedroom. No one said anything for a few seconds until another of the walls sustained a massive bashing, bowing it inwards.

"We've all got to get out. Come on!" Sara yelled. Luanne jumped onto the bed, stepped over Lonnie and reached up and unlatched the skylight. "Gonna need a boost."

"I got you." Sara got up onto the bed and moved into position next to Luanne. She interlocked her fingers together and Luanne put her sneakered foot into them. She pushed up until she could open the skylight hatch all the way back. Then she put her arm up through the opening onto the roof of the RV and pulled herself up and out.

A couple of seconds passed before they heard her call out, "Holy sheeeeeiiit!"

"If there's a sixer of PBR up there, it's mine!" Lonnie croaked.

"Yeah, tell that to this fuckin' monster!" she came back with.

"Where is it?" Sara yelled up over the commotion of the door being wrecked behind them. There was no doubt as to where the second 'pede was, mere feet away on the other side of the thin door and walls.

"It's on the ground out here but it can reach its head up to the roof!"

At that moment the door caved in and about half of the head of the centipede already inside the RV jutted into the room, almost to the foot of the bed. Rebecca had to jump out of the way to avoid being hit by it.

"Let's get up there, come on!" Sara screamed. She jumped up on the bed and stood below the open skylight. "Hand me up that chair," she said, pointing to a plastic chair in front of a tiny desk in the corner. Lonnie picked it up and gave it to her, suddenly roused into action by the appearance of the monster. Sara stood on the chair without waiting for anyone to steady it and pulled herself up through the skylight onto the RV's roof. Rebecca followed and lastly, Lonnie managed to haul himself up.

The four of them stood on the RV's roof and surveyed their surroundings. Desolation reigned, with no one else around except for the marauding centipede circling the RV, with another now inside the vehicle below them. It shook the entire RV with its rumbling.

"What's our plan?" Rebecca wanted to know.

In response, Sara raised her walkie-talkie to her lips. "Unit 33 to Dispatch, requesting urgent immediate assistance, do you copy, over?"

If there was a response, it was overpowered by the crunching of fiberglass and wood as the megapede outside and below repeatedly bashed its Yugo-sized head into the RV. Sara thought she heard the static-ridden beginning of a radio reply when the impact pitched her forward and almost over the edge of the roof. She landed on all fours, with her hands gripping the edge while she stared down at the marauding arthropod. With a sick realization of failure and dread, she watched as the walkie-talkie bounced off the beast's head and landed on the ground somewhere under the RV.

"Don't try and get it!" Rebecca cautioned.

"Not going to," Sara replied. She pushed herself up and away from the edge but remained sitting for stability while the RV still rocked. "But we have to get out of here. The two of them are bashing this thing apart from inside and out!"

Indeed, the RV was undergoing a dual assault from outside and inside as the external walls were repeatedly rocked at the same time as the inner structure was being subjected to untold destruction by the centipede in there.

"We could make a run for your truck," Rebecca suggested to Sara.

"How far is that?" Luanne peered around the campsite at the bog behind them and the line of trees bordering a lonely stretch of black top in front of them.

"Too far," Sara summarized. "Not doing that."

The RV shook again, this time with enough force to knock all of them off their feet. A tearing, ripping noise was heard that lasted for a few seconds, and then the various appendages of the second centipede were visible beyond the edge of the RV. Rebecca checked for the second centipede and sure enough—there it was. That could mean only one thing.

"The second centipede fell through the floor of the RV!" she told the others.

Sara pointed down at the ground close by the big vehicle. "Yes, I see it—it's on the ground!"

The others crowded along the side of the roof to get a look at it, as if to see for themselves that there really were two mega-pedes on the loose. As they gathered, the 'pede that had just fallen out of the RV rippled along the ground on spindly appendages away from the vehicle toward the other colossal segmented beast.

"I've got an idea!" Sara yelled.

CHAPTER 9

"Does the RV run?" Rebecca asked Luanne and Lonnie as they huddled together as a group, now on their feet, on the roof of the battered recreational vehicle.

Lonnie nodded. "Hell yeah. Engine's good as gold. Can't say much for the rest of it." He nodded down through the skylight, referencing the destruction that must have happened below when the centipede fell through the floor. "We'll have to make sure we have ground clearance from the flooring that fell through, and that the tires are still good. But the engine won't let us down."

"Unlike you," Luanne jabbed.

"Let's stay on track here," Rebecca said, her eyes resolute. Sara's plan was a good one. "Why walk when you can ride, right?" she said, voicing her enthusiasm for the plan after finding out the engine was in operational condition. Given the state of the vehicle's owners, that wasn't something she would have placed a whole lot of faith in.

When both centipedes were perhaps twenty feet away from the RV, and beginning to entwine with each other, the humans filed back down through the skylight into the RV, with Sara leading the way, then the kids, followed by the RV's troubled owners. Lastly, Rebecca followed suit after a final spot check on the oversized centipedes.

"They're still about in the same place they were before, doing some kind of dance."

"Great, looks like they're mating, more on the way," Sara speculated.

"Let's hope not," Rebecca called. "I'm coming down. How's the floor down there?"

"Bedroom's fine, but the hallway leading to the cab is gone completely. Can't see the cab from here." Rebecca dropped down through the skylight, where the others had left a space for her. She could see now that making their way up to the cab would not be easy. The entire floor was missing save for one or two small isolated sections at least halfway to the cab.

"Tell you what," This from Lonnie, whose raspy voice belied his two-pack a day cigarette habit, "there's room for two up front. I'll run up there—along the ground, fast—jump in the cab and start it."

"Keys?" Rebecca asked.

"In the ignition," Lonnie said, before continuing. "So I drive, and one of you comes with me to tell me where to go to get to your truck. Everybody else stays back here."

A beat of silence passed while they thought about this. Rebecca and Sara made eye contact. "I'll go up front with him," Sara said. "You stay here." Rebecca gave no argument.

"Let's get this shit show on the road!" With that, Lonnie jumped down out of the bedroom to the grassy ground, the two walls of the camper still on either side with the roof overhead, like a tunnel. As his feet trammeled across the earth toward the RV's cab, Rebecca watched the centipedes outside through the bedroom window.

"They're turning around!" she said, tension evident in her voice. "They sense the vibrations! Hurry, Sara, go!"

Sara launched herself after Lonnie. As a young, fit and sober person, she was quite a bit faster than Lonnie and easily caught up to him before he reached the cab. "Keep going," she told him. "We're almost there."

"That's what she said!" Lonnie joked as he reached the cab. Being on the ground, it was a big leap up to reach the intact floorboard of the cab. Lonnie managed to perform a standing jump that took him high enough to perch both elbows up onto the floor of the cab. She didn't relish it, but Sara bear-hugged his jeans-clad lower legs and pushed him upwards until he was able to crawl onto the cab's floor. She then jumped high enough herself to pull up unassisted.

The two of them took quick stock of the cockpit. Still littered with fast-food wrappers and open soda and beer cans, it appeared well travelled and yet functional. Sara took the passenger seat but did not put her seatbelt on, preferring to be able to exit quickly should it come to that. Lonnie took up position behind the wheel, pulled the key down from the visor, and turned the ignition over without fanfare.

Sara pointed through the windshield. "Head out there and then take a right onto the road."

"You got it. Hold on back there!" Lonnie stepped on the accelerator while turning the wheel and the RV lurched into motion.

"They're coming towards us," came Rebecca's cry from the bedroom.

"They can suck my tailpipe!" Lonnie growled as he pressed harder on the gas. The big RV rumbled and bounced over the uneven ground toward the road. They had nearly made it across the campsite when they heard the children screaming in the back, and then multiple legs clacked onto the upper right portion of the windshield. Sara retracted in horror. Realizing her window was still open, she pressed the switch to roll it up.

It was almost shut when the tip of two legs protruded inside. As they were chopped off by the window closing into the frame, the two body parts dropped onto Sara's arm, still twitching and jumping though severed from their body.

She was embarrassed to let out a little shriek of horror as she brushed the leg tips down into the foot well. But no one heard it, for Lonnie was preoccupied with driving the RV while one of the big 'pedes blocked nearly the entire windshield with its body. He had to stick his head out of his still unrolled window to see anything in order to drive.

"Make a right out on the road!" Sara yelled.

"Hold on, we don't wanna take this thing with us, right? Watch this."

Lonnie suddenly stomped on the gas and the RV lurched forward, accelerating sharply. When he reached the road a few seconds later, he shouted, "Brace yourself!" and then slammed on the brakes. The centipede that clung to the front of the RV, blocking the windshield, was flung off into the thick foliage on the other side of the road. It quickly disappeared into the vegetation.

"Everybody okay back there?" Sara called back.

Rebecca's reply came from the rear of the RV. "Only one of us is still in the bedroom now, but I don't think any bones broke."

"How much farther up is your ride?" Lonnie asked Sara. She pointed off to the right. "It's right behind that clump of trees there."

"A little farther then." Lonnie prepared to put the big vehicle back into gear.

"Everybody get back up in the bedroom!" Sara yelled back. "We've got a little farther to go and there's at least one of the centipedes still in fighting condition!"

A commotion ensued at the rear of the RV while the three kids, Rebecca and Luanne clamored back up into the bedroom and took more fortified positions.

"All set!" Rebecca yelled up front. But Sara pointed ahead of them, where the long, raised form of a massive centipede crawled across the road in front of the RV. Before she could say anything, Lonnie floored the accelerator and aimed the front of the vehicle at the body of the trundling 'pede.

"I got this! Ya'll just hold on. I'm gonna take his ass out!"

Scanning the roadside vegetation, Sara was relieved to see no signs of the other centipede. At least there was only one to beat. She white-knuckled the hand rest and braced her feet against the footwell while the RV picked up speed. If the massive arthropod sensed anything was headed its way, it showed no concern. It continued to slowly trundle across the road as if it had all the time in the world, its many legs pitter-pattering across the ground like a precision machine.

Lonnie muttered unintelligible curses while he maneuvered the big vehicle across the uneven ground toward the ginormous 'pede. As they neared the strange creature, it stopped in its tracks, antennae curled eight feet skyward, frozen in place. Any hopes they had of simply driving over the beast were quashed as its mega-body filled the windshield. It was at least as tall as the RV itself, if not a little taller. No way they could drive over it.

"The body—" Lonnie was saying to Sara, now. It took her a few seconds to register that he was no longer talking to himself, but was asking her for information. "Is it hard like a lobster or soft like a caterpillar—can we drive through it?"

Sara's mind flashed on what she recalled of centipede anatomy. It wasn't enough to say for sure. She was a ranger, more of a naturalist, an ecologist who knows about how the overall ecosystem works as opposed to a zoologist who studied the details of individual animals.

"Dr. Trout back there is the one to ask." She turned around to shout but Lonnie said, "I got this," before pressing a button on the dash. "Intercom." He spoke into a microphone on the dash: "Yo Luanne, show the Doctor back there where the intercom button is. We need to know if we can drive through this centipede or if it has a hard shell."

A couple of seconds later, during which the RV continued barreling toward the megapede, Rebecca replied. "Hard exoskeleton shell. Maybe we'll crush through it, maybe not."

"Great!" Lonnie seemed to take this as good news. He stomped even harder on the gas pedal, sending the recreational vehicle surging forward even faster. The beastly arthropod stopped moving and turned its gargantuan head toward the oncoming vehicle. Lonnie T-boned the creature with his foot still on the gas. Fortunately for them, as the creature turned its head, a gap opened between the plated segments which meant that rather than bearing the full brunt of the impact, the RV penetrated past the animal's armored plating. This extra travel distance reduced the forces on the passengers as the RV slowed drastically within a few milliseconds.

Lonnie smashed into the steering wheel and the airbag deployed, throwing him back against the seat headrest.

Meanwhile the centipede was cut in half, the windshield and windows offering a reddish-brown kaleidoscope of arthropod gore as the vehicle hurtled through the dismembered being. Somehow, through it all, Lonnie kept driving. Never even took his foot off the gas, just clawed frantically with his hands to rip aside the airbag until he could see enough to drive.

But by then it was too late.

"My truck!" Sara was screaming. "Look out!"

And then they experienced another impact, this one metal on metal, glass on glass, as the RV crashed into the parked pickup truck, devastating the driver's side cab, crumpling the metal into the seat, triggering the airbag of the pickup and finally tipping the truck up onto its side.

The RV continued past it, Lonnie somehow able to steer it onto a dirt road that crested a swampy hillock before leading deeper into the seemingly endless expanse of wet grass. A field of tall, reed-like shoots emerged from shallow water for as far as the eye could see, with only a narrow crest of dirt serving as a roadway through it all. To the practiced eye, patches of low, dry ground were visible here and there, dotting the wet landscape, but to most people it was simply a never-ending field of wet grass.

"Stay on the trail!" Sara shouted, unsure of how familiar Lonnie was with the Everglades. He could be a South Florida local who camped frequently in the 'glades, or he could be a tourist from Alabama here visiting for the first time. She could not afford to take chances by assuming what he knew or didn't know about her workplace. But at least his words were reassuring.

"I see it, I'm on it," he said through gritted teeth while two-handing the wheel this way and that to bump along the raised dirt trail. It was mostly straight but would occasionally jog left or right before resuming its former course.

"Slow down!" Sara trilled, as the top of her head slammed into the ceiling.

"Working on it!"

They jolted over a depression in the trail and the front right tire rolled off the dirt into the bog. Instantly they felt the vehicle slow, and they were pitched sharply forward. Lonnie gunned the engine and the RV's momentum was sufficient to carry them back onto the precious sliver of dry land.

"Just slow down and stop when you can!" Sara said.

Lonnie didn't reply, but began applying the brakes. Before the road jogged left again, he was able to coax the big roller to a stop. He studied his rear view mirrors. "I don't see any of those damn things. Let's take a look." He opened the door while Sara turned around and looked to the back of the RV. She couldn't see any of the others.

"Hey, how is everybody doing?"

"What happened?" Rebecca appeared in the bedroom doorway and jumped down to the ground where the RV's missing floor used to be.

"We just stopped when we got far enough away from the centipedes," Sara shouted back.

"Where are we?" Rebecca looked apprehensively off to her left, through a window.

"Middle of fuckin' nowhere, that's where." This from Lonnie, who now stood outside next to the RV's cab. "Whole lotta grass as far as forever. Behind us, the woods where the centipedes are."

"There's a small building way in the distance," Sara said, as the kids and Rebecca filed out of the RV's side door.

"Can we get help there?" Rebecca asked.

"No, I think it's just an unmanned weather substation or something like that."

The group convened in front of the RV. After a quick look around, they discussed their options, with Lonnie expressing himself first. "There's no way to turn this thing around, road's too narrow. And backing up all the way we came would be a bitch. Take forever. So is there anywhere we can get to by continuing ahead on this road? We got gas."

Sara furrowed her brow as she stared out across the sea of sawgrass, past the lone block cement structure in the distance. "I honestly don't know. This is not a normal part of the park or my patrols. I'd say it goes at least to the utility building, beyond that, I don't know. It could go all the way across to Flamingo, where there's a small town."

"I say we go for it," Lonnie said. "Any objections?"

CHAPTER 10

Coral Gables Police Station

Detective Rene Bravia dropped his desk phone into the cradle with a sigh and a shake of the head. He'd just gotten off the phone with Dr. Landis' ex-wife. He had broken the news of her ex-husband's death to her, without citing too many specifics, in case she was somehow involved, which he doubted. Her response was typical for an ex-spouse who hadn't been married to the person of interest for many years. "I hadn't heard. What's this got to do with me?"

Bravia explained that Landis was found dead in his home of apparent suicide. At this she expressed some mild sorrow but still remained mostly unemotional. They hadn't spoken or had anything to do with each other in over a decade, she said, not even staying in touch over social media once their son turned eighteen, some eight years ago.

Bravia had called the son as well, which, while a much more emotional call, had offered the same dearth of information relating to the case. He seemed to have no knowledge of his father's specific work, knowing only that he was a university professor specializing in biology. He claimed to know nothing of his work with BioGen. He was in Seattle, as Alvarado had told him, himself a university student majoring in music. So much for like father, like son, Bravia thought. So where did that leave him in terms of exhausting all known contacts of the deceased?

*BioGen...BioGen...*Bravia rubbed his temples as he thought about the company and the emails he'd read from Landis' hard drive. *What about that lady professor, what's her name, Landis' colleague, Trout?* She'd offered to help make sense of that weird BioGen file he had.

He dialed Rebecca's number, hoping to give her a gentle reminder that she'd offered to help, but it went straight to voicemail. Now what? He supposed he could call BioGen and ask to speak to one of the contacts mentioned in the emails. But he'd sure like to hear what those files had to do with from Dr. Trout before he made that call, since if there was anything less than above-board going on, it would put them on edge.

Lt. Bravia drummed his fingers on the desk as he thought about his next move. He could just wrap the case right now, he knew. In all probability, it was a suicide. A strange one, yes, given the weapon used and the decedents' line of work, but a self-inflicted death, nonetheless. On the other hand, it was no big deal to wait on one more contact—Dr. Trout—to see what she said about Landis' files. That settled, Bravia took a deep breath and tried Rebecca's cell number one more time.

CHAPTER 11

Everglades National Park

Rebecca frowned as she glanced at the display on her cell-phone which told her she was currently in an area with no service. *Zero bars, dang it.* Not that she really expected otherwise. She didn't spend nearly as much time out here as the park rangers did, but still, being a South Florida resident and a zoologist to boot, she'd had quite a few occasions over the years to visit, and she knew that much of the park was out of normal cell service zones.

"Can we go any faster?" one of the kids yelled up to the front. After surveying the wilderness for signs of more centipedes, and declaring the way forward clear for now, they'd piled back into the damaged RV and struck out on the narrow dirt road that bisected the immense sawgrass swamp. Only the squat concrete building in the distance broke up the vast wilderness. The going was bumpy, making it difficult to read her phone, but when Lonnie had to stop to clear a fallen log out of the path, she'd had the chance. Now back behind the wheel with Sara in the shotgun seat, the RV lurched forward again.

"Hold onto your asses!" was Lonnie's reply, to which Luanne shot him a silent middle finger from her place on the bed. They could see the blades of grass whipping by in the space between the bedroom and cab, where the floor was missing. One time a small bird, startled out of its resting place nestled in the grass, flew up to avoid the moving RV, but found itself trapped under the roof and between the walls. The kids screamed while it dashed around, smacking into the sides, then darting back to the bedroom where it hit the roof and fell onto the bed. Rebecca swaddled it in blankets and held it. "Its wings aren't broken, it'll be okay. Next time we stop, I'll let it out the window."

They drove on at the slow, sedate pace the dirt track demanded. Bottled water and bags of chips were shared with the kids while Rebecca did her best to keep their mind off of the situation by caring for the bird. After a time they felt the RV start to slow and then lurch to a bumpy, rough stop.

"What happened?" Rebecca called up.

"Obstacle. Gonna be a while. Everybody can hop out to stretch."

Rebecca, Luanne and the kids jumped off the bed and filed along the ground between the RV's walls until they reached the door. Luanne opened it and they stepped out onto the sliver of solid ground before the terrain gave way to pure swamp on either side of the RV. Sara and Lonnie exited from the vehicle and the two groups met right in front of the cab, where the problem was evident.

Ahead of them, the roadway was washed out for about a ten-foot section, creating a watery gap they needed to somehow ford to continue along the road. Lonnie stood on the very edge of the water, staring down into it, trying to gauge its depth.

"I don't reckon we try to just roll through that," he concluded. "We'll bog down in that muck."

"Agreed," Sara said. "Do we have any boards or logs we can use to build a bridge across?"

"Not from the environment here." Rebecca cast a doubtful eye around at the flat, grassy, wet landscape. "It would have to come from inside the RV. Do you have a firewood supply, maybe?"

Lonnie chuckled in response. "We have a few pint-sized logs, yeah, but that ain't gonna do it." He stared at the RV while stroking the stubble on his chin as if in deep thought for a moment before continuing. "Tell you what, though. This thing is shot as it is. It's got no floor, and we're okay, right? What do we need the walls for?"

At this he grinned and then cackled like a madman as he walked to the door in the main body of the RV and then entered the damaged vehicle. Outside, the group could hear Lonnie rummaging around inside, opening and closing cupboards, stomping around and cursing, until he said, "All ya'll stand clear of the sides!"

With that, the sound of a hammer smashing through the RV's siding commenced. A series of well-placed blows cleared a large hole in the right side of the vehicle, and then Lonnie was able to rip away the rest of the vinyl siding in one large rectangular piece.

"Help me drag this over to the gap."

The three women helped Lonnie to drag the unwieldy piece of material over to the front of the RV. Once there, they were pleased to see that it did indeed just barely stretch all the way across to the other side where solid road picked up again.

"Now for the other section," Lonnie said, as he trotted back into the RV, now completely open on one side. He repeated the process as before, with another flurry of hammer blows soon raining down again. When he had a sufficient opening, he ripped away the siding until it came loose in one long rectangular piece as before.

"Hopefully this'll do it," Lonnie said, dragging the additional material around to the front of the RV with the help of Rebecca and Luanne. "I might be able to get a little more of it, but not as big as these two."

"I think it might work if we just lay it on top of the other one," Sara said. She stood on the edge of the watery obstacle, staring into the water as it washed over the first piece of siding. "It's not that deep, we just need to keep the wheels from sinking into the mud, and these should hopefully do that."

She grabbed hold of one end of the new piece and together, the four of them pulled it into position, placing it on top of its twin. "It looks good but we should test it. Who wants to walk across? Because if we can't walk across it, we're sure as heck not going to be able to drive across it."

Silence ensued from the group, followed by nervous laughter.

"I'm serious," Sara pressed. "If it won't support a person's weight, how's it going to support the RV?"

"She's right," Lonnie voiced. "Only the driver should be in the RV when it goes across, anyway. Lighten the load as much as possible. Everyone else should walk across."

"I'll drive, then," Luanne said.

"I drive." Lonnie was resolute, as if stating an incontrovertible fact.

"Cuz you don't know how to swim," Luanne sneered.

"Bitch, you listen here—"

"Hey!" Rebecca's voice was sharp enough to stop both of them. "Settle down! There are children here! Your children! What's the matter with you!"

This seemed to calm them both down enough to proceed with a rational conversation, so she continued before things could get out of hand. "Just let Lonnie drive. He's been doing a fine job of that so far, no reason to change it up now."

"The driving is risky, too," Sara pointed out. "If the siding doesn't hold up, the RV and it tips over sideways, you could get trapped..."

"Great, let the bastard drive!" Luanne spat.

Lonnie glared at her along with a menacing lip snarl, but said nothing as he climbed into the RV's cab and got behind the wheel. "Ya'll get across and I'll meet you over there."

Sara addressed the remaining group outside the RV. "Since this was my idea, I guess I'll go first." There were no arguments, so she stepped up to the edge of the brackish water, where the white vinyl siding sloped underwater, still highly visible beneath up to four feet of water at the deepest point. She silently hoped that it was resting on the bottom at that deepest point, otherwise this gap could be impassible for the RV.

She lamented the fact that she was not geared up for water work, wearing normal hiking boots rather than hip waders, with jeans. But she had no choice about that, and so she stepped onto the RV siding in the water. It made for a slippery surface, and she waved her arms around in an attempt to balance as she adjusted to the odd footing. Step by careful step, she eased herself deeper into the water as she descended the ramp of siding. So far it was reasonably stable, with the material easily supporting her weight. When she reached the deepest portion of the span, the water was up to her chest. She jumped up and down lightly a couple of times to test the stability of the platform—it wouldn't be able to stand up to the RV, after all, if it couldn't take this—and was pleased to feel ungiving bottom beneath the siding. She continued, walking up the vinyl slope now, slipping a couple of times, and dunking her head once, but ultimately making it to the other side of the road bank. She staggered out of the water and turned around to face the group, giving them a thumbs up.

"I think the RV will make it. Who's next?"

Rebecca spoke up. "How about if I go next, and then the kids go as a group. Luanne follows up after them."

Everyone agreed and Rebecca waded across the water to the road on the other side, standing beside Sara while she did her best to squeeze the water from her clothes. "At least it's not cold," she offered those still waiting to cross.

Luanne rounded up the three kids and held the two younger ones, the girls, each by a hand, while she had the boy walk immediately ahead of her so that she could grab him if necessary. This crossing was more difficult and took longer than the others. While they made their way, Rebecca scanned the surroundings for any signs of human activity—a plane, an airboat, anything that would signal the presence of someone in a position to offer them assistance. The sky was clear, so she turned her attention to the sawgrass swamp, slowly turning her head from west to east. She was about to look back to the progress of Luanne and the kids crossing the gap when a ripple of water caught her attention.

It was small, not like a wave, but the fact there was currently no wind whatsoever made her look twice, since a disturbance like that could indicate the presence of an animal in the water. She pulled on her polarized sunglasses, which sometimes helped her to see below the water's surface. *There*! She caught sight of a dark form moving fast toward the RV from the marsh off to the right.

What's that? Kind of big, whatever it is. Could the centipedes be back? But as she observed the disturbance some more, it became apparent to her that the movement was all wrong for it to be one of the megapedes. This creature, whatever it was, moved in a straight line, not a sinusoidal

S-curve type of motion. Which ruled out a giant snake as well, Sara thought. She glanced quickly back over to the water gap to check on their progress. They were almost there, and she didn't see signs of creatures in that direction.

She whipped her head around to look back at the aquatic anomaly. Same ripple, still there, slowly spreading outward in two directions. *Alligator or croc?* She pondered the possibility while staring at the moving wake. She couldn't rule it out. Alligators also had sort of an S-type of locomotion, though. She watched the water intently while the first of the kids reached the edge of the other side of the road and took Lonnie's hand.

She decided that the ripple was caused by a very large 'gator, if that's in fact what it was. It could perhaps be a crocodile, she thought. She was pretty sure it wasn't a giant centipede, though. She'd take a big gator over that any day. She recalled the old saying she knew that doctors sometimes used: "If you hear hoofbeats, think horses, not zebras," or something like that. In other words, chances are it's the more obvious thing.

Alligator, she told herself. Maybe a croc. She turned back around to the road in time to see Rebecca and the other two children climbing out onto the strip of dry land. When she turned back around, her heart stopped.

Her brain was flooded with attempts at categorization, and yet she did her best to shove these aside as she simply gawked in disbelief at the monstrous creature now reared up in the swamp by the road. The sheer size of it was disconcerting, yes, but more than that, whatever *it* was--some kind of lizard, she supposed--was even more alarming. Once she temporarily ignored the fact that this animal's tail looked to be about forty feet away from the head, she was able to focus her attention on the head, which made absolutely no sense to her whatsoever.

She felt dizzy just looking at it, like it was somehow shattering her very perception of reality, for the head was that of a dinosaur. Not in a crocodiles-are-living-dinosaurs kind of way, either, but an actual iconoclastic dinosaur...a *T. rex* head on the body of a crocodile or alligator. The forelegs were extremely stout, thick as hardwood tree trunks, propping the front end of the beast up above the water and reeds. Forty feet away, the tail swished back and forth above the water.

And yet even this wasn't the most arresting aspect of the spectacle, for in the mouth of the obvious predator squirmed and writhed one of the centipedes that had tormented them so, now a victim in its own right. As Sara watched, the jaws of this croc-dinosaur hybrid clamped down hard on the megapede, severing its frantically wriggling body into two halves which dropped into the swamp. The T-rex' head reared back as it easily chugged down the log-sized piece of centipede trunk that it had chewed on. In the water, the two separated halves of the 'pede body flailed around mindlessly on their own, peppering the water with chaotic splashes.

At this, the rest of the group on the road turned toward the commotion and promptly began to scream and yell incoherently. It instantly dawned on Sara that Rebecca, Luanne and the three kids had nowhere to go, no shelter of any kind. Lonnie, meanwhile, honked the RV's horn, adding to the cacophony. Sara waved at him to stop. The noise wasn't helping anything. This monster of a dinosaur-croc was still preoccupied with eating the still-writhing centipede pieces, wolfing them down in agitated fury, and so Sara decided she better take advantage of that distraction now before it was too late.

Channeling her high school swim team days, Sara dove headfirst out into the middle of the gap over the white RV siding, knowing that as soon as she hit the water she'd be halfway across. Lonnie was waiting for her to take the RV across, and it made her nervous to be standing near the huge vehicle with Lonnie behind the wheel. What if he panicked at the sight of the monster and floored it without concern for her safety? It's not like she knew the guy, after all, and what she did know about him painted anything but a pretty picture.

She closed her eyes for the impact with the water but opened them soon after. She saw a flash of white—the RV siding—but did not hit it. She stayed underwater as long as possible, allowing the momentum of her dive to carry her slicing through the water, where she was not visible to the predator from above, and also reduced splashing which would attract predators. When her gliding slowed and she surfaced for a breath, she was pleased to see she was already almost to the other side of the road. She started windmilling her arms and kicking fast, sacrificing stealth for speed, knowing she didn't have far to go. The weird T-rex gator was still out in the swamp, gorging on the severed megapede.

When the ranger felt her hands come into contact with the spongy swamp bottom, she pushed to her feet and then grabbed Rebecca's outstretched hand. Once standing on solid ground again, Sara turned to look out to the water, where the odd beast continued to thrash about in about the same location, devouring its mega-meal. She looked back to the RV.

Lonnie revved the engine, signaling he was ready to go.

Sara figured now was the time, since there was no telling what the freakish predator would do once it finished with its food. She waved him on as the group backed up from the edge of the roadway. Lonnie stopped gunning the motor in neutral and let it die down to an idle before slipping it into forward gear.

"Come on Lonnie, you sonofabitch, you got this!" Luanne bellowed.

The driver of the RV stuck his head out the window and hollered back. "Be right there, sweetheart!" And with that, Lonnie rolled into the water onto the RV's former siding.

CHAPTER 12

The flurry of curse words erupting from Lonnie's mouth almost drowned out the revving of the RV's engine as he accelerated into the water. The front end of the vehicle landed on the siding, and immediately the entire RV canted left. He gunned the engine some more to try and gain stability and traction, but the result was to drive the vehicle deeper into the water, pressing the siding down into the mucky bottom. Looking through the windshield, he registered the looks of worry on Rebecca and Sara's faces, just before the amber tinted water washed over the glass.

Lonnie pulled the wheel to the right, but he no longer had any traction. He felt the RV being buoyed by the water, and even with the cab door closed, water started to flood in.

"How damn deep is it?" he shouted to no one in particular. He pressed on the gas pedal, hoping that sufficient speed would push him through. Yet all it served to do was barrel the cab deeper down into the siding. His windshield filled with white, and then a flurry of brown mud particles as the siding was pressed into the mud by the weight of the RV. Water started flooding into the cab through his open window and he realized the cab was tipping to the left.

"Goin' over!" he yelled before abandoning ship. He shimmied through the open window but the cab rolled over on him, pinning him to the wet ground. He was shocked to see that he had almost made it! The dry ground of the other side of the road was only five feet away, but it did him no good. He kicked his legs but felt the weight of the cab pressing down on him.

It wasn't a hard and fast crush due to the water taking most of the weight, but he still found himself pinned by its formidable mass. Making matters worse, he found that because he was lying on top of the smooth RV siding, that he was unable to get any purchase with his hands to try and pull himself away from the cab. His hands and fingers simply slid along the slippery surface. Fortunately, his head was barely above water, but to take a breath he had to turn his neck painfully at a certain angle.

And he knew that the RV could sink lower into the muck at any time.

"Help! Help me!" he screamed, realizing the dead-seriousness of his predicament.

Sara and Rebecca were first to rush to the cab, wading out into the shallow water, while Luanne remained on the road with the children, keeping an eye on the T-rex croc.

"Watch out," Sara told Rebecca, "the RV could still shift in the mud."

Rebecca knelt and took stock of Lonnie's situation. She tried not to let her face betray the sense of fear that enveloped her on seeing his circumstances. He was pinned from the waist down by the cab, his head barely above water. She planted her feet and took hold of his upper arms, more to see how tightly he was pinned than that she thought it would really work.

"Gonna try to pull. One, two, three…" She gritted her teeth and grunted with the effort, straining her muscles for all she was worth. Lonnie grimaced and moaned also, but to no avail. His body did not move an inch. The RV had already begun to settle into the muck atop the piece of plastic siding, pushing the siding itself into the muddy bottom. She looked at the man with a mixture of pity and resolve. He was in a very serious situation indeed, and try as she might she was unable to force from her mind a vision of him drowning as his head sunk below the mud.

"Please help!" he sputtered. "Get it off me! There's a jack in the back!"

Rebecca shook her head. "Ground is way too soft to use a jack, Lonnie." She shook her head silently as she considered how dire his situation was. Even if they had direct communications with the Coast Guard this very moment, she wasn't sure they would be able to save him in time. Would a helicopter even have enough lifting power to raise the recreational vehicle enough to allow the man to slip out unharmed? She didn't know, and worse than that, she knew it didn't matter because no such help was forthcoming. His fate depended on three women and three kids stranded in the middle of nowhere, with next to nothing outside of the RV that was lying on top of him.

Rebecca looked back down at the trapped man and the vehicle, the siding, the mud below that, the water. She was trying to think of something that at least might represent a solution enough to be worth trying when Sara's pleading voice dashed her thoughts to pieces.

"It's coming this way! The thing that ate the centipede! It's moving fast!"

"What?" It was so horrible she just had to get confirmation that's what she really said.

"It's coming this way!"

She couldn't put off this new reality any longer. She looked down at Lonnie whose face was now a mask of abject terror as his neck muscles cramped and his face went underwater. Rebecca reached down and pulled his head up, twisting it sharply, knowing it must hurt, but also still not reaching the water's surface. Finally, with a little more pressure, his mouth broke the surface and he gasped, inhaled, gulped air greedily.

A new sound grew louder: Splashing. Then Sara's voice again.

"Rebecca! It's almost to the RV!"

The zoologist looked down at the trapped man. "Deep breath, Lonnie. I'll be right back with something to help, just a second." She could see the protest wild in his eyes, but she left before he could reply.

She rose and walked around the front of the RV cab, and then she saw it.

The T-rex-croc hybrid, or whatever it was. It was swimming fast in a prone position, its strange dinosaur head protruding above the waterline. It moved straight toward the RV without hesitation, as if beelining in on the out-of-place object. On the continued section of road, Luanne had the children huddle on the far side of the land strip, hunkering down low so as not to be highly visible to the rampaging predator.

Rebecca ran up to Sara, who was pointing at the oncoming beast, not far from the RV. "Sara, he's pinned under there. I don't know what else to try. Can I have your belt? Maybe I can pull him out with that. Any other ideas? He's going under soon."

Without a word, Sara removed her leather belt and handed it to Rebecca. "I'll go with you."

The two women ran over to the fallen RV on the side where Lonnie was trapped.

"Oh my god, his head is underwater!" Sara screamed, but no sooner had she completed her sentence than his nearly bald dome of thin, wispy black hair broke the surface. He sputtered and croaked before going under again. Sara and Rebecca knelt in the muck by his side, and Rebecca pulled his head above water.

"We're going to try something with a belt to pull you out. It might hurt, but we've got to move fast."

He made meaningful eye contact with her and nodded ever so slightly.

While Rebecca slipped the belt underneath Lonnie's armpits and pulled it through, Sara went back around the front of the RV. The monster was right there, coming in fast towards them. Glancing left to the other section of road, Luanne and the kids were huddled low and nearly out of sight in the tall sawgrass on the edge of the roadway. *Good.* She ran back to Rebecca and Lonnie.

Rebecca looked up at her as she arrived. "Like ten more seconds and that weird thing is going to be here!" Sara spat.

"Not sure he has ten more seconds," Rebecca said, while Lonnie's head slipped underwater again. She nodded to the belt cinched through his armpits. "Take this end and help me pull!"

Sara took one end of the belt while Rebecca kept the other. "On three…" They jammed their feet deep into the mud and then pulled with all their might, straining their muscles and tendons to the breaking point. Just as Rebecca was convinced she was about to pass out from the effort and give up, a gurgly sucking sound ensued and Lonnie slipped a good eighteen inches out from under the RV. He was still stuck beneath it, but at least they had moved him. It was possible!

But their celebration was short-lived. "It's here!" Sara yelled, staring off to her left, where over the hood of the fallen RV was the most fearsome head on any animal she had ever seen. Rebecca turned to look, expecting to see a big alligator or something like that, and found herself wholly unprepared for the psychological impact the monstrosity had on her psyche.

What in God's name is that thing? What is *it? Is it real? Is it fake? Does it matter?* These thoughts drove around Rebecca's mind like a freight train, slow to turn and not very fast, but barreling with mass and momentum that simply could not be ignored. She forced herself to take one second longer to look at the animal—if that's what it even was—objectively, as a professional scientist. *Definitely reptilian…*But that was the extent of her surety, for the rest of it made no sense whatsoever to her. It had characteristics of both alligator—or was it crocodile?—and some sort of gargantuan dinosaur, like a T. rex or possibly an Allosaurus, she thought, shaking her head as she pictured the dinosaur textbooks she'd devoured as a child. She was not a paleontologist and did not specialize in dinosaurs or other prehistoric, extinct species as a zoologist.

The fact that it was so large meant that it was nearly impossible for it to be a previously undiscovered species. That was the troubling thing. Even hiding in the Everglades, it would have been sighted by now. So that left only one possibility she could think of at the moment, under extreme duress—that of some kind of genetic manipulation. Because it seriously looked as though someone had taken a T-rex head, bulked up the shoulders and forelegs of a crocodile and stuck the head on top. And somehow it was functional. She looked at it now, snapping back to the moment, the jaws of the head snapping viciously as it lunged forward in that S-shaped croc run. It'll be here in about five seconds, her brain told itself, a warning to disengage from the analytical thoughts.

As if to corroborate this intuition, the splashy footfalls of Sara backing away from the pinned Lonnie reached Rebecca's ears even before she started moving. The monster was about to be upon them. Rebecca turned and looked to the road, where Sara was heading. She put herself in motion, only to slip and fall face-first into the mud, face spiking on sawgrass painfully on the way down. Not allowing herself to wallow in pain, she jammed her arms into the soggy ground and forced herself to her feet.

Now she could hear the oddball megafauna that charged toward them. It made a wheezing, braying sound, extremely high-pitched, that seemed to come from deep within its body before being modulated by the mouth. She knew at this point that she needed to move away from Lonnie or she would likely be the target of this creature's aggression, whether it be for a meal or an attack out of fear or territory protection—it didn't much matter. She was utterly helpless against this creature.

And that's when she heard the first shot.

Sara—Ranger Cliff-- standing on the road, in the classic shooter's stance, feet shoulder-wide, service pistol in a two-handed grip. Rebecca heard the thud of the bullet smack into the leathery hide of the croc-rex, and yet if the creature noticed, it wasn't evident. Rebecca turned to look at Sara's gun. What was that little peashooter going to do to that gigantoid creature? It didn't even *annoy* it! Maybe if she scored a direct hit to the eyeball or in the open mouth to the throat? Short of that, she didn't see how it could help.

The monstrosity continued toward her at its same pace and course. Rebecca was about to dive into the water when she checked the impulse. *Don't do it! It'll get you!* Open water gave the animal far too many advantages over her—speed and lack of hiding places for starters. She would stick out like the sorest of thumbs. She eyed the tipped-over trailer and decided that the RV itself offered the best chance of shelter. She watched Lonnie as she ran away from him and the monster, continuing around behind the RV. Running along its side until she reached the open portion, she jumped inside the open space. She landed on the ground inside the RV with a wet thump, hoping it wouldn't cause the creature to investigate. But from the sounds of Lonnie's hopeless wailing as she ran toward the back of the RV, she didn't think so.

Rebecca walked as quickly as she dared while still remaining quiet toward the back of the RV. When she reached the bedroom, the only place save for the cab that still had four walls, a floor and a roof, she glanced left out toward the swamp. Nothing in sight save for a stump of dead centipede jutting up out of the sawgrass. She heaved herself up and into the bedroom, hoping that this flimsy shelter would be sufficient to save her life.

From her position on the bed she peered down the length of the ruined RV just in time to catch a glimpse of the croc-atrocity through the windshield, rounding the cab toward the side Lonnie was trapped on. Lonnie was making noise now, she didn't know what to call it—crying? Blubbering, choking, sobbing, sputtering, all at once. She thought she made out the word, "Help," but couldn't be sure. She was overwhelmed by a sense of helplessness in her inability to help the man, to help any of them, really.

But especially Lonnie.

#

Sara dared to poke her head above the sawgrass in order to get a peek towards the RV. The croc-beast was there, right where Lonnie was trapped. She didn't know what else she could do. She had fired a shot and hit the giant lizard, but it didn't seem like it had had any effect. She told herself to try again, that a man's life was at stake. But at the same time…what if the bullets drew the beast to her? Luanne and the kids were here. Could she afford to take that chance? She thought of that classic moral dilemma with the train tracks, where the participant is given the choice to take no action and let the train hit four people tied to the tracks, or divert the train to a parallel track where it will run over one person tied to the track. Deciding she could not allow harm to come to multiple people, she ducked back down into the grass and turned to Luanne.

"I need you to stay here with the kids, okay?"

"Where are you going?" Luanne hissed.

Sara held up her service firearm. "I'm going to try to take another shot at that thing to scare it away from Lonnie, but I don't want to risk drawing it over here to us."

Luanne screwed her face up in disbelief. "Lonnie? Screw that low-life bastard. Don't even waste another bullet on his sorry ass. He got what's coming to him if you ask anybody who knows him."

Sara shook her head and shrugged. "That may be, but it's my duty to try and save him. Stay put."

The ranger stayed low in the grass while she crept toward the front of the RV. Every few feet she raised her head enough to see the monster. On the third such check, Lonnie began emitting a blood-curdling screech, or howl, was more like it. A guttural yet pathetic sound that seemed to come from his entire body at once. Sara rose enough to see what was happening and felt a mini-bomb of adrenaline explode inside her. The T-rex creature was raising its massive head, and smashing it down on the trapped man like a hammer of doom. Over and over again, clubbing the man to death with its closed maw, while he lay pinned beneath the RV, the water level right up to his upturned face. He was utterly helpless, and Sara had never felt so sorry for anyone as she did for this man now in her entire life.

She rose and took aim with her gun. The head of the predator was almost sideways to her in a perfect profile, affording her a shot at the right eye. She knew that would be her best chance of deterring the attacker, so she held her breath as she had been trained at the shooting range, lined up her aim and slowly squeezed the trigger until it fired. For some reason the loudness of the blast jolted her, more than the first shot had. Perhaps it was the great concentration she had employed in order to take careful aim this time. If that was the case, it was worth it, for the round smacked dead center into the elongated lizard eye, clouding it on impact and sending a trickle of red blood sluicing down the reptile's ungodly face.

The animal squealed, a hideous braying noise that was ten times worse than nails across a chalkboard if you asked Sara. But it raised its head from the victim and pushed its entire body up higher on its front two legs, at least temporarily abandoning its prey to see what had caused it such harm.

Sara ducked back into the grass, deciding that another shot that would not hit such a vulnerable spot was not worth the risk of giving away her position. It terrified her beyond measure to think of that dinosaur-headed alligator waddle-running over to her in that way they charged on land.

What she heard next was the tearing and ripping apart of bone and cartilage together with the most pitiful, agonizing outburst she had ever heard uttered from a human, his voice bubbling with the water, or was it his blood? She couldn't take it anymore and stood up, aiming her pistol.

She blasted two more rounds into the creature's gorging, bloody head, but it didn't even look up. Its hide was too thick for the lead projectiles to penetrate. She told herself not to waste any more ammunition, that there were other creatures that it might still be effective against. She looked at the RV lying on its side, at Lonnie's body rapidly disappearing into the gullet of the freakshow predator, which had taken thorough advantage of his predicament.

They were trapped out here now, after all.

CHAPTER 13

Sara shrunk back down into the sawgrass in fear while the predator finished consuming Lonnie's remains at its leisure. Wet smacking and tearing sounds, interrupted by occasional nasal exhalations were the only audible noises while the humans hunkered down around the RV and the road. The ranger was beyond mortified, certain that she would need post-traumatic stress counseling. How could she be exposed to such hideous violence on her first day on the job? She did her best to put those thoughts from her mind and concentrate on more important matters...

...such as how to get out of here if and when this monstrosity decided to leave. At least while it was here, it was no doubt keeping the remaining centipedes at bay, as well as the usual complement of dangerous Everglades predators: crocodiles, alligators, snakes, big cats, bears, sharks, and who knew what else? Sara knew that she, of all people, ought to, but clearly that was not the case. Even the phrase, "God knows what else" seemed not to apply here, for that T-rex croc was beyond natural.

At any rate, they were not out of the woods yet—quite literally—she knew. They were now stranded out here with no working vehicle, no means of communication, and not much in the way of gear or supplies, with three children. Just as the overwhelming odds were frustrating her to breaking point, she heard a splash from the direction of the dino-croc. She slowly stuck her head above the grass until she could see Lonnie's position. She was just in time to watch the beast slip into the water and slide out toward the wider sawgrass prairie.

She waited and watched for five full minutes to be certain the animal wouldn't return. She didn't want to make any noise that would encourage it to investigate a possible prey item. Thankfully the other group on the road was being quiet so far, too, but she knew that couldn't last much longer with the three children.

She stood to her full height and watched the dino-croc swim away before she slowly spun 360 degrees, checking for anything that could either help or hurt them. Aside from the departing predator, she spotted nothing new of interest. She eyeballed the distance along the road they had paid such a high price to access---the squat bunker-like building perhaps a mile—or was that two, three?—away. Distances could be so deceiving out here in the vast, flat landscape. It didn't really matter, though, she reflected darkly, since walking back the way they came took them past the surviving centipedes, if there were any, and it was now further than the remaining distance to the building. She wasn't sure which degree of uncertainty offered more hazards. She was the ranger here, though, so it was up to her to make the best educated guess that offered the group—the remaining group—the best chance of survival.

She stood up and faced Rebecca, Luanne and the children. "Okay everybody, I think we can regroup now. The croc-thing is gone. For the time being, anyway."

"Thank God!" Luanne exclaimed, rising from the weedy reeds. The others followed suit, brushing bits of plant matter and dirt off of their clothing. Sara trudged through the shallow water to the road where the others stood. She pointed to the concrete utility building in the distance.

"I see two options: one, we walk over there, see if it offers shelter, communication, supplies or all three. No guarantees, since I don't actually know what it is. Or two: we walk back the way we came."

"Past the centipedes?" Luanne squeaked.

"At least we know there's one less of those now," Rebecca said.

A few moments of silence passed as they considered the options. At length, Sara offered, "The building is closer, but I'm not sure what it offers."

"No more centipeedies!" the youngest of the children said, appearing as if she were about to cry.

"The truth is we don't know what's out there anymore than we knew these strange creatures were here in the first place," Rebecca said.

Sara stared out towards the concrete building, where the sky was beginning to redden overhead. "I'd say we have a couple more hours before we're going to need to make whatever camp we can come up with for the night. Actually, I can think of three options. Let's vote. One: We stay right here and use what's left of the RV as a shelter for the night. Then we make our move—in either direction—at first light tomorrow. Two, we go back the way we came, having to camp out in the open somewhere along the way on the road, probably, with whatever gear we can salvage and bring with us from the RV. Or three, we head for that building in the distance, the goal being to reach it before it gets dark and camp there tonight. What do you think?"

"I don't like the idea of spending the night on this little strip of land," Rebecca stated.

"Me neither," Luanne added. The kids remained silent.

Sara continued. "So then it's either camp here for the night in the relative comfort of the RV, or we strike out soon for the bunker over there." She looked in that direction before turning her gaze back to the RV, where Lonnie's fresh bloodstains marred the wheel well.

"I don't like the idea of staying here all night because the predator already killed here, and it could return to see if it can find another meal," Rebecca stated flatly. "It might even be able to smell us from wherever it is now, a mile away."

Sara looked at Luanne. "Any objections to heading for the building, then?"

The RV woman shrugged and shook her head slowly while staring at the ground. "Nah. Whatever you think is best."

Sara eyed her for a moment. She looked utterly defeated, literally a beaten down woman, physically and mentally. "Are you sure?"

Luanne looked up and made eye contact. "Yeah. There's things I can't say right now in front of the kids, but let's just say that what happened to him..." she nodded to Lonnie's bloodstains before leaning close to Sara and lowering her voice, "...that's not exactly the worst thing that could have happened to us, you hear what I'm saying?"

Sara nodded, taken aback but trying not to let it show. She flashed on the condition she found the couple in when she first opened the RV's bedroom, and supposed she shouldn't be surprised. "All right then, it's settled. Let's take some time to go through the RV and gather up any supplies or gear that we can carry. I'm talking about backpacks or bags to carry things comfortably on the hike. I'm talking about food, water, camping gear, tools, weapons, lighters or things to start a fire—anything that is small and light enough to carry that also serves a purpose out here. Any questions?"

One of the girls raised her hand. Sara nodded at her. "Go ahead."

"Can I bring a toy?"

"Me too, I want a toy!" the other girl said. And then the first girl started to cry, bawling that she wanted to bring a toy. Sara spoke up above the bawling. "Yes, each of you can bring a toy. Let's all go and gather our things now. Be quick about it, daylight is wasting." As if to underscore this fact, she glanced nervously off toward the west, where the sun was already lower in the sky.

Sara fell into stride with Luanne as they walked toward the RV. "There must be a tool kit and a first aid kit in the RV, right?"

Luanne nodded without emotion. "Used to be, anyway. I'm sure we have something. I'll take a look."

"Thanks."

Luanne entered the cab of the vehicle by being boosted up to the overturned window by Sara, while Rebecca and the kids headed for the bedroom. Sara remained outside the RV, keeping watch against predators while also looking around for anything salvageable that might have been thrown from the vehicle when it flipped over.

She had nearly completed one full circuit around the RV when she heard Rebecca call out from inside, what sounded like in the bedroom.

"Sara, got something here that might help!"

The ranger made her way to the back of the RV and entered through the open side, dropping into the bedroom. Rebecca handed her a small yellow plastic walkie-talkie. "The kids gave it to me. I know you lost yours, so I dunno, I guess it might not be that good but it's better than nothing?"

Sara nodded and took it. "FRS/GMRS frequencies, different than what the Park Service uses, and lower transmit power too, but better than nothing. Might have the NOAA weather band, too. I'll check it out, thanks." She pressed the power button and watched the tiny display as the unit came to life. "First, I'll step outside and then do a scan of the channels, 1-22, to see if there's any activity. I doubt we're in range of anybody, but let's find out. How's the supply gathering going?"

"Good," Rebecca said, hefting a backpack laden with gear. "We've got a good balance of utility vs. weight, I think. See you out there in a few."

Sara left them in the bedroom and ventured back outside, eyes sweeping the landscape for potential predators, an action that was fast becoming a habit. The wetlands surrounding the RV were strangely quiet considering the carnage that just transpired. Still, she would take strange over more carnage any day of the week, and so set about scanning the walkie-talkie's channels for any signs of radio activity. Hearing nothing, she broadcast her own message: "Channel 15, anybody copy? Ranger Sara Cliff here in Everglades National Park; anybody copy, over?"

If anyone did, they weren't responding or in range to respond. She continued scanning for a few more minutes until the rest of the group exited the RV and gathered around Sara.

"No activity, as expected. I'll keep it on scan mode and call out periodically as we move," she said, clipping the device to her backpack strap. "Everybody ready? We've got a decent hike ahead of us." She stared out down the strip of land that cut through the vast marsh. The concrete bunker stood like an island in the middle of it, before the road continued on toward the distant landform of Flamingo.

"It's going to be best if we travel single file," Sara said, pointing to the narrow track of land. "I'll take lead, then Luanne, how about you next with the three children behind you, and Rebecca, you bring up the rear. Everybody okay with that?"

No one said they weren't. "Okay, then. Let's get this show on the road!" She did her best to sound upbeat, but deep down, she was highly concerned. They were woefully unprepared for a night in the open 'glades should they either be unable to reach the building for some reason, or if they did but found it offered no shelter. But she was putting the cart before the horse, as her mother was fond of saying, and so the only thing to do for now was to move out.

The group fell into place as arranged, Sara in the lead. She deliberately walked a pace that was brisk for her, knowing they only had a couple of hours to walk if all went well. She dared not move faster than that because of the children. She didn't know what she could do if they gave up and refused to move any more. Two of the three of them were too big to carry for any real distance. She had checked their shoes, though, and found them to be decent, and all of them seemed reasonably healthy. Between them they carried one four-person tent, and that would have to be set up on this sandy track for the night if they couldn't reach the building.

She watched the sun sink lower in the sky as they marched towards it, the inevitability of its setting contrasting sharply with the unsafe bet of their own fate.

CHAPTER 14

Everglades Ranger Station

Senior Ranger Ben Offstead frowned as he watched his Dispatcher, Kevin Hardison, turn away from the radio transmitter and shake his head. "No reply again, sir."

"I assume you also got her cell-phone number from Admin and tried that, too, just in case?"

Kevin nodded. "Of course, sir, but no luck. I did leave a message asking her to check in as soon as she gets it."

"What about other rangers in nearby sectors—you contact them? Maybe they heard something?"

"I spoke with two of them, sir—Strasberg and Valenzuela—and neither had any information. Naturally I let them know the situation so they can put the word out."

"Okay." Offstead glanced out the window while rubbing the stubble on his chin. "Be dark soon. I'm going to start mobilizing a search party. Meanwhile, if you hear anything—either from her or about her—make sure you let me know right away."

"Of course, sir." Kevin turned back to his table of radio equipment while Offstead strode purposefully from the room.

This wasn't good, not good at all, Offstead reflected. A rookie ranger out alone on her first day of service not returning by the end of her shift, with no contact. His thoughts went to the strange animal attacks, and he felt weird. Not scared, but just…strange, like an odd sensation he couldn't quite explain. It must have something to do with it, he thought. *It must.* But regardless of why she was still out there, she was still out there and he needed to go find her.

Offstead saw one of his veteran rangers walking into the office up ahead and he called his name.

#

Everglades

The ground got soggier over the last half-hour. It made the walking more difficult, harder on the feet. Sara thought she could feel a blister forming and made a mental note to pack a moleskin as part of her daily kit. She'd expected to mostly drive, but still. She was a ranger, she was supposed to be good in the outdoors, right? And if she felt this way, what about the others? So far no one had complained, but could that be far off? She eyed their destination ahead, still somewhat distant, though closer than it was when they'd left.

Two more miles? Three? Luanne's voice behind her broke her out of her thoughts.

"Sara, the kids are asking if we can stop for a quick break?"

Sara kept walking while answering. *And so it begins.* "We should keep moving, guys. Look at the sky, it's getting dark. We want to reach the building before the sun sets, otherwise we'll have to walk in the dark, and that's too dangerous."

As if to underscore her point, she took a giant stride over a wet hole in the ground.

"The bugs are god-awful, too," Rebecca pointed out as she swatted at her face. "Who has the bug spray?" They only had one can between them, and without it, faced a long night of misery if they were stuck outside. Even with it, the pall of insects becoming active around sunset still found flesh to their liking. Luanne passed Rebecca the can of DEET. "It's getting light. Go easy on it."

Rebecca sprayed her clothes and hat down lightly and passed the can back up. The group trod along the slim, soggy dirt track that represented the only raised ground for miles around, marching toward the squat gray building. They were close enough now to see a small forest of antenna bristling on top of the structure, the highest of which was adorned with a blinking red light.

Up front, Sara continued to put one foot in front of the other, maintaining a resolute pace that she hoped the group would tolerate for another hour or so. She thought that would put them at the building. The bugs kept up as dusk set in, and Sara had to apply insect repellent as well. She monitored the walkie-talkie scanning but no transmissions were picked up, so she periodically put out one of her own, asking if anyone copied. No one did, so onward they marched. Around them, the sounds of the swampy prairie lit up the early evening—the buzzing of insects, the chirping of unseen birds, even the throaty croaking of alligators unseen out in the bog.

As she walked, she tried not to mentally revisit the horrible death of Lonnie. She still couldn't believe her first day on the job had gone so awry, and that led to thoughts that she might be fired, founded or not, which of course only compounded her stress, so she did her best not to think about that, too, by putting out more radio broadcasts that also went unanswered.

But the time did pass with each footstep, as did the distance, and when she next looked, the squat concrete edifice was not more than a football field away, a welcoming beacon in the rapidly descending darkness.

"Almost there!" Rebecca called out from the rear of the procession.

"Good job, everyone!" Sara said, hoping to rally the troops. "I knew we could do it!"

The kids asked variations of, "Are we there yet?" which Luanne did her best to field in an optimistic way without lying. The group bunched closer together as they approached the building. But as they neared it, they saw that there would be at least one more obstacle to overcome, for the track on which they had walked, which had become increasingly muddy although still solid, now gave way completely to shallow swamp water.

A light rain began to fall as Sara held an arm up not fifty feet from the building, indicating they should stop to assess the situation. Another water gap, she told herself, thinking about how wrong the last one went. And this time there was no vehicle to even try to ford it with.

"It *looks* shallow, at least," Rebecca said, pointing to a small wavelet breaking over the ground, glinting in the light of a rising moon. Sara shone her small flashlight on the same spot and nodded in agreement.

"Hopefully it's reasonably solid all the way across. If not, we'll just have to swim, if it's deep enough for that." She aimed the beam of light across the span to the raised mound of dry land which the building occupied. *Is it even worth risking the crossing?* she asked herself. *Good question.* After what happened to Lonnie, it would be stupid not to consider it, right? She took one step out into the water, which was only an inch or two deep, but would the ground hold or give way into a quicksand-like bog?

Sara kept some weight on her back foot, still on solid ground, while she pressed down into the wetness with her forward foot. The wet ground was spongy for about an inch but then held solid. She took a tentative step with her other foot, so that she was standing with both feet in the water a couple of feet from the dirt track, and held firm.

The others in the group started walking over to her but she held out a hand for them to stop. "Let me cross first. No reason for all of us to venture into the unknown together. Plus I could use some extra eyes. Tell me if you see anything I should watch out for."

Rebecca produced another small flashlight and shone its stingy beam on the watery ground a few feet in front of the park ranger. Luanne kept watch out on the surrounding wetlands for any large predators that might be active during the crepuscular period.

Sara took another step forward, again testing the firmness of the ground before trusting it with her full weight. Still good, she ventured forward a little quicker, eagerly eyeing the solid ground only ten feet or so away. Then rapid, sinewy movement caught her eye off to her left. After a startling adrenaline dump, she followed it with her flashlight only to find it was a small fish, perhaps a juvenile redfish. Harmless. She continued on, cautiously testing each footfall before putting her full weight down.

In such a fashion she forged her way across the liquid plane, pleased to find that it did not become deeper as she progressed. In fact, the ground actually had no water over it, although it was still wet, the last few feet up to the dry hillock of land on which the building was situated. She stepped up onto the dry dirt and turned around to face the group.

"It's safe to cross! Take the same route I did though, because we know it's solid. Go one at a time the same way. Who knows if it gets deeper or quicksand-like off to the side?"

Rebecca insisted that Luanne go next, with the youngest child right behind her. While she watched them cross to make sure they didn't go astray, Sara turned her attention to her new surroundings.

The squat building was about fifty feet away, at what might constitute all of five feet elevation at the foundation. She could see no vehicles of any kind, nor hear any signs of human activity. Looking up, the blinking lights atop the antennae silently warned aircraft, she supposed, not to fly too low. But what signals were these antennae broadcasting or receiving? Or were they merely towers to hold the lights?

Impatient to find out what the building might offer for them, she turned around and lit the path in front of the others, who made their way carefully across the flooded plain until they stood beside her. Then, after waiting for one of the kids to tie her shoes, they set out as a group toward the unknown facility.

CHAPTER 15

Everglades

Ben Offstead flicked on the high beams of his 4x4 SUV as he turned on to the same state road where the fatality occurred with the chameleon collectors. Seated next to him in the passenger seat was veteran ranger Sam Gumshoe, a swarthy complected go-getter with a handlebar mustache. Three other vehicles, each staffed with a pair of rangers, had also been dispatched to other areas of the park to widen the search net.

"Don't see any vehicles up ahead," Sam said, pointing out that if Sara had left her patrol vehicle at the scene of the chameleon collector deaths, it wasn't here. Offstead nodded.

"Let's take a look at the actual site." He pulled off on the left side of the road, as far as he could go before the ground was too thick with vegetation. He aimed the SUV at the site of the earlier carnage and left the high beams on.

"No vehicle here, either," Gumshoe said.

"Okay, back off the state road into the park and we'll follow the route she was supposed to have taken today." Offstead put the SUV into reverse and drove them back along the state road until reaching the narrow thoroughfare that led back into the national park. He turned right onto that, keeping the brights on, and drove slowly into Everglades National. From the passenger side, Gumshoe swept a handheld Q-beam spotlight out along the road and beyond, searching for anything unusual. Offstead picked up his radio transmitter and informed the other search patrols that they had found nothing at the one site they searched so far, and gave their heading. The other patrols acknowledged the report, stating they were just leaving the station.

Offstead looked over at Gumshoe as he picked up a tumbler of coffee from the drink holder. "Good idea to bring these along. I have a feeling it might be a long night."

#

Everglades

"It's locked." Rebecca's voice carried the same dejection that all of the group now felt. They had walked around the building entirely, which was nothing more than a single-story, rectangular concrete block. There was a concrete pad that extended two feet on either side of the building, and the antennae array on the roof, and that was it. Starkly simple and profoundly disappointing at the same time, it seemed to offer nothing in the way of help or aid other than blocking the wind from one direction.

The door in front of them was a no-nonsense metal affair with not even a knob or handle, only a lock set flush into the door.

"I don't suppose you have the key?" Rebecca looked to Sara, who shook her head. "I know I'm a ranger, but no, the only keys they gave me were to the ranger station outer door and to my patrol vehicle." Rebecca made prolonged eye contact with her without saying anything, and so Sara tried her station key in the lock anyway. It didn't fit.

"We'll have to figure out something else," Sara said. "Some other way…" She trailed off as she began looking around the building, craning her neck to look up.

"There's nothing else to check out," Luanne said. "We walked all around already."

"There's the roof," Sara pointed out. "We need to look at everything."

"I agree," Rebecca said. "Who wants to be the one to get boosted up there?"

"I'll go first," Sara volunteered, "and see if there's anything we can do from up there to get inside."

Rebecca and Luanne stood opposite to one another and interlocked their hands held low to form a basket. Sara placed the boot of her right foot in the basket and then pushed up as they boosted her. Sara was able to grab onto the lip of the roof and then haul herself up from there.

As she pushed up to her feet, she was confronted with a thicket of wire poles, some basic aerials while others were more complex towers supporting antennae at their tops, some thirty feet above the roof. The tallest three of these featured the red and white lights which blinked against the now dark sky, ostensibly to warn aircraft of the obstruction.

"I'm up," Sara called down and began to walk around the crushed gravel rooftop. She had just turned around when she caught movement in the air, perhaps fifty yards away from the building, farther out into the swamp.

"What's up there?" Rebecca called up, impatient. "Is there a way in?"

"I don't know yet," Sara answered. "But I see something out over the marsh. That way." She pointed and Rebecca and the others walked around the building to see in that direction.

"I can't really see anything," Rebecca said.

"Me neither," Luanne concurred.

"It's moving. It's big, whatever it is. Either one big thing or lots of little things, I can't tell yet."

"Oh I see something now, too," the boy said, pointing. "Birds?"

"Biggest birds I ever seen!" Luanne said.

"And there's a lot of them!" one of the girls pointed out. Indeed, a flock of birds darkened the sky not far from the utility building, flying their way at low altitude. They flew as a silent unit, and when the lead bird turned, the others shifted effortlessly in the same direction, flocking together in tightly coordinated fashion.

On the roof, Sara resumed her search for a way inside the building. "There's a skylight up here!" she said.

"Does it open?" Rebecca asked from the ground.

Sara's reply was immediate and decisive. "Negative. No hinges or anything. Hard plastic, tinted dome. Gonna have to break it somehow, then we can drop down inside. We'd have some shelter for the night."

"Can you smash it open?" Rebecca asked. They heard some thumping—the sound of Sara's boot heel repeatedly crashing down onto the skylight.

"Nope. Maybe if I had a big rock?"

Rebecca addressed Luanne and the kids. "Everybody, let's find big rocks, okay?"

"How big?" one of the boys asked.

"As big as you can find," Rebecca answered. "If you can't pick it up, show me or your Mom where it is."

They split up around the building to locate smashing implements. As Rebecca turned the corner of the building, she froze in place. Up ahead, the flock of birds was much closer, and lower to the ground. Coming in fast.

From the roof, Sara said, "Hey everybody. I don't like the look of these birds. They're coming right at us!"

All of them stopped what they were doing to look over at the airborne animals flocking their way.

"I'll head them off," Rebecca said, breaking the silence. "The rest of you, keep gathering rocks to break the skylight. We need to get into this shelter." Then she stepped out to the side of the building and hefted a softball-sized chunk of rock she had found. She waited for another second while watching the animals fly toward them--still unwavering in their course toward the building, right at roof level—and hurled the rock at the middle of the formation with all the force she could muster.

The projectile fell just short of the triangular front of the formation, but was close enough that it still had its intended effect. The creatures broke formation and splintered into a disorganized group rather than the purposeful phalanx it had been.

"That should let them know they were headed for an obstacle," Rebecca explained. Then she turned her attention back to the task at hand as she turned to watch the sun sinking low on the horizon. It would soon be dark.

"How are we doing on those rocks, people?"

"Got a good one here!" Luanne said, lifting a football-shaped mini-boulder from the earth.

"Toss it up," Sara said, moving to the corner of the roof nearest Luanne and holding her arms out. Luanne met her there and threw the rock up to her, which she was able to catch. She took it over to the skylight.

"Careful, Sara, if you throw it down on it, it could bounce back up and hit you."

"I'll be careful. First I'll see if I can just hold it and smash..." She knelt over the skylight, gripped the big rock in two hands and brought it down in a swift motion onto the middle of the clear plastic dome.

"Ow!" The rock impacted the plastic and bounced off, still in her hands, causing a jolt of pain to resonate through the joints in her fingers with the impact. To her dismay, there was only the barest scratch on the skylight.

"They're regrouping and circling back!" Luanne's voice sounded harried and frightened, ragged. In the same tone, she added, "Something's not right with these things!"

Rebecca called up to Sara. "Keep trying, Sara. I'll check this out down here."

"Will do!" Sara went back to work with the rock, considering how to apply the rock to the skylight, while Rebecca focused her attention on the aerial disturbance.

Something was atypical about these animals, she realized, while eyeing one of them as it wheeled around only ten feet away. For a flight-capable bird, it was on the very large size, even for a raptor, yet it possessed an odd-textured body and wings. And then, in the chaos as the animals struggled to regain formation while they flew chaotically around the site, two of them collided in mid-air. A series of angry squawks reverberated off the building walls and then one of the birds dropped to the wet ground only a little way out into the marsh with a wet *plop*.

Luanne hucked another stone into the swirling birds, which caused them to separate again and fly away from the building. Rebecca took the opportunity to run over to the fallen animal and examine it.

She knelt next to the grounded beast, its beak opening and closing slowly as it gasped for breath on its side, the one eye she could see wide open. Normally the sight of an injured animal would fill her with sadness, but in this case, her scientific curiosity overwhelmed her emotions. What was this creature? *So odd...*

Its wings were characterized by a leathery texture more fitting to...*dinosaurs*...Rebecca thought. *Pterodactyls?* And yet unlike pterodactyls—at least anything the paleontology community understood to date—the creature also sported feathers. Its head was decorated with an exotic-looking array of colorful plumage—red, pink, yellow and vibrant green, some short and densely packed, while others were stalked. Then there was sparse feathering on the legs, too, sort of a carpet of greenish-purple down. But the wings—they were definitely not feathered, but leathered. And the beak was very long and pterodactyl like.

Rebecca knew she was dealing with something different here. Something strange, like the other animals she'd encountered since coming out to the Everglades. *What was going on?* But screams from the kids and a flurry of winged activity just above ripped her out of her thoughts.

The birds were back. Only now the paleontologist was quite sure that they weren't really birds. Not really dinosaurs, either, but some sort of hybrid. She was trying to think of how this might help her, how characteristics of each might influence their behavior, when she saw something drop from the mouths of one of the animals from about ten feet up. A wriggling prey item landed on the ground at her feet, bloody and damaged from its ordeal.

But the most startling thing about it was that Rebecca recognized it from before. One of those strange lizards that had killed the chameleon collectors! *What was going on here? The entire ecosystem seems to changing before my eyes...*

And then she felt a sharp stabbing pain in her side. She looked down a split-second after feeling the leathery wing of one of the ptero-birds brush against her shoulder, and then saw the thick, two-foot long beak that had glanced off her side. But not before doing damage. It didn't penetrate her skin, thank goodness, but she had felt the snap of bone and knew that one or more of her ribs was at least fractured, if not broken.

This was getting way out of hand, she thought. She had to get this group to safety and herself to a hospital, and then she had to figure out what was going on out here. She called up to Sara again, this time wincing with the pain in her ribs as she shouted.

"Sara, how's it going up there?"

Her answer was a sharp crack followed by a whooping holler. "Making progress! The key is to hit the corners. The birds are distracting me though."

"They're not birds."

"What?"

Rebecca realized she was only distracting Sara further. "Never mind, I'll tell you later. We'll try to fight them off for you long enough to break that skylight."

But the latter statement was rapidly proving to be easier said than done. Around her, the tiny building site was turning to chaos as the three children and Luanne alternately heaved rocks at the ptero-birds and ran for cover against the side of the building while the aerial creatures became more aggressive toward the humans, darting down on them and dipping low to slap a human head with a heavy leathery wing at speed.

Rebecca darted out into the riskier open space area so that the others could all see her at once. "Everybody, we need to drive these birds away from the roof so that Sara can work on getting into the building." She didn't bother not calling them birds; that would only complicate things and scare everyone. Birds was close enough.

The children threw smaller rocks while Rebecca and Luanne pelted larger missiles at specific winged attackers. It was exhausting labor, but it did have the desired effect of scattering the ptero-birds. When they regrouped, they were farther out into the marsh. They didn't leave the area, but flew around in a loose circle that grew into a tighter squadron with each pass. They were gearing up for another attack.

"Sara, now's your chance! Do it now before they come back. I don't know if we'll be able to hold off a second wave!" Indeed, they were now out of rocks, and those that remained to be found on the ground were smaller and fewer. On the roof, Sara went back to work. She kept pounding on the same corner of the skylight, having spiderwebbed the plastic a long time ago, and now actually denting it in. She raised the rock high above her head in two hands yet again. Brought it down full force, even harder than before. This time she was rewarded with the tempered plexiglass giving way.

The rock broke through, but unfortunately her fingers scraped against the broken edge of the skylight. She screamed in pain as the skin was torn, the rock plummeting through the created opening. It landed with a loud thud onto a concrete floor, but she couldn't hear the impact over her wail of agony. When she opened her eyes, her screaming had stopped, but now she could hear the others calling up to her.

"You okay?" Rebecca yelled first.

"What's up?" Luanne wanted to know.

Sara held her breath, afraid to look at her fingers. Each hand was in pain and she could feel blood dripping off of both of them. Looking down into the room, she could see only darkness, but she swore she could hear the pitter-patter of her blood landing on the floor below.

And then she heard a different kind of pitter-patter, this one preceded by a loud thump. On the roof. She turned her head and saw one of the ptero-birds flexing its wings on the corner of the roof, stamping its feet as if testing whether it could walk on this surface. And then another landed, this time on the opposite corner. While it stretched its own wings and hopped in place, the first lander began to walk on two feet towards Sara.

Ignoring her hands for now, the ranger knew she had to act fast if she was to avoid further trauma. She wasn't particularly afraid of birds—she'd befriended a large emu at a local tourist attraction fruit stand by feeding it oranges—but the purposeful movement of this creature, along with the fact that two of them had gone out of their way to land on the roof and investigate her—put her on edge. And they looked like no other bird she'd ever seen before, either.

Down on the ground the skirmish raged on, with crude projectiles flying, curses bellowing, ptero-birds screeching and squawking. Sara kept her focus and balanced on one leg as she raised her right foot at the knee, bringing the hiking boot up. She slammed the heel of her boot down square in the center of the skylight, watching the second of the ptero-birds start to teeter towards her, upright on two feet.

She lost her balance as her foot protruded through the plexiglass and she suddenly had nothing to stand on. She put her hands out on the roof to keep from smashing her face into the edge of the skylight. Caught a glimpse of the underside of one of the bird-beasts running, almost to her. Sara pushed up with her hands, noticing with rising dread the bright, bloody handprints she'd left behind.

But the skylight was mostly smashed through, leaving jagged sharp edges all the way around. Enough room to drop through, Sara hoped. She would have liked to take the time to remove the frame of the skylight completely, but with the creatures rampaging toward her, there was no time for that. She repositioned herself to be able to drop through. She wasn't worried about the height of the drop since the height from the roof to the ground wasn't all that much. If she hung down from the roof, her feet would have one or two feet of clearance from the ground at most.

Now the closest ptero-bird leapt into the air, opting to take flight to cover the remaining distance to its intended target: Sara. The park ranger screamed as she jumped, setting her body vertical like a beanpole, arms pressed tightly against her sides. As she dropped through the narrow skylight opening, she felt the creature's beak rustle through her hair, knocking off her wide-brimmed ranger's hat. The ptero-bird flew off with the hat clutched in its beak, not yet realizing its "prize" was not edible. Perhaps it would make suitable nesting material, Sara thought fleetingly on her way down.

Sara cried out in pain as a protruding shard of broken plexiglass gouged a hole in her right side, and then she was falling through open air, briefly, until her feet contacted the concrete floor below. Her knees buckled and she tumbled to the floor, putting her arms out to protect her face. Pretty sure she had landed without breaking anything, Sara rose to her feet and looked up at the skylight. The other ptero-bird's head appeared in the opening, and its beak opened up to squawk at her as it released frustration at losing a probable meal. Sara didn't think the bird creature could fit through the skylight—they were wider than she was— but wasn't one hundred percent sure of that. She decided to get the door to the building open before the bird thing dropped down and she was trapped in this dark space with it. She shivered at the thought.

Almost dark outside, with the bird blocking the skylight, it became near pitch black inside the little utility building. Fumbling through her pockets, Sara found what she was looking for—the little keychain flashlight she carried. She turned it on and took her first look around the space. There were rows of both mechanical and electrical machinery lining the walls of the building, and no furniture of any kind. A purely functional utility station, designed to protect equipment from the elements and, no doubt, meddling humans. DANGER HIGH VOLTAGE signs were the only wall decorations.

From outside she heard shouting and screaming with renewed urgency, so she moved to the door. She saw a silver latch style handle and turned it. She pushed and nothing happened, so then she pulled and to her epic relief, the door swung open inward, flooding the inside of the room with the dim twilight that had taken hold outside.

"Come inside, everybody! It's open!"

CHAPTER 16

Everglades

"Let's check the campground and interview people, ask if Sara might have stopped by earlier," Ben Offstead suggested as he slowed the SUV to a stop.

"Haven't seen her anywhere else," Sam Gumshoe said. "Haven't seen much activity at all, really." It was true, the park was in the off-season and had its lowest number of visitors this time of year. Driving around, they'd not seen a lot of other vehicles or people at all. The campground represented a high concentration of visitors. One of them might know something.

Offstead called into Dispatch that he and Gumshoe were leaving their patrol vehicle to check the campground, and then he switched off the engine. He and Gumshoe walked casually into the grounds. This particular area was designated for tent camping only, no vehicles, which meant it could only be reached by hiking or backpacking. This tended to keep attendance down, in addition to the fact that permits were required for overnight stays.

He could see the concern of the campers as they walked onto the grounds. Were they checking for permits? Underage drinking? Fishing and hunting violations? Perhaps it was the smell of marijuana in the air. But right now, the pair of rangers cared about only one thing, and that was finding one of their own.

The first people they approached were an extended family of Cubans occupying a picnic table strewn with beer cans and liquor bottles, and various food items including a birthday cake. A few of them looked over at the rangers, but the loud chatter did not stop. Offstead walked to the middle of the table and introduced himself. He spoke in Spanish, to ward off the "*No Inglés*" he would inevitably get if he started in English. Sometimes Cubans would be surprised a Caucasian could speak Spanish, and Offstead used to enjoy that, but now, after so many years on the job, it was simply the way it was.

He produced Ranger Sara Cliff's hiring photo and showed it to the group while asking if any of them had seen her. All quieted down and took a look at the picture before shaking their heads and uttering a collective "no." Gumshoe handed out a few business cards, asking them to call the station should they see or hear any information about her, to which they nodded and said they would.

The two rangers continued further into the campground, where numerous small cooking and campfires blazed and barbecues smoked. They veered toward one fire from which the sound of acoustic guitar music wafted. The pair walked up to a cluster of grungy-looking younger people singing along with the musician, who was seated on a log next to the fire. He stopped playing when Offstead nodded and clapped, approving of his performance.

"Can we help you sir, or you just digging the tunes?"

Offstead smiled. "I'm digging the tunes, sure, but we have an important situation to tell you about that maybe you could help us with before you get back to your music." Joints were hurriedly extinguished, alcohol set down.

"Look," Offstead said, "right now you don't need to worry about any of that stuff. We're not here to issue citations or looking for violations. This is about something much more serious than that." The group of revelers relaxed visibly and listened more intently to Offstead, who continued. "We're looking for one of our own, a federal park ranger on her first day on the job who hasn't been seen in a concerning amount of time." He proceeded to explain who they were looking for, to describe Sara and her intended route that day, but again, no one claimed to know anything about Sara's whereabouts, nor had they seen any rangers at all that day, until now.

"You said it was her first day," the guitarist, a long-haired man in his late twenties said. "Maybe it was, you know, a take this job and shove kinda thing?" This elicited laughter from the rest of the group, but Offstead and Gumshoe waved them down.

"No, no, no," Offstead said firmly. "This isn't like a greeter job at Walmart or something that someone would just walk away from without a word. She went through a months-long interview and selection process to get here, it's a career milestone for her—"

"She was excited and enthusiastic to be here, as of today," Gumshoe interjected.

Offstead nodded in agreement. "Absolutely, in fact—"

He was interrupted by a loud rustling of foliage somewhere behind them, on the periphery of the campsite. Everyone including the rangers turned to look, but in the dark, nothing obvious stood out.

"Any of you know what that could be? Somebody taking a leak over there or something like that?" Offstead asked. He'd seen it all during his tenure as a ranger and was not easily spooked, nor was he complacent about situational awareness.

"It's not anyone from our group," the guitarist said, and the rest of them nodded in agreement. Gumshoe produced a small but bright tactical flashlight from his utility belt and aimed its beam toward the source of the ruckus.

"I don't see anything," one of the campers said, but by the time she had finished speaking, the rustling happened again, even more pronounced this time. Offstead added his own flashlight beam to the area in question.

Then the campers began to scream.

CHAPTER 17

Everglades

Sara, Rebecca, Luanne and the three children huddled inside the small concrete bunker. Overhead, the full moon was visible through the broken skylight, which also let in a wisp of breeze. They had closed the door, preventing the ptero-birds from entering that way, but now the open skylight was the biggest concern.

They could hear the stomping of the cryptid beasts on the roof, and now and again one of the creatures would jump across the open skylight. So far none had tried to fit through or even look into the opening, but none of the humans held out hope things would stay that way for very long.

Sara switched on her penlight, bathing the industrial space in feeble white illumination. Rebecca switched hers on for an initial inspection of the room, but then quickly turned it off, much to the chagrin of the kids, who lamented it was too dark.

"They're used to sleeping with night lights brighter than this," Luanne said.

"Sorry," said Rebecca, keeping her light off, "but for one thing, too much light might attract those things up there. We don't want them getting curious and coming down through the open skylight. And for another thing, the only lights we have are this one, and the little one Sara has, so I'm thinking it's best to conserve battery power."

Luanne and Sara agreed. They found an open space on the floor, put a couple of blankets down and had the kids lie down. While Luanne comforted them and tried to get them to fall asleep, Rebecca and Sara moved to the opposite end of the room, near a bank of electronic equipment, to confer.

"I think the first order of business," Rebecca led off, "is to somehow block off that opening up there so that we don't have to worry about those creatures getting in here."

"Absolutely," Sara concurred. "That way we can get some sleep in here. Believe it or not, I'm freakin' bushed."

"I hear that." The two women smiled at one another for a moment before Sara continued, looking around the room. "I don't see anything we can readily use for that, though; you have any ideas?"

Rebecca stared up at the light, where the underside of a ptero-beast was visible for a second passing over. "Even if we can't find a hard surface, like a board, to place over it that will physically stop them from coming in, simply covering the top with something soft—like a blanket or jacket or something—so that they can't smell us down here as easily, or even see that there's a gap—would be better than nothing."

Sara nodded. "Okay, but I know that I don't have anything suitable in my little backpack. Yours?"

Rebecca shrugged. "I'll check my pack and ask Luanne to go through her stuff, while you check the room to see if you can find anything useful in any capacity."

"Sounds good." Sara began moving about the room with her weak light while Rebecca retreated to the far side of the room to take inventory of their belongings. She started by illuminating her light on some sort of control panel on the wall nearest her. Fairly simple, with no computer screen, only a few switches and a couple of knobs, with some exposed multi-colored wires running here and there between them.

"No idea what these are for," she mumbled to herself while walking along the array of equipment against the wall. She continued her tour of the small facility, perusing the equipment and trying to determine its purpose while keeping an eye out for something that could be used to create a blockade for the skylight or for communications. The room was free of clutter, unless one considered the equipment itself to be clutter, that much was clear. No rubbish or storage items or discarded material of any kind could be seen. She continued to walk the perimeter of the room while considering what the equipment was for. She pictured the roof of the building, with its large tower that supported radio antennas and what she supposed were aircraft warning lights.

But looking around the room she saw no conventional radios of any kind—no console with a microphone like a ham radio or anything with a keypad or something like that. There was a solar power charge controller for the panels on the roof, panels that supplied power to the lights and whatever telemetry signals were being sent out, she supposed, for the meteorological station. Also on the roof was an anemometer measuring wind speed, a barometer, thermometer and humidity sensor. Maybe some other stuff she didn't know about; she wasn't a meteorologist, after all, but knew that the park service employed them and had cooperative projects with fellow federal agencies such as NOAA's National Weather Service.

The door side of the room was bare, so she moved to the other small end wall, past where Luanne was trying to bed the kids down and where Rebecca was kneeling over a pack, rummaging through its contents. Overhead, she still heard the disconcerting trampling of ptero-bird claws and the occasional squawk. On this wall she found only structural supports that ran through the roof to support the towers, steel legs that ran all the way to the floor where they were cemented in place.

Sara moved to the last wall, the other long side of the building. The first part of it featured bundles of cabled wiring, snaking up through the roof and laterally along the walls to other components inside the building. Nothing she could do with that, so she kept moving along the wall.

"Nothing solid in my pack we can use to barricade the skylight," Rebecca announced, standing up. "One more pack to check." She walked over to Luanne, who told her she could check her pack while she was cooing softly to the kids to try to get them to sleep.

Sara found nothing else of interest along the long wall until she neared the far end of it. Here there was a large plastic case mounted on the concrete wall. She noted that it had a hasp to insert a padlock, but that no lock was in place, so she opened it. Inside she was surprised to see a modern computer screen. At first, she held out hope that she might be able to use it to access the Internet and get a message out, but a frown took over her face as she stared at the controls. In lieu of a standard QWERTY keyboard was a proprietary control pad with a series of directional arrow pads only. She'd never seen anything like it, but fortunately there were labels above each pad.

A label centered over the first two pads read TWR 1, while one pad was labeled PERIOD RED ON (along the horizontal left-right axis, and the other PERIOD RED OFF, along the top-bottom y-axis. The second pad was the same except substituted "WHITE" for "RED".

Then the second two pads had a TWR 2 label centered over them, with both pads labelled exactly the same as for the first set of dual pads. Sara pondered what the meaning of this was while she thought about this building's main purpose. Almost all of the wiring led up to the roof, which supported the solar panels and the two large towers. And then she knew.

TWR! *Tower. Two towers, 1 and 2. But what's this other stuff? Red...white...*She looked up out the skylight, and saw a flash of red from the left, and then a white pulse from the right side of the roof. *The lights! Period...*Sara counted the interval between flashes of the red light, which seemed to be more frequent. *One...two...three...four...five!* It was off for five seconds before turning on again for...She understood now, and counted softly to herself the next time the red light came on. *One...two...OFF...two...three...four...five...That's it!* The directional pad

L-R control dictated the period, in seconds, for how long the light stayed on, while the Up-Down controls determined the period for how long the light stayed off.

To test her theory, she thumbed the right-side directional pad five times. If she was right, this should cause the red light to stay on now for ten seconds, twice as long as it had been set for. She looked up at the red light and held her breath while it was in the OFF cycle. *If this works it should take effect on the next ON, I guess*...She counted: *three...four...five...six! ...Seven! ...ten*...And then the light blinked off and stayed off for five seconds, before staying on again for ten more seconds.

"Yes!" She'd been so caught up in what she was doing that she hadn't realized she had spoken—nearly yelled—the word aloud. And now the whole room was staring at her expectantly.

"Sorry guys," she said sheepishly. "It's just that I didn't expect to really figure this out, but apparently I did."

"What'd you figure out?" Rebecca wanted to know.

"How to control those tower lights on top of the roof. You know, the blinking red and white ones."

Rebecca sighed wearily as she stood up from rummaging through the pack. In her hands she had a blue nylon windbreaker. "That's great, Sara, but how does it help us get out of here?"

Undeterred, Sara went on. "So I think we may be able to set the tower lights—one of them, anyway—to send on S.O.S. message, instead of the normal aviation warning pattern they're set to now."

At this, Rebecca and Luanne cocked their heads to look at Sara more closely. "Say again?" Rebecca said.

Sara took a deep breath before continuing, realizing that she now had the rapt attention of a college professor who might have taught a course equivalent to the ones she had completed as part of her own ecology degree to become a park ranger. "The way I see it, since we're going to spend the night here anyway, we may as well try to signal the outside world that we're here by altering the pattern of the tower lights. I could have them stay on all the time, for example, or off all the time, which might also get their attention; now that I think about it, although of course I don't want an aircraft to hit us—but even better would be an S.O.S."

Rebecca took the few steps over to where Sara stood and took a quick look at the controls in the wall-mounted cabinet. "And you think you could really do that?"

Sara did her best to summon confidence in her voice. "I think so, yes. The buttons here control—"

"You don't have to explain it," Rebecca cut in. "Just do it."

"Yeah," Luanne agreed.

Sara relaxed a bit. "Okay." She looked at the jacket in Rebecca's hands. "Is that what you found to cover the skylight?" Rebecca pursed her lips.

"Yes, couldn't find anything solid. This will have to do."

"Okay, but wait until I get the lights changed. I need to be able to look up there and see how the lights are reacting to what I'm doing down here."

Rebecca nodded and took a seat against the wall. "All right. I'll just take a breather, then. Let me know if you need anything." Likewise, Luanne went back to laying down with the kids and trying to get them to sleep.

Sara turned back to the light panel controls. S.O.S., she thought. *You got this.* She thought about her task for a few moments while staring up through the skylight. The ptero-birds were still up there, but seemed to have calmed down a bit. No longer did they jump over the skylight, at least. She forced her mind away from them and concentrated on the task at hand.

She only needed one of the lights to send the message, she realized. Ideally, one light would be turned all the way off, while the other flashed the S.O.S. She wasn't sure if it was possible to turn them all the way off, but if not, she supposed she would set the ON interval to as short as possible—one second—and then the OFF interval to as long as possible. But which light should blink out the cry for help, red or white? She ruminated over this for a minute while listening to the smallest of the children start to cry. White was probably visible for the longest distance, she thought, but red was more of a distress color. In the day, she supposed red might even be more visible than white, though of course she hoped they were long gone by full daylight.

Deciding to go with red, Sara went to work on the controls. After some experimentation, she found she could get the white light to essentially turn off by having it off for fifty-nine seconds and on for only one second. Good enough. So then she worked on the more complex task of setting the red light to blink the desired pattern. Then she realized that SOS—three short pulses followed by three long and then three short again, would be impossible to program with such a simple ON then OFF mechanism. What had she been thinking?

And then she forced herself to calm down, thought about it, and decided that any pattern at all that was obviously different from how it normally was ought to attract the attention of those who were familiar with it. Especially if they were looking for her, which she had absolutely no doubt that they must be by now. The thought of a search for her filled her with embarrassment—what had she gotten herself into? But also made her smile a little as she pictured her boss, Ranger Offstead, yelling at his people to coordinate a search. And of course Kevin, dispatching it all to coordinate.

So she bent to the task and programmed the red light to blink one second ON and one second OFF—the shortest possible periods. After looking up through the skylight—this time with a jumping ptero-bird blocking her view—and being satisfied that the resulting pattern was suitably attention-getting—she opted to go ahead and set the white tower light in the same manner. Why not? With such a short interval, it would have almost a strobe effect, and therefore be very arresting, certainly not a normal pattern, together with the red. So she set the white tower light to blink one second on as well, and then stared up through the skylight at her handiwork.

Pleased with the results, she turned around to face the others. She explained to Rebecca that she couldn't set an actual SOS, but instead changed the pattern to something abnormal, to which Rebecca was about to reply when a loud scuffle up at the skylight demanded their attention.

It was Luanne who voiced the concern first. "The birds! They're coming down!"

Suddenly Sara knew it was true. They had waited too long to cover the skylight while she was rigging the tower lights, and the ptero-animals had finally figured out they could get down through the small opening. Down to the prey that waited below.

"Open the door!" Rebecca shouted. "We need a way out!"

"Got it." Sara ran to the building's only conventional door and shoved it open.

"Oh no!"

No one answered her, because the first of the big ptero-birds had dropped inside the building. But outside, Sara could see, was just as bad, if not worse. An entire flock of the bipedal creatures had been waiting on the ground, just standing around on two feet as if they knew the door would open at any time.

Sara pulled the door shut. She'd rather fight the beasts inside as they came in one at a time through the narrow roof bottleneck than outside where they were far too numerous to mount a viable defense against.

"There's a whole flock of them on the ground right outside the door!" Sara told the others.

But Rebecca and Luanne were too busy to answer, because the ptero-bird that had dropped to the floor was now going berserk, jumping and flapping its impressive leathery wings while lashing out with its foot-long hard beak. Sara noticed the windbreaker Rebecca found on the floor and snatched it up. While Sara and Luanne danced around their adversary, with Luanne trying out a high kick on it, Sara crept up behind the beast and tossed the jacket over its head. Still holding the jacket by its arms, she yanked hard on it, pulling the beast to the floor, where it proceeded to thrash its head side to side. In this process it hurt both itself and Luanne, who took a gash to the ankle from the beak, right through the fabric of the jacket.

Sara saw the blood splatter on the concrete floor. She was about to kick the beast in the head when a second ptero-bird fell through the skylight. Now what? She didn't see how they were going to win this unless they found a weak spot in these creatures' fighting. The kids were now all up and screaming and crying, huddled in a far corner of the room, as far from the fight as they could possibly be in the close quarters, but not actually all that far.

Another bird-monster plummeted down through the open skylight, but this one dazed itself by striking its head on the floor, and Rebecca was able to quickly immobilize it by stomping on its neck and cracking the vertebrae. With this third animal, and also the first bird incapacitated, the three women now faced only one ptero-fighter. They circled around it warily, dodging its quick beak-lashes and wing flaps. But this animal-fighter was not giving ground; in fact, it was pushing the three women toward the opposite long wall of the building. It hadn't connected with any of them yet, but Sara soon found herself backed up against the door. Rebecca struck out with a right hander of her own, but she was clearly the weakest of the three human fighters, and her blow missed, putting her off balance for a moment. The ptero-bird took advantage of this and struck with a kick of its own that landed high on Rebecca's left thigh, spinning her around while pushing her back into the door.

The strange animal assailant saw the chance to do some real damage and moved in. Sara saw it lower its head and start to move its feet, knowing it meant to charge Rebecca while her back was to the wall. Except that Sara realized the wall was actually the door, so she acted on impulse, not knowing if it was the right thing to do but also having no other recourse. Sara charged Rebecca herself and grabbed the zoologist with one arm, gripping her into a hug and ripping her away from the door. With her other hand she opened the door handle, shoving it open with her foot.

It opened just wide enough that the charging ptero-bird, expecting to collide with the flesh of its prey, instead passed through the doorway into the open air outside. Sara let go of Rebecca who fell to the floor while Sara pulled the door shut. She caught a glimpse of the waiting flock of ptero-birds, now suddenly on alert, and shuddered at the thought of what that many of the beasts would do to them.

Rebecca rolled over and got up from the floor, ready to defend against more oncoming ptero-birds, but for now, at least, there were no comers. Sara picked up the jacket they were going to use to try and cover the skylight, but it was now tattered into shreds as a result of the battle. She eyed the skylight, where she caught movement of more of the monsters, although none were attempting to come down at this moment. She looked to the inert ptero-bodies on the floor, two absolutely still while one twitched weakly as it lay on its side.

"Maybe we could stuff their bodies up into the skylight and block it like that?"

"How would we get them up there?" Luanne asked.

Sara stared up at the skylight. Fortunately, the ceiling was low, only about six feet. She nodded slowly as she stared up at it. "I think that's worth a try."

Together, the three women hefted one of the dead creatures and stuffed it up through the skylight so that half of its body was up on the roof, while the legs protruded down into the opening, partially blocking it. This drew the interest of the other pteros however, which began gathering at the skylight and pecking at their fallen comrade.

Rebecca had an idea. "Maybe we should distract them while we set up the body blockage by opening the door and throwing rocks at the ones out there."

"Do we have any rocks?" Luanne asked.

"No, but maybe I can gather one or two right by the door. Just by opening the door, we'll probably distract them. I'll try it while you two continue setting up the blockade, okay?"

Sara and Luanne agreed to this and they set about putting the plan into motion. "Let us get in position with the next body before you go out there," Sara said. She and Luanne dragged the other completely dead ptero under the light. When they began to heft it, Rebecca put her hand on the door.

"Here I go." She opened the door and stepped outside. The ptero-bird flock was still there, perhaps a little farther from the door now, milling about, pecking occasionally at the ground. Rebecca spotted a fist-sized chunk of rock about five feet from the door. She ran to it and picked it up. By now most of the creatures were frozen in place and staring at her. She hurled her rock into the midst of them while running back to the door. What she was not expecting was one of the animals on the roof to come flying down at her.

One of its toe claws raked down her back, ripping her shirt and drawing a thick red line from between her shoulder blades to the small of her back. Shrieking with the sudden forceful agony, she continued her path to the doorway and ducked inside, slamming the door shut on the ptero-beast that was right behind her in hot pursuit.

Half expecting to see a prehistoric melee unfolding in here as well, Rebecca was relieved to see Sara and Luanne hoisting another dead body into place up in the skylight, effectively blocking most of the space. Only one ptero-bird body remained, the one that still twitched.

Sara turned as Rebecca entered. "How'd it go out there?"

"Rough. I got injured." She turned around to show her back, eliciting gasps from Sara and Luanne. "We'll patch that up as best we can," Sara said. "But first let's get this body outta here. I don't think we need it for the skylight. It's good and blocked."

"It's still alive," Rebecca noted.

"I don't have the heart to kill, do you?" Sara asked.

Luanne walked over to the bird and stomped hard on its neck with the heel of her boot, causing it to go totally limp.

"Never mind," Rebecca said. "But hold on, before we take it outside, I want to get a sample." She went to her pack and withdrew a small plastic container like the one she'd used to collected the tissue sample from the strange chicken-velociraptor hybrid animals that killed the chameleon collectors. From this animal, she both plucked a small feather and used a nail file to scrape a small piece of skin from one of the legs which she deposited into the sample container. "Good to go, thanks. I'll get the door, you guys drag it out?"

With some trepidation, Rebecca returned to the door while Sara and Luanne lugged the dead body over. "On three," Rebecca said. "Careful, they could be out there."

After the count, Rebecca swung the door open and yelled, "Clear but not for long!" Sara and Luanne heaved the body out of the door, barely enough to clear it before ducking back inside.

Safely ensconced within the concrete bunker, the clan of survivors set about cleaning their wounds and bedding down for the night while above and around them, the ptero-birds milled about in confusion beneath the rapidly blinking tower lights.

CHAPTER 18

Everglades

"Everybody calm down!" Ben Offstead demanded. His tone was firm, but Sam Gumshoe could see that his gun hand wavered a bit as he aimed his pistol at the as yet unseen disturbance. This was proving to be quite a last couple of days—the deaths, the strange animals, the missing rookie ranger, and now this—whatever this was. Gumshoe drew his own weapon, just in case. It was probably some drunk kids coming back from taking a piss or making out or something like that. But his boss drew his weapon, so…

"What is it?" a young woman seated by the campfire asked, voice trembling.

In response, Offstead bellowed toward the vegetation. "Federal ranger here. Slow down and come out with your hands up! I repeat…"

"If it's a panther it won't listen!" one of the campers joked to subdued cackles. But he was right, Offstead mused. Not that he expected a panther—he knew just how rare they actually were. But it could be something formidable; there was a small population of bears in the Everglades, or even a pack of feral dogs would be no picnic. He'd seen it before.

But the next few seconds would make it all too clear that this was no dog, or bear or panther. The very first thought Offstead had was that somehow an alligator had gotten up into a tree—high up. They did sometimes climb a little ways up if the branches were big and low enough to the ground. But the scaly reptile body he saw moving through the leaves was way, way up in the trees, much higher than a 'gator could normally get. So what was it?

Like him, Gumshoe and the campers concluded that they didn't need to be this close to find out. All of them backed away, nobody running yet, but all of them moving backwards at a steady pace. The guitarist still carried his instrument, and a couple of the campers still clutched bottled beers in foam coozies. All of them were here for different reasons, and all now had a common purpose: stay safe in the face of this unknown danger.

So far only the scaled body was visible, but it was large, Offstead thought. But there was something else, too, something that was really oddball about whatever the hell this thing was. He hadn't gotten a view of the head yet, so he wasn't sure what he was dealing with, but when part of the body passed through sparser foliage near the treetops, he could swear that the skin of the creature changed color. It was green, and then it was blue and white—matching the sky!

Offstead shook his head to clear the ridiculous thought. *I must have breathed in some of these campers' joint smoke!* But then, as the campers collectively let out a *whoa!* he got a glimpse of the whole creature, and he *saw* it change color before his very eyes. As if the rapid color-changing ability wasn't enough, what the creature actually was floored the experienced park ranger even more.

He still didn't get a very clear view of the head, but he saw the entire body leap from treetop to treetop, and in those few seconds, Offstead clearly saw the shape of the animal. The sailfin was the most distinguishing characteristic. *Like one of those dinosaurs I used to like when I was a kid*, he couldn't help but think. *The ones that look like a giant dragon but with a big spined sail running along their back.* It was the sail that changed colors—from green to blue and back to green as it passed in front of different colored backgrounds. *Amazing*! He couldn't help but think. Truly astounding, but now what to do about it? His entire park was turning into some kind of weird cryptozoological zoo.

But first and foremost was the safety of his guests. "Everyone!" he yelled. "I need you to stay calm. Stay quiet, do not antagonize this animal."

"What is it?" a girl asked in a panicky voice.

"I don't know yet. Some sort of reptile, perhaps a crocodile (*liar*), we really don't know at this time. So please give it space."

Gumshoe added, "If your vehicles are close by, I recommend going to them and getting inside, roll up the windows and stay there until we issue an all clear."

At this, a few of the campers began to straggle away toward the nearest road, which was not close. A couple more emerged from their tent, curious as to the commotion outside.

Meanwhile, the massive creature—about the length of a full-sized limousine—continued hopping through the treetops toward the campsite area.

"It's like one of those sailfin dinosaurs!" Gumshoe said incredulously, allowing his gun hand to fall by his side. What good would his little pistol do against such might?

"We need to evacuate the entire park!" Offstead said, snatching up his walkie-talkie. He spoke to Dispatch back in Headquarters. "Kevin, I need you to put out a bulletin to close the entire park ASAP due to…just call it 'unknown animal threats', over."

Kevin's voice came back over the radio asking for clarification. Offstead responded while watching the color-shifting reptile lumber through the treetops toward the campsite. "Look, Kevin, I understand there will be questions on this, but now is not the time, okay? I'm staring at some kind of fucking dinosaur right now, okay?"

"Its head is like a snake! No, it *is* a snake!" Gumshoe's observation, even though his voice was low and calm, cut right through the radio conversation to Offstead's brain. He saw it too, as the creature lumbered over the top of one tree and leapt to the next. Its head *was* like a snake— rather than being connected directly to the body, like a Komodo dragon, it was attached to an elongated, skinny neck that had its own controlled movements, like a snake, extending perhaps six feet out from where it attached to the main body. As he watched, a black tongue slid out of the small mouth, no doubt sensing chemical signals in the air. The color of the whole body and sail changed back to green as the creature descended lower into the canopy.

"Keep going, everybody! Please get to your vehicles and leave the park immediately!" Gumshoe prodded.

"What about our stuff?" a young man asked, pointing to a tent.

"You can collect it later. Your stuff will be fine, it's your personal safety that is the highest concern right now," Gumshoe said, pointing to the living dinosaur lumbering across the treetops. It was now almost at the edge of the camp clearing. The tent guy and his friends backpedaled rapidly toward the trail that eventually led to the road, keeping an eye on the beast in the trees.

"Here it comes!" Offstead's warning came at the same time as the impossible creature fell out of the trees and into the edge of the camp clearing, its two front feet landing on the dirt, and then the back two crashing into the edge of the foliage behind. The creature stood there frozen, its ridiculously small snake head on the end of what looked like a python attached to the main lizard neck, its flicking tongue its only movement. Offstead and Gumshoe were frozen in place too, awed by the sheer spectacle of the thing that should not be. As they gawked, the snakehead, neck and front two legs of the creature turned brown before their very eyes, to match the color of the dirt below it, while the rear half of the animal remained green to blend with the foliage.

Offstead aimed his gun at the dirt a few feet away from the beast and squeezed off two shots. He didn't want to hit the animal and risk provoking an attack when so far it had not done that, but at the same time, it had gone out of its way to drop into their camp and he had no idea what it might do now. Hopefully a loud noise popping up dirt near it would cause it to move off.

But the actual result was far different from this hope. The oddball lizard launched into a full-on dead charge, straight for Offstead and Gumshoe, who also fired off a warning shot which did nothing to deter the marauding quadruped.

"Time to go, Sam," Offstead said, trying to keep his voice low enough that none of the park visitors would hear him and perceive panic. He and Gumshoe turned and ran, leading by example. *Run calmly*, Offstead thought. *Run in an orderly fashion to your vehicles.* For the most part, the campers adhered to this mantra. A few of them stopped by their tents to scrape up a backpack, cellphone, or perhaps the keys to their vehicle, but by and large there was a quick and steady exodus away from the campsite to the trailhead leading to the nearest parking area.

With the exception of this guy, Offstead thought sourly, observing an obviously inebriated young man walking toward the monster with a lighted torch in his hand and an open bottle of whiskey in the other.

"Sir, federal ranger here! For your own safety and the safety of others, I need you to back away from the animal. Back away now!"

But the man kept walking toward the sail-finned being, in fact, if anything he picked up his pace to a near trot as he continued toward it.

"I said stop!" Offstead yelled. But the crazy guy kept going, waving his burning stick.

The dinosaur thing lowered its weird snake head to look at this new…threat? Person of interest, anyway. Offstead wasn't sure a skinny human with a glowing stick represented a threat to this massive mega-beast. And then the color of the beast started to change…to red. Its long neck and skinny head turned first, followed by the majestic sail on its expansive, sloping back. And finally, the body itself. The whole thing turned a deep shade of red in a few seconds' time. Offstead had seen chameleons change their shade to match their surroundings, but that was a slow and gradual process with more muted hues. This was so much more impressive. It suggested a physiology that was little understood, Offstead knew that much. He also knew that this kid was in grave danger, from the sheer size of the animal he taunted if nothing else. He had no idea as to its disposition, or if it even ate meat, or what. But no living being liked to be messed with like this. This kid was asking for it.

"Get away from the animal! You're in danger!"

But instead of listening, the man began to run the remaining distance to the sailfin dino. Stopping short by only about twenty feet, about one body length of the ginormous creature, he then proceeded to huck the flaming torch up onto the creature's body, where the sail joined the back.

At first the dino had no reaction, but after about five seconds, its tiny head reared up on its snake body and turned itself to look backwards, ostensibly where the source of the pain was. It emitted a shrill, very high-pitched gasping sound.

Offstead thought the kid was done. The giant lizard's tiny head roped back around until it faced its attacker, and then suddenly it began moving toward the torch thrower. Not running, but just walking. The torch began to slide down its back, and Offstead could see that it wasn't really going to harm such a big animal. Until that is, this crazy kid produced a plastic bottle of lighter fluid that had been used earlier to start the campfire, pointed it toward the approaching beast and waited until the thing was damn near on top of him. Then he squeezed the bottle and directed a strong stream of clear accelerant up onto the creature's back where the torch was.

There was a *whooosh* noise as the flame met the lighter fluid, and then suddenly the entire animal's right side was in flames. Weirdest of all, Offstead couldn't help but notice, was that the lizard's skin—the part not actually on fire, that is—actually turned orange to match the color of the flames, so that the whole animal was adorned in rapidly flickering orange tones, making it even harder to tell which part of it was really on fire. The guy unscrewed the cap to the lighter fluid and chucked the open can up at the side of the lizard before backing away himself.

Again, he was on target and a new gout of fire cropped up, this time on the lizard's underbelly. The lizard brayed a horrible wail of agony and reared briefly up on two legs before charging forward at his fire assailant. The young man turned to run but tripped on an exposed root and went sprawling face first onto the dirt. Offstead and Gumshoe could see what was about to happen and they did their best to stop it, both of them firing their service pistols into the chest of the death-charging monster. But it did nothing to stop the giga-lizard.

The man on the ground rolled over in time to see the immolated mega-beast walk over him, and then, underside still aflame, lay down on the ground, smothering the man with its full flaming weight. Both rangers were now firing their weapons into the animal's side, but it had no apparent effect. The man's terrified screams soon stopped and then, to the horror of Offstead and Gumshoe, the slender snakehead rose up high and then swung out to the right—looking in their direction as they raised their pistols yet again.

"Get back, get back!" Offstead yelled. Gumshoe was already back-stepping before he finished, well aware that this animal, now literally on fire, could move plenty fast, and that their weapons were pitiful against it. The lead might be doing damage that would take its toll later, but that didn't help them now.

But, adding to its unpredictability, the dinosaur creature moved forward instead of toward the pair of shooting rangers. It jumped ahead a bit and then slowed to a walk, flames now beginning to die out as it lumbered through the campground. It walked right over an eight-person tent, crushing it beneath its four feet and long, dragging tail.

Offstead tapped Gumshoe on the shoulder. "Watch that thing—cover me while I check this guy." He nodded to the downed young man who still lay unmoving where the dinosaur had trampled him.

"Copy that, I got your back," Gumshoe responded, eyes already on the sailfin dinosaur. It stamped over another tent, continuing to plod its way across the campground. It dragged a nylon tent stake line that wrapped around its right rear leg behind it as it walked.

Offstead reached the comatose man, took a look toward the middle of the camp to make sure the beast was still moving away from him, before kneeling next to the man. He could see right away that the prognosis was dire. Blood streamed from both corners of his mouth, and one ear. He made a disturbing rasping sound as he breathed, and as he watched, a thin bubble of blood formed between his lips until it popped, splattering tiny droplets on Offstead's cheek. Besides all that, which probably resulted from the humongous lizard sitting on the man, Offstead noticed that he had severe burns on his torso. The fabric of his shirt was actually charred right into his flesh in some spots. He shuddered as he reached for his walkie-talkie and placed a call to Dispatch.

"Kevin here, Ben, what's—"

"Kevin, 911, we need an ambulance right away out to Campsite 17. Severely injured visitor."

"Okay, calling now. What happened to him, over?"

"Crush and burn injuries from a large animal, over."

Offstead could hear the confusion in Kevin's voice. "Crush *and* burn?"

"That's right. Make the call, please."

"It's dialing. What kind of animal?"

Offstead looked over at the camp in time to see the lizard's sailfin—all that he could now see of the beast—turn midnight blue as it blended in with the night sky. He depressed the transmit button on his radio and spoke. "A fuckin' dinosaur. No, don't tell them that, they'll think it's some kind of prank. Just say a big lizard."

"An alligator?"

Offstead sighed heavily before replying. "Yeah, sure. Tell 'em it was a massive 'gator. How's that park evac going?"

"Gotta talk to the 911 operator, Ben. Evac is in progress. Talk to you later. Stay safe, over."

"Over and out."

He looked back to Gumshoe, who stared intently in the direction the lizard had gone, but now stood more relaxed with his gun down.

"Sam, ambulance on the way."

"Good. I can't see that dinosaur anymore, but it went that way." He pointed to the road where the campers had walked to get their vehicles. "How is that guy?"

"Alive but barely. Unconscious. I need to stay with him until paramedics get here. Can you hike up to the road and monitor the evacuation—make sure everybody gets into their cars and leaves?"

Gumshoe hesitated before answering. The implication was clear: to do that meant to follow the path the dinosaur had last taken. Still, the ranger vehicle was that way also, and it represented safety. Offstead would be alone here with no backup until paramedics arrived, probably by helicopter.

"You got it, boss." Gumshoe checked the action on his pistol, chambered a round, and moved off in the direction of the campsite parking.

Offstead knelt by the side of the gravely injured young man. "Help's on the way buddy. Hang in there." He didn't know what else to say. Never in his career as a ranger had he seen such an injured person. He'd recovered several dead bodies over the years—a drowning victim, an ATV accident where the guy wasn't wearing a helmet and struck a tree, even a hunting accident where a man had been accidentally shot in the head. But somehow this was so much worse than those. This kid was likely to die, and in such horribly spectacular fashion, at such a young age. It didn't seem fair. Such a random thing, a giant lizard rampaging out of the woods…*When it's your time to go, it's your time to go, I guess….*

Offstead was suddenly ripped out of his thoughts by the radio squawking at his hip. He recognized the voice of one of the rangers he'd sent out on search patrol looking for Sara.

"Ben, Steve here in Patrol 4."

"Steve, where are you? We've got a hell of a situation here. Park ordered evacuation."

"Copy that evac, Ben. We've got something we might want to check out, wanted to run it by you in light of the evac, over."

The young man on the ground started having a mild seizure, coughing up foaming bloody white stuff. Offstead turned his head to the side so that he wouldn't choke on it and did his best to hold him down so that he didn't hurt himself any worse, but he felt like it was pathetically little that he could do. *Where were the dammed paramedics?*

"Be quick about it, Steve."

"OK, so you know the antenna installation out on the marsh, over?"

"Yeah."

"So the tower aircraft warning lights on that thing have gone berserk, blinking all crazy, not in their usual pattern. We're thinking maybe we should check it out. That was before the evac order, though, I know there's a lot going on now."

"We've got freakin' dinosaurs and other weird crypto-animals roaming around the park killing visitors, Steve. And no, I don't want to add planes crashing to that list, either, but you said the tower lights are still on, right, just in a different pattern?"

"They're still on, yeah. But I was thinking, the beginning of the access trail out to that utility building isn't far from the edge of Sara's route today. You think it's possible that she ended up out there and changed the light pattern as a signal that she's there?"

Offstead could think of a lot of other things his ranger could be helping out with right about now: the situation right here at this campsite could use some backup, for example, before more visitors got trampled by this humongous lizard. On the other hand, he'd made zero progress with his missing rookie ranger, and so maybe it wasn't a bad idea to start searching outside of her intended route. Not only that, Offstead reflected, but now that it'd been brought to his attention, if he ordered him not to check it out and it turned out she was in fact there...

Well that was just about the last thing he needed, wasn't it? But there had to be a quicker way. It would take hours for Steve to drive out there and back, and if it turned out to be nothing more than some technical glitch...An idea came to him and he spoke into the radio with renewed vigor.

"Steve, listen, it's a long way by ground. Why don't you requisition air support and have a chopper take you for a quick hop out there to check it out, over."

"If it's available, I'll do that."

"I know it's available. I stopped in at the hangar earlier today, they just finished up a fire suppression run up north and were going to be back doing maintenance. There's somebody there who can fly you to the antenna installation. Listen, I'll radio them myself and direct them to have a bird waiting for you by the time you drive over there. So go ahead and get moving. I've got to go myself and direct the paramedics. Over and out."

Suddenly the young guy spasmed and heaved up a gob of black stuff from deep within his body, then went still. "Come on, buddy, stay with me!" But the light in his eyes was out. That glazed-over stare would haunt

Offstead for the rest of his life, he already knew that. And then the sound of a siren reached his ears, the paramedics approaching the campsite.

You're too fucking late. Offstead switched channels on his radio to make the call into the aviation branch. Hopefully this wouldn't be too late, too.

CHAPTER 19

Everglades

Sleep did not come easy for Sara that night. After cleansing and dressing their various wounds as best they could, then creating makeshift bedding and conducting a final security check of the bunker to keep out the ptero-birds, eating what few snacks and drinking what little water was available, the group bedded down for the night, absolutely exhausted. Luanne snored like a dog, which didn't help matters, but Sara knew that wasn't it. Nor was it that at least one of the kids had to be soothed back to sleep every so often. Nor even was it the clouds of mosquitos that plagued them inside the bunker. She would have thought that with all of the ptero-birds out there, the bugs would have feasted on their blood, but perhaps their hides were too thick to penetrate? She had applied bug spray but now wondered if they were actually attracted to the stuff. And then there was the general heat—oppressive, water laden, ever-present, a force to reckon with unto itself. The walls of the bunker meant that they did not get the benefit of the slight breeze that wafted across the marsh.

But even with all that, what it really was that kept her from sleep, Sara knew, was that come morning, if no one had seen her light tower signal and come out here to rescue them, they would have to get themselves out of here. On foot. On their own. Because they did not have the food and water to last here another night. The marsh itself was brackish, partially salty and not suitable for drinking. It would probably rain some, but still. There were children here who needed food.

She listened to the strange sounds of the ptero-birds chortling on the roof—they were definitely still up there. She half-wondered if it would be possible to sneak up there and take them all out in their sleep by bashing them in the head with a heavy object, but supposed that after the first one or two, the rest would wake up and overtake her. *Unless all three adults tried it....*

No, she thought, it was definitely asking for trouble. And besides, she knew from opening the door a crack earlier to take a peek outside that there were about fifty of them waiting on the ground, all sleeping standing up with literally one eye open. *No thanks. Please, universe, let someone see the tower lights and send help for us by morning.*

She lay down on her makeshift bed of a jacket, a backpack for a pillow, and did her best to shut down her mind. She'd read an article once about how the U.S. Army had a foolproof method for falling asleep anywhere in two minutes that soldiers used in battle, something about relaxing your facial muscles, breathing heavily out, imagining yourself in the midst of tranquil, sensory-deprived scenes….but ten minutes later she was still awake, listening to prehistoric toenails scrape on the concrete ceiling while the partially blocked tower lights blinked far overhead, their red and white lights filtering down into the bunker.

When sleep finally did overtake her due to the sheer enervation of the day, it was a fitful, disturbing rest punctuated by start-and-stop nightmares full of gnashing teeth and bloody body parts and, oddly enough, being broke while searching for a new job. It was the worst sleep she'd ever had, and after a while even a prolonged nightmare was a welcome respite because it meant she remained asleep.

In the nightmare she was being chased by an amorphous dinosaur-like monster, something with four huge legs and a body that towered somewhere high above in a dense fog. She was running as fast as she possibly could, but the beast galloped toward her, increasing its pace, moving very fast for something so large. Its feet clopped on the hard earth as it ran, not a clackety sound like horse hooves on pavement, but more of a dull rhythmic thumping, a *whump whump whump whump* as its four feet pounded the earth. Though she ran as fast as she had ever run in her life, the monster soon overtook her, and just as it was about to trample her into the dirt, to grind her small body into insignificant meaty pulp, she awoke with a start.

"Sara, Sara!" Rebecca was saying urgently into her ear as she shook her awake. Sara was embarrassed, thinking she had been crying out in her sleep during her nightmare. She rubbed the sleep from her eyes and rolled over. But something was wrong. Very wrong.

She could still hear the *whump whump whump whump*, loud and very near.

"Sara! There's a helicopter here!"

"Huh, what?" She propped herself up on an elbow.

"Your tower light thing must have worked! There's a helicopter hovering right over us!"

And then they heard a male voice booming from a loudspeaker issuing from above: "Park Service Aviation here. Ranger Sara Cliff, we are looking for you. If you are inside, please open the door. There are animals there so don't step outside, just open the door, and we will set down. Or radio us on VHF channel 10. I repeat..."

The airman repeated the message through the loudhailer while Sara got to her feet. Everyone else in the room was already up, including Luanne, who was helping the children to pack up their things. "We're getting out of here, kids, time to go. Come on..."

"Be careful opening the door!" Sara warned. Her vivid bad dreams of being chased by unknowable monsters still haunted her.

"We need to let them know we're here or they could leave! I don't think they want to land with those pterodactyl animals out there," Rebecca said, moving to the door.

"Just be ready to close it quick," Sara said.

Luanne shepherded the kids over to the far corner of the room in preparation of the door opening. Rebecca put her hand on the door handle. "I'm gonna peek out there and make sure the creatures aren't right outside. If they're not, I'll swing it open. It's still sort of dark outside, so I want you to take your flashlight and shine it out there for the helicopter."

Sara's fingers flew over the zipper of her backpack and she extracted the light and turned it on. The beam was better than nothing, but not powerful.

"Okay, on three, here we go..." The chopper lowered even closer to the building and she had to shout to be heard above its beating rotors. "...two...one...now!"

She cracked the door open and peeked outside, checking to make sure no beasts lurked immediately outside. She didn't want to fling it all the way open and have a flood of them pour inside. But the doorway was clear. Outside, a few feet away, however, the pack of ptero-birds hopped around on two feet like kangaroos, heads craned up to stare at the mechanical bird in the sky.

Sara wasted no time shining the light out the door. It stabbed weakly through the rapidly fading darkness. Sara guessed it must be between 5:30 and at the latest, six in the morning.

Suddenly the voice from the helicopter boomed again. "We have a visual. We will set down in the clearing outside the door. Stay inside until we land. The animals should disperse as we set down. Stand by..."

Rebecca ducked back inside the building as the chopper appeared over the open grass outside. The ptero-birds hopped and ran around, but did not leave the area. The chopper pilot stabilized the craft into a hover over the center of the open area, then began a slow, controlled descent.

But the pteros did not scatter as was hoped. They stood their ground, even while buffeted directly by heavy rotor wash. They ran around in circles or else stubbornly knelt and held firm in one place. Those on the perimeter could take to the air, and a couple of these were unfortunate enough to get close enough to the 'copter to be dashed apart by the tail rotor. It was a wake-up call for Sara and Rebecca when they were sprayed with reddish blood, a thick piece of leg bone narrowly missing them and smacking into the bunker wall. It was also a wake-up call for the pilot, who had to stabilize his craft as it canted wildly to one side after striking the creatures. A recovery was made, though, and then the chopper skids contacted the ground and all hell broke loose.

"Oh my God, I see something else out there!" Sara screamed. "You're not going to believe it!" she finished, ducking back inside the bunker.

"What?" Rebecca asked. "At this point I don't think there's anything I wouldn't believe." Behind them, the children huddled with Luanne, sobbing.

"It's one of the centipedes."

"Ah, our good friends, *Arthropleura.*"

"Who?"

"*Arthropleura.* A genus of extinct prehistoric millipedes, actually. I was thinking about what those things might be overnight and that's my best guess at this point."

"I envy your ability to think about anything other than how we're probably going to die, which is what I did all last night," Sara admitted.

"I'm a zoologist," Rebecca yelled over the chopper noise. "Prehistoric millipedes come to life is what we live for! Are we gonna make a dash for that 'copter or what?"

"I guess so. Are they going to open the door for us, though, or what?"

"I think they're scared. Too many animals out there. They're probably waiting for us to come to them."

"Can't say I blame them. Maybe we should start running out there and then they'll open the door?"

"I think we should all go as one big group. We'll be more intimidating that way to the animals. Also, the first run out might catch them unaware, but if we go one at a time, or in smaller groups, they might catch on to what's happening and go after the second group harder because they missed the first."

Sara nodded. "Good point. I'll see if Luanne and the kids are ready. Here, take my light and wave it at the pilot to try to get his attention, let him know we're coming." She handed the light to Rebecca and moved to Luanne, whose kids were holding hands around her body.

"Luanne, we're going to make a run for that helicopter. You want me to help carry one of the kids, or how do you want to do it?"

"I asked them if they can run. They say they can," Luanne said, teary-eyed. "Right, darlings? We're going to run to the helicopter and it's going to take us to safety, okay?"

All three kids nodded through wide open, tear-filled eyes.

"All right, way to go, gang!" Sara said, doing her best to sound upbeat. "We've got this! Just a few feet out the door and we'll be in a cozy aircraft going home. Who's with me?"

The kids nodded silently without taking their eyes off their mother. "Come with me to the doorway, then. Just right over here..." She led them to the door, which was being held open by Rebecca, who stood just outside, waving the flashlight. "Stay inside, don't come out yet."

Suddenly Rebecca whirled around from outside and shouted inside to the others. "A cluster of the ptero-birds are attacking one of the millipedes. I say we go now while some of them are distracted!"

Luanne looked back to Sara, as though uncertain. Sara looked outside at the helicopter, which was still on the ground, rotors spinning, engine roaring, doors closed.

"Give me one of the girls. I carry one, you carry one, the boy can run. Rebecca's running point to be able to fight off the animals if necessary." Sara said this last part quietly enough that she didn't think Rebecca would hear it, since she wasn't sure how she would feel about being unilaterally nominated for such a task, but she was out there already, Sara thought, so it was kind of the default.

Luanne nodded and handed the older girl to Sara, who hefted the child up over one shoulder facing backwards. Sara looked outside again, and now saw that Rebecca was about halfway to the chopper, its doors still closed. On the edge of the cleared area, a swarm of ptero-birds still battled one of the megapedes, but movement off to the right caught Sara's attention. Another massive milli writhed up out of the swamp and wriggled its way toward Rebecca. This did not bode well. Rebecca had time to make the chopper before it reached her, but the rest of them might not.

She felt the impulse welling up inside her, the one telling her that doing something was better than doing nothing, that going *now, now, now,* was the right thing to do rather than summoning an iota of patience and waiting to see what might happen next. *Go, go, go, now, now, now!*

"Rebecca, behind you!" She had to give the warning even though, predictably, Rebecca paused to turn around. On seeing the new multi-legged threat, she spun back around and started to run toward the chopper. But during this brief pause of forward motion, a pair of ptero-birds that had been cast off from the pack devouring the downed megapede turned their long-necked heads toward the zoologist. As if on the exact same mental wavelength, both primitive beings launched into a run toward her at the same time, and in the same cadence. It was clear that they would be on her in seconds.

"Run, Rebecca! Chopper, now!" Sara screamed. Rebecca was already in motion, waving the little flashlight in her right hand, trying to get the attention of the 'copter crew. For it was a crew, Sara could see now. In addition to the pilot, there was also a co-pilot, who now opened the rear door of the Bell Jet Ranger helicopter about two seconds before Rebecca reached it. Luckily the door slid to the side to open, for if it had opened outward, Rebecca would have been slammed in the face since she did not stop her sprint. She dove headlong into the helicopter's interior, the ptero-bird duo mere feet behind her.

The helo man did his best to haul her inside, but Rebecca could see him eyeballing the pair of ptero-birds that also appeared to have no intentions of stopping. The creatures hopped effortlessly into the open craft, proceeding to stomp and kick and peck at everything inside. Even over the engine noise and rotor wash, Sara could hear the awful screams. And then, miraculously, she saw a human hand appear on the 'copter door—the airman's—and then the door was sliding shut—catching the neck of one of the ptero-avians between the frame and the door itself before the door bumped back, slightly ajar. The predator went limp and sagged in the door frame, its legs hanging outside while its limp neck and head were still inside the cabin.

The other assailant was still fighting, however, and in its throes, kicked its fallen brethren outside of the craft. The dead body plopping to the ground must have caught the attention of the surviving megapede, for it now charged straight toward the lingering aircraft. Sara barred her arm across the doorway, not wanting the standing child to run on his own. She knew Luanne wouldn't go before her.

Inside the helicopter, the battle of two men and one woman versus one strange but very heavy bird-like reptile raged on, with the dino-creature hopping and kicking all over the aircraft. Sara could see the pilot's arm lash out from the console seat and then, above the din of the motor, she thought she heard a gunshot. She told Luanne, who was asking her what they were going to do, to hush. "Is that a gun? Did you hear that?"

Both of them listened some more and the same sound was heard two more times in close succession. Before Luanne could answer, the ptero-avian was kicked out of the 'copter to hit the ground hard. Barely alive, it twitched and bled on the dirt next to its partner-in-crime who had fallen before it.

Sara's impulses welled up more powerful than ever, overflowing to the point she felt she would burst if she didn't act. Both animals out of the copter, Rebecca inside the 'copter. She turned to Luanne, eyes wide.

"Let's go, now! Come on!"

Sara left the safety of the building first, hugging the girl tightly against her as she fell into a run. She could hear Luanne behind her, the smallest child clutched in her arms, while the oldest child, the boy, ran on his own between Sara and Luanne. Even as she clumsily ran toward the waiting aircraft with the child, Sara couldn't help but look to the right, at the mega-millipede. It was there all right, scuttling across the open flat area, its feelers twitching like crazy as they tried to process an overload of sensory data for the primitive nerve bundle that served as its brain. The fear of seeing it distracted Sara from the physical process of running with a toddler and she stumbled.

The toddler landed on two feet and somehow continued running toward the chopper. Sara, meanwhile, had semi-twisted her right ankle and fell again when she tried to stand, crying out from the jolting pain. From her position on the ground, Sara watched a male arm reach out of the still-open door, beckoning the child, who continued to move forward rapidly on two unsteady feet, her own arms outstretched before her. By the time Sara struggled to her unsteady feet, the mega-millipede was only about ten feet behind her.

With a yelp of surprise at seeing how quickly the arthropod had closed the distance, she bolted for the chopper. But there was more she couldn't see, on the other side of the aircraft. A new flock of ptero-avians had grouped together and moved in concert toward the opposite side of the helo.

Luanne actually passed Sara on the way to the chopper, since she never faltered. She plodded resolutely onward, the wailing girl held firmly against her breast, while her son ran along beside her. Sara looked to the left as the three of them passed her up without so much as a sideways glance.

It started to pour down rain. A rare, instant hard rain where there was nothing and then there was a deluge that began turning the ground to mud. They sloshed through it toward the chopper. Sara caught sight of Rebecca's concerned visage shouting unheard urgencies at all of them. She kept going.

The boy reached the open door first. He was hauled in easily by the male crew member who then turned around and held his hands out again, this time for Luanne's baby girl. The mother handed up her baby and then started to climb in herself without waiting for the airman's assistance.

Sara moved up to the aircraft to push Luanne up if necessary but since that was not needed, she turned around to get a look at the monsters on her tail. The megapede was flinging its massive head to and fro, about halfway to her, distracted by warring with ptero-birds on the way.

But suddenly the chopper canted sharply toward Sara, lifting up off of one skid. She had to roll backwards to avoid the rotors, one of which nearly hit the ground. When she came to a stop, Sara was looking away from the helicopter at the marauding megapede, a riot of twitching, jittering appendages. By the time she turned back around, which wasn't more than a couple of seconds given the death threat looming her way on a thousand legs, she was mortified to see the chopper lifting off into the air.

"Wait, stop!" she waved her arms. She was certain it would set back down, that the pilot just needed to regain his balance of the craft after being almost knocked over by the ptero-avians, but to her utter dismay, shock and, yes—horror—the mechanical bird continued into the sky.

Its loud hailer offered little comfort. "Seek shelter in the building. We will come back for you. It is too risky for the aircraft to stay. Take shelter now and help will be back for you!"

Sara watched the helo lift up higher into the sky and then turn and fly toward its distant headquarters. She felt anger threatening to overtake her, How could they do this to her—leave her behind like this when she had helped all of them?

But the sound of excited clucking, screeching and other more indefinable noises removed her attention from the chopper and made her realize that she had no time for anything other than reaching the shelter of the building. She heard the loudspeaker again as she pushed to her feet and started to run.

"Dropping supplies to help…" She didn't bother to turn around to get a look at the small red boxy object that dropped from the chopper to land on the ground near the edge of the clearing. She could feel the beasts trammeling the ground right behind her, pounding after her. She saw the open bunker door and ran for it in great leaps and bounds, willing herself not to trip, knowing that to stumble or fall or otherwise slow her forward motion in any way would almost surely mean certain death. Being eaten alive or trampled to death while being pecked apart was not the way she wanted to end her young life. Her brain dimly registered the otherworldly, ethereal sounds of the *Arthropleura* somewhere back there, too, but she concentrated on reaching safety.

And soon she was at the doorway, that small rectangle of blackness that signified shelter and protection. It would have been easier to sprint right through it, like a marathon winner triumphantly bursting through the ribbon at the finish line, but she knew she had to be able to stop to close the door behind her lest the beasts follow her inside and trap her there. Summoning her childhood softball skills, she went into a slide as she crossed the threshold of the doorway, which slowed her progress enough to enable her to grab the edge of the door on the inside and fling it shut.

She heard and felt the impact of the ptero-avians as they crashed into the unexpected barrier. She stood quickly and pulled on the door handle to make certain the door was really closed all the way. It was. Now she could relax.

That door was the only way in. Except for the skylight, she reminded herself, looking up. The makeshift cover of the dead ptero-avian bodies was still in place. But also still in place were the living ptero-birds up there on the roof. Not as many, since some of them had gone to ground to participate in the action there, but she could see at least a couple of them still on roof patrol.

And above them, the flashing distress beacons of her programmed tower lights. *At least they know I'm here*, she thought. *At least they know I'm here. Now I just have to find a way to survive until they come back for me.*

CHAPTER 20

Coral Gables

Detective Rene Bravia had watched with interest the local news piece on television, about a helicopter rescue that had just taken place in Everglades National Park. Something was indeed afoot in the 'glades, he noted to himself. Strange animal attacks requiring evacuation, park closure--not normal, not normal at all. And all of it happening in the wake of Dr. Landis' curious death.

Local TV news had live footage showing the chopper landing, with that zoologist colleague of Dr. Landis exiting the aircraft to a waiting cluster of local reporters. Bravia had wasted no time in placing a call to Dr. Trout's cell-phone, knowing she would now have service. To his surprise, she had answered his call, explaining that she would be heading into work at her university lab after stopping at home for a much needed shower and lunch.

Now, as Bravia waited out a red light before crossing onto the Florida University campus, he hoped that she would be able to help him with the BioGen files he'd gotten from Landis' home computer. She had reached out to him by phone earlier, after all, to tell him about the strange animal attacks on the chameleon collectors, so she was apparently concerned, as well.

Bravia parked in the lot for Trout's building and entered through double glass doors on the ground floor. Took the stairs up to the second floor and walked down the hall to her lab, the door to which was wide open.

"Hello, Dr. Trout?" he said by way of announcement.

"Come on in," came the female reply from somewhere deep in the lab. Bravia entered and walked back between the rows of lab benches until he found her seated at a stool in front of a complex-looking piece of equipment.

"Dr. Trout, thanks so much for seeing me on such short notice, I really appreciate it. Please, don't get up, I know you've been through a lot in the last twenty-four hours." He extended a hand and she shook it without getting up.

"You're right about that. And that poor ranger, Sara, is still out there!"

"I assume they've mounted a rescue for her?"

"As we speak."

"She'll be in good hands, then."

Rebecca nodded, but her mind flashed on the ptero-birds, and how the poor girl must still be hunkered down in that concrete bunker, and she shuddered. "I have no doubt."

Bravia handed her a computer flash drive. "I have the files from Dr. Landis' computer on here."

Rebecca took the drive and inserted it into an open laptop on the lab bench next to the machine. "So you said these are files having to do with Archie's consulting work with BioGen Corporation?"

"That's right. I have no idea what they mean, or what they even have to do with. But since, as you say, this was private consulting, not a publicly known grant, and also based on email correspondence that revealed possible tensions between Landis and those he was working with at BioGen, and given what's been happening in the Everglades, I decided it's worth it to have you look at them."

"Sure. Let me take a look right now, I can probably tell you what they have to do with, at least."

Rebecca finished running the virus scan on the flash drive and opened a folder showing its contents.

"Only thing on there are the files in question," Bravia clarified. Rebecca nodded and opened one of the files, a spreadsheet.

"Okay, so here we have a csv. file—that's comma separated value—usually used to store data that's been exported from some other program, like maybe a spreadsheet. In this case…" She leaned in closer to the screen and squinted while scrolling through the data. "In this case I'd say these are base pairs from some gene—all the characters are one of four letters, A, C, G, or T. And here we go, the header up top has what is the name of the gene, 'Taq 41C', which means nothing to me personally off the top of my head, though that doesn't mean much. And as you can see, there are multiple tabs in this file, I'm guessing one for each sequenced gene…"

She clicked on a couple of the other tabs to open it, look at the header, and then nodded. "Yep, each tab has a different header that names a different gene. The actual data is the arrangement of the As, Cs, Gs and Ts that make up the gene. Let me take a look at the other file."

Bravia nodded. "I see. And there were many other files just like this one, I just chose one at random to show you to get an idea of what they are."

"Okay, let me see what we have in this other one here…" She paused while opening the other file. "Okay, this is a proprietary math program used a lot for statistics, called MATLAB."

"Ah, I was wondering what that file extension was," Bravia said.

"Yeah if you don't have the program it won't open, but I do have it, since I use it sometimes for my own work, so let's check it out, it's loading…"

In a minute she was scrolling through columns of data in different colored panes. "Let me just try something here…" She hit a key that triggered a pop-up message reading, "Running simulation…"

Then the columns of data below changed. "Okay, so what they're doing is running successive generations to see the result of the genome, like if they mated two animals and instead of waiting for them to give birth to see the genome of the second generation, they're just simulating it here, mathematically, based on genetics and statistics."

"So it's a computer generated offspring?" Bravia queried.

"A computer generated genome of an offspring, yes. Its genetic sequence. So it's like they're trying to see what they might make if they combine two different genomes—that is, if you have the DNA from one organism, and combine it with the DNA of another, what will you get? Well, this lets them take a stab at it without having to actually mate the two organisms and then wait for them to reproduce to see the results. Oh, here we go!"

"What?"

She pointed to a play button on the screen. "Phenotype projection."

"Huh?"

"Phenotype is what the physical manifestation of having a certain *genome*—the genes—will look like. For example, if you cross two blue-eyed people, the phenotype for the inherited genes of the offspring—"

"Would be blue-eyed also."

"Most likely. So, here we have a movie of what these two genomes would yield if they reproduced, which is good because I don't see a species name anywhere on here, though it could be in the code somewhere as a comment, perhaps. But let's just check it out."

She clicked the play button and they watched as an animation began to run. "Oh wow, here we go!" Rebecca enthused as the video began to play. "American Crocodile, male." The video was animated, but rendered in sophisticated anatomical detail. The animal itself had a silhouette of a man standing beside it for quick size reference, although complete measurements including length and weight were also listed in a corner of the screen. Then the screen transitioned and a new animal appeared on its own pedestal, one that elicited a gasp from Rebecca.

"Looks like a T-rex?" Bravia said, sounding confused.

"It is. *Tyrannosaurus rex*. Let's watch."

"Gee, no Netflix and chill for you, am I right?" Bravia smiled.

Rebecca chuckled. "This is pretty good viewing if you ask me. But I'm concerned where they're—uh-oh. Oh my god!"

"What the heck is that thing?"

Rebecca's eyes opened wide as she stared at the screen. "It's a—we were joking when we called it a Croc rex…it's a cross between a T. rex and a crocodile."

"Wow. Far out concept. Kind of like the stuff I used to draw on my notebooks when I was bored in school."

"Yeah except this isn't a concept, Detective Bravia. It's real. They actually did this."

Bravia looked puzzled. "But how'd they get the DNA sample from a T. rex? Like, how'd they know what genes it had?"

Dr. Trout shot him a respectful look. "Good question. Lately in the news there was a lot of hoopla about a T. rex leg bone found that was only partially fossilized and contained soft tissue—collagen, if I'm not mistaken. Add to that the presence of iron-rich blood and a rapid onset fossilization process, and *voila*—65 million years later we have Tyrannosaur DNA." She glanced at the laptop screen. "And obviously, BioGen found a way to get hold of it. Probably a Sotheby's auction or something like that. However they did it, it doesn't matter because I know for a fact that it worked."

Now commanding the detective's full attention, Rebecca went on to explain how she saw the T. rex crocodile hybrid—in the flesh—in the Everglades the previous day. She made prolonged direct eye contact with Bravia. "You've done it, Detective. You established a direct link between what Dr. Landis was working on with BioGen and the strange creatures now running amok in the Everglades. Thank you."

Bravia actually blushed. He was unused to compliments from the public related to anything but the most obvious cases, such as returning a missing child alive or apprehending an armed and dangerous suspect. To have someone note that he had gone above and beyond the line of duty in his investigative work did make him feel good. But still, his decades' old skills honed on the job wouldn't let him be derailed by a little flattery. *Now what?* The voice inside his head asked. *What does this mean for the case? Can we close it?*

He needed to think on it some more, but unfortunately the answer was leaning towards the negative. While Rebecca continued to play with the computer program, Bravia reflected on what this new development meant for the case. It certainly appeared that Landis was mixed up with BioGen in a way that could have negative repercussions for him. Bravia thought back to the email messages on Landis' home PC, doing his best to recall the gist of them.

Lab work with animal DNA markers...out of your hands now...contractually bound. You were paid handsomely......performance bonus...concludes our business....

And then there had been some pushback from Landis: *I have a right to be informed of the results.... full disclosure clause.* To Bravia this suggested that although Landis helped BioGen with some kind of lab work, he might not have known exactly what he was doing, nor what the intended end result was, or the final application of the work. Or at least if he did, he was unhappy about his ending compensation or felt that he had been misled in some way? Then Bravia almost laughed out load. Landis was unhappy all right. *Guy ripped out his own jugular with a dinosaur claw.*

Why would he do that? So this company owed him some money, maybe, or took his work in a different direction than expected—was that a reason to take your life? Here was a successful professional, near retirement, financially well off. He didn't need anything from BioGen, not really. *So then, why'd he do it?*

Rebecca's next words ripped Bravia from his line of mental inquiry. "Oh no, no, no! I see what they've done here."

"What's that?" Bravia asked, now focusing on her laptop screen.

"They've deliberately combined genes of various animals—reptiles and others—in such a way as to produce viable offspring. These creatures are neither of the original organisms that contributed DNA, but rather a new hybrid animal that the world has never before seen."

"Is that..." Bravia hesitated, choosing his words carefully. "Is that bad?" He felt a little foolish, knowing he was in the presence of a professor of zoology, but then again, she was the expert here, so it would be foolish of him not to ask. It reminded him of his own grade school days, when the teachers would say, "The only stupid question is the one you don't ask!" *Right.*

She looked at him like he was asking if it was okay to rob a bank. "Is that *bad*? Oh I don't know, if you think it's okay for anybody to start their own freaking Island of Dr. Moreau on public lands, then it's not bad. Because we're not talking about computer simulations and theoretical combinatory genetics, here, Detective. I thought we were—that's what any rational scientist would think."

She then pointed to the animation on screen. "But no, I *saw* one of these creatures with my own eyes in the Everglades yesterday. That means these are no longer just simulations—they have gone ahead with creating them in real life!" Then, as she clicked through the MATLAB program, her eyes lit up as she recognized a creature in an animation.

Her gaze moved from the screen to the machine, a large boxy affair with a glass window in it, which she had been working with when Bravia entered. It was a DNA sequencer; a sophisticated piece of technology that determined a DNA sequence from an actual tissue sample. Prior to Bravia's visit, she had placed the tissue sample she had collected from one of the ptero-avians in the bunker into the DNA sequencer. Eyeballing the machine's progress now, she saw that the sequencing had been completed only minutes ago. On the laptop screen, she clicked a link under the animation that read, "Genomic sequence." She had noticed that some of the animations had this link, while others did not. She hoped that didn't mean what she thought it did.

On screen, a very long sequence of the genetic base pair letters—A, G, C, T—was displayed in text form. She picked up her laptop and then carried it over to the machine, standing so she could hold the screen next to the DNA sequencer's display. "Oh wow. Just as I feared."

"What?" Bravia asked, leaning in closer to both screens.

"They're the same. Exactly the same sequence. As much as I can see, anyway. It's dozens of pages long so, to be sure I'll export the genome file from the sequencer and then do a text compare on the laptop of both genomes. Then we'll know for sure."

As her hands moved purposefully over the sequencer's controls, Bravia asked another question. "What will we know for sure?"

She clicked a button with a flourish and then went back to her laptop. "That the animated freak of a creature in this video was not only conceptually conceived of, but actually created or spawned, if you will, in real life, as a living animal."

"By Dr. Landis and BioGen?"

Rebecca looked away from the laptop with a frown. "Yes. But I still can't imagine Archie would intentionally do something like that. Especially releasing it to the wild. No way can I imagine—oh, hold on, here it is." She pressed a few more keys and closely examined the message written on a new window. "One hundred percent match," she said, eyes gleaming with intensity. Then the display on the gene sequencing machine changed color and Rebecca grimaced as she looked at it.

"Hold on, what's this…" She squinted at the message, then opened her mouth wide in surprise. "Oh my God…"

"What now?"

"I've been hacked."

"Hacked? Your computer, or the gene machine?"

"The actual gene sequencing machine, it's been hacked."

"Well anything connected online can be hacked. I even read an article about how this guy's car was hacked as he was driving—"

"No, I know, but this machine is *not* connected to the Internet."

"It's not?"

"No, and it was still hacked."

Bravia stared at the gene machine like it was from outer space. "How?"

"The only possible way is that the code itself that it sequenced told it to execute certain instructions."

"But I thought this DNA code came from living animal tissue—a specimen you collected yourself from the park?"

"Right. That's what makes it so scary. Whoever did this *knew* that people would be looking into what these animals are by sequencing their genes, and so to make that investigative process more difficult, they encoded the genes with an artificial sequence of bio-malware that actually infects the machine doing the sequencing."

"What'd it actually do to it?"

"Read that."

Bravia leaned in closer to the display and read the message that was in simple block text:

What are you looking at? Stop looking at my code! This code is proprietary and protected by US Patent Office No. 883763669375. Your machine will now shut down. Do not run this sequence again under penalty of law! You have been warned!

Suddenly the display froze up, turned a blue color while the message disappeared and was replaced with a hexadecimal error code. Then, one by one, all of the machine's lights blinked out, a hum was heard as it powered down, and then it remained dark and silent.

"Blue screen of death!" Rebecca said matter-of-factly. "Wow. As mad as this makes me, I'll probably be able to publish a whole paper on this in the leading bioinformatics journal. Living organism DNA arranged to run malware in the machines that try to sequence them. Good lord! That means those dinosaur things walking around out there have encoded into their cells useless junk DNA that serves no biological purposes for them.

It's only there to hack the machines of anyone who tries to sequence those genes. Incredible!"

"I'll say. What it means to me is that I need to pay a little visit to BioGen. You'll back me up on this as a witness, I presume?"

Rebecca nodded earnestly. "Oh yes. As a scientist I find this kind of behavior reprehensible."

"And let me ask you, aside from this hacking activity, what specific laws have been broken by creating these hybrid animals, as you call them, and releasing them into the wild as appears to have been done here?" Bravia wanted to know

Rebecca's sarcastic laugh filled the lab. "Oh I don't know, for starters, the Invasive Species Act, the Endangered Species Act, possibly the Animal Welfare Act, various FDA Genetically Modified Organism restrictions..."

"Okay, so we'll need to bring this to the attention of Park Services and FWC."

Rebecca nodded. "Not sure what they'll be able to do about it, but yes. They need to know what's happened here." She went back to her laptop and then clicked on a new video animation. Bravia eyeballed the screen in horror as he watched the hyper-realistic animation of a terrifying monster parade around on screen.

Rebecca studied his reaction and said, "We can only hope and pray that some of these other creatures never made it past the modelling stage."

CHAPTER 21

Everglades

Ranger Sara Cliff checked that the door to the utility building was shut for the tenth time that morning. Her nerves were so frayed she didn't trust anything she did anymore. But it was closed, securing her from the prehistoric beasts that loitered right outside. Looking up, she could see that the skylight opening was as secure as could be, too, though she thought the ptero-bird corpses might be beginning to decompose. She couldn't hear or see signs of the creatures on the roof, but that didn't mean they weren't there. She was trapped in here, trapped like a rat in a cage, she fretted. Like a morsel of living food in a larder for these animals to break into and eat when they became hungry enough to go to the trouble.

She knew she was being melodramatic with herself. She should be happy, after all, for simply surviving the last twenty-four hours, and knowing that now help must be on the way since they knew exactly where she was. Even if she could, she told herself, leaving this place would be a mistake, since this is where the rescue team would return to find her. She had to simply fortify this bunker and hunker down as best she could until help arrived.

But passing the time wasn't as easy as she thought. She was tired as could be after the fitful night full of tossing and turning and bad dreams, but she was afraid to fall asleep now for fear of missing her rescuers. She didn't want them to think she wasn't in here, after all. They might think she had taken it upon herself to leave the building for some reason, maybe if the animals had broken in....

She forced herself to stop thinking about all the things that might go wrong and to focus on what she could do to ameliorate the situation. People had died, after all, and she was still alive. She had that to be thankful for. She liked her job, she realized. She was a ranger and proud of it. Proud to help people experience this wilderness that she was so fond of herself, even with its unpredictability, its discomforts, and yes, even its deadly dangers. But that didn't mean she would take risks for no reason.

She wanted to see what was outside, but the flat ground outside the door was out; simply too risky. The roof was her best bet—it offered a better vantage point from which to see what was happening outside, and, as far as she could tell, the ptero-birds had largely abandoned it in favor of the action on the ground. Looking up there now, she couldn't see any of them. Still, there might be one or two, she couldn't say for sure without at least poking her head through the skylight.

Sara climbed up on some of the wall mounted equipment until she could pull herself up through the two dead ptero-birds that they had used to cover the opening. It was disgusting to have to shimmy her head between the two leathery hides, and she held her breath as she did so, fighting back the beginnings of a bout of retching. Noise was the last thing she needed to make. She felt elation at seeing a clear, empty roof, except for the towers and infrastructure equipment that was supposed to be there, until she turned her head and saw it. At least there was only one, she told herself. It could be worse. A lot worse. A single ptero-avian, standing on one leg like a stork, gazing down on its associates as they milled about in the clearing below.

She pictured herself sneaking up onto the roof and running full force into it, knocking it off the rooftop. She could probably do that, she realized, but then what? It would just rile up all the others on the ground, and then they'd all hop up here on the roof. They might possibly even be so incensed at that point that they'd figure out how to get down through the grotesquely blockaded skylight, and then it would be all over for Ranger Sara's first day, wouldn't it?

She did not kid herself that she had the skills to stealth kill it—to stalk up on it and wring its neck until it died a silent, gasping-for-air death that none of its flock noticed down below. One back-kick from the thing would probably smash her sternum and knock her to the ground in one fell swoop, ironically "killing two birds with one stone" for the ptero-avian— incapacitating her and getting her off the roof. She realized that she would have to settle for acting like a prairie dog, thrusting her head above the skylight while the bipedal predator was facing the other way, so that she could get a quick glimpse of what was happening in any given direction. Right now, she was facing the road back to where they had come from.

An eerie quiet pervaded the scenery as she watched the road while the ptero-birds clucked and kicked their toes into the ground. A light wind rustled the sawgrass. She could just see in the distance the ruined RV, where Lonnie had made his last stand. It would be a difficult drive even for an off-road vehicle, she thought, looking at the road to the building, with its washed out sections, one at the RV and one surrounding the building like a moat. Were they going to send another helicopter? She quickly swiveled her head to look back in the direction of the clearing where the congregation of two-legged creatures stood around. The helo landing hadn't gone so well last time, she thought. Maybe they were afraid to try it again?

She looked back to the road, to try and visualize a convoy of Ranger Service vehicles making its way toward her, but when she turned around, she nearly had a heart attack.

The ptero-avian now stood not five feet from her, having silently traversed the roof while she faced the other way. She had totally underestimated their capability for stealth. Staring silently at her, neck bent so that its head was eye level with hers, she felt frozen in place, immobilized by the sudden shock-inducing appearance of the predator. She told herself not to make any sudden moves, certainly not to go on the offensive. *Don't even blink.* She knew that the animal could lash out at her with what for it would be a casual motion, but for her would translate to catastrophic injury. *It could peck my whole face off right now with one little movement of its neck....*

She unhooked her fingers from the edge of the skylight, and did the only thing she thought might save her life: slid her elbows off the edge of the opening in the roof and allowed herself to drop straight back down into the room, do not pass Go, do not collect two hundred dollars, but do pass two dead ptero-birds guarding her entrance into safety. She slithered past the odious corpses and landed on the cement floor with a loud thud, instantly going into a backwards roll in case the creature was dropping in after her. But when she was on two feet again, she looked up to see only the skylight—even the two ptero-birds were still in place.

So now what? She dared not go back up there now, that was for sure. Not only that, but she'd had a look out there and there had been nothing to see or hear that had to do with her getting out of here anytime soon. So she set up a little nest in the corner of the room farthest from the skylight, sat down and tried to at least rest as best she could without actually falling asleep.

Fifteen minutes later, she was snoring.

CHAPTER 22

Everglades

"We're not gonna make the same mistake again!" Offstead said to a roomful of park law enforcement and rescue personnel. They were gathered in a semi-outdoor room that was open-air but had electricity and furniture, which served as a staging area for ground and water vehicles.

"The helicopter landing was too risky. The road out there is too narrow and washed out."

"And it's blocked by the recreational vehicle she somehow got out there in," Offstead's field partner, Sam Gumshoe said.

"Right," Offstead said, picking up the reins again. "So these swamp boats are the ticket. We'll be able to launch near the start of the same road they used to get out there, but then boat across the sawgrass and come up on the antenna installation on the far side of the building. It should attract less attention for the animals than a chopper. Thoughts?"

Gumshoe checked the action on a 12-gauge pump shotgun. "Pistols ain't gonna do it against the frickin' dinosaurs that are out there. What else we got to make sure we can stand up to a confrontation if need be?"

Offstead nodded to the shotgun. "Long guns have been distributed—rifles, shotguns, we also have heavy-duty tranquilizer darts, net guns and even tasers at our disposal."

At this, several of the rangers broke off into excited chatter about weapons and fighting strategy. Offstead raised his voice to continue.

"But I will reiterate, as more media attention falls onto our little neck of the woods, the world will be watching. We do not want to kill these animals if we don't have to. We will be working in cooperation with scientists from an alphabet soup of agencies to determine the best course of eco-remediation. Our job today is to keep the *people* in our park safe, not to kill animals, unless killing animals is the only way to do our job. Is that clear?"

A chorus of affirmative responses erupted around him as weapons and gear continued to be loaded into a pair of swamp boats. The craft were shallow-water aluminum, open boats with a giant fan motor on the back that allowed them to be able to travel over extremely shallow water that would be impassable for a regular boat. Offstead once remarked that they could run on top of a wet sponge if need be, and while an exaggeration, they were the perfect vehicle for navigating the Everglades' many miles of shallow bogs, flats and creeks.

Offstead glanced at a clock on the wall. "Team A, you're the swamp boat group in charge of rescuing our new ranger. Should take about an hour to reach the antenna installation. Sara Cliff needs our help. Make sure we get her out of there safely, am I understood?"

After a roomful of enthusiastic replies, Offstead continued. "Team B, you're in your regular patrol vehicles to escort visitors from the park and combat the unusual wildlife we've been seeing, *if necessary*. I repeat: *if necessary*. This is not a carte blanche to go off on some half-cocked safari, do you understand? I need you out there to help people, to keep them safe, and to uphold your normal duties as a park law enforcement officer. If we need a specific animal team, one will be assembled at my discretion. Until then, it's people first, and you are to leave the wildlife alone unless it won't leave you alone. Clear?"

Everyone said they were. "Then let's go get 'er done!"

The room broke out into a hive of activity as the two groups readied their respective vehicles for field operations. Offstead turned to Sam Gumshoe. "Sam, I'll be staying behind at headquarters to oversee things and handle the media. I'm putting you in charge of Team A. Three men on each boat; you're captain of one, I want you to pick two more captains and your crew, then roll outta here STAT!"

"You got it." Gumshoe waved over another ranger and pointed to one of the swamp boats, while Offstead stalked off to talk to one of the team B rangers. The thought of that sailfin dinosaur lumbering around the campsite still had him on edge, and he told his employee so. "I want you to patrol that campsite, and then, after the visitors are taken care of—that is, escorted off the park premises—I want you to keep tabs on the whereabouts of that gigantic lizard."

"You got it." With his teams readying themselves for imminent deployment, Offstead left the staging area and headed over to his HQ office. His admin staff had been pestering him about a lot of phone calls coming in, media requests for interviews, including one from a national news network. *Here we go*, he thought, climbing into his pickup truck. *Should be one helluva shitshow.*

CHAPTER 23

Everglades

In this nightmare, Sara Cliff was running after a helicopter, a hovering helicopter that never quite descended low enough to pick her up. It was pouring rain with lightning and thunder, and yet she stood on a road with fire burning on both sides. Even in this strange scenario, it was the smell that stood out the most. A horrid, charred flesh odor that pervaded her nostrils and made her cough and choke. She hacked and dry heaved until she was saying "help" in her sleep, until she thought she was going to pass out, and then she woke with a startled spasm.

Eyes fluttered open, she felt a sense of *deja vous...I've been here before....*because she had not only been here before, but actually woken up here before, and also after a bad dream. And this time, she hoped there would be a helicopter outside like there was last time. The 'copter was in this dream—nightmare—too, she thought optimistically as she rose to her feet. But after walking beneath the skylight, she didn't see one.

She could hear the rain though—it dripped through the skylight, running down off the slowly putrefying ptero-bird bodies. And she could see the lightning, and hear the thunder. *So that part of the dream was real,* she thought. *That's the part that got me to wake up.* Just to be certain she wasn't keeping a chopper waiting outside, she moved to the door and put her ear against it. She was terrified that she'd open the door and a dozen ptero-avians would bull their way in and trample her to death. It could happen, she knew. No one was here to stop it. She was completely on her own and had to be cautious for herself. So like a housecat that pauses on the doorstep before going all the way outside, she very cautiously opened the door a crack and peered out.

She started to cough, just like in the dream. *Smoke.* Heavy currents of it wafted into the little building. *What's going on?* She took a deep breath and then looked outside again. *There—what's that?* A flicker of orange behind a thick curtain of black smoke not far from the cleared area around the building.

The sawgrass field was burning!

Sara knew there could be fires in the Everglades, but had always thought they would happen in the drier environments such as the hardwood hammocks, the stands of pines and palms, not the swampy sawgrass fields. But the grass could burn right down to the water, and burn it did, she saw. As another mighty cloud-to-ground lightning fork split the sky frighteningly close by, it occurred to her that this was most likely how the fire started. A light wind fanned the flames from one area to the next, catching the tips of the grass on fire first, then burning right down to the water.

Sara shut the door again, grabbed her backpack and put it on. She wasn't sure if she would be able to stay here. The building seemed fireproof enough with its concrete blocks and single metal door. But there was the skylight, she thought, looking up, where the shadowed form of a ptero-bird could be seen jumping across the opening. Wisps of smoke wafted down through the opening, but it was nothing compared to when she opened the door, since the fire was burning at close to ground level.

Up above, more ptero-birds gathered on the roof. She could hear them now, clucking and warbling frenetically as the fire neared the cleared area where the building was. She didn't think they would fly off in the direction of the fire, which meant that, like her, they might stay here for a while. Sara went back to the door and opened it a crack. She had to know what was going on—was the fire getting closer? Was it only on one side? What she could see right away was that not as many of the creatures were out here now, many having flocked to the roof. This gave her the courage to open the door a bit wider and then to step outside. She wasn't going up on the roof again, that was for sure, so to see around the building she would have to physically walk around it.

She crept around, hugging the wall and doing her best to make zero noise so as not to draw attention to herself. Of course she didn't want to be mauled to death by animals, but she also didn't want to be fried to a crisp in a brick oven, which is what she was afraid might happen to the building. It might not actually burn, but what if, after being overtaken by flames, it simply heated to unsafe temperatures? To avoid this fate for sure, she needed to know if the fire was on all sides of the building, or just the one. Was escape even an option, for the animals and her?

She held her shirt up over her mouth and nose, filtering the smoky air she breathed while she walked. Reaching the corner of the building, she looked back to the clearing and the ptero-avians. They stood on the far side of it from the fire, in a tight-knit group, stamping their feet. Then as the wind shifted, blowing the smoke right into them, they began to leave. First one, then two, then four, then all of the ones on the ground started trotting over to the same road that the RV had travelled on to get here.

Sara glanced up at the roof and saw that there were a few up there, perhaps a half-dozen, standing stock still as they watched the others depart the area.

The fire was massive, consuming the sawgrass swamp in every direction; only the muddy road remained free of flames, but thick clouds of black smoke wafted that way. She began to cough and choke out here, with the air currents carrying the smoke right into her lungs. She decided she would be best waiting inside the antenna building for her rescue rather than take her chances out here in the smoky air and monster-filled wilderness. She turned to walk back to the bunker, but then, with a sinking feeling that literally caused her knees to start shaking, she saw one of the ptero-predators drop through the skylight into the antenna building. The front door of it was closed, so there was no way it could get out unless she opened the door. And then, as she watched, another, and then another two-legged lizard-bird dropped through the skylight. While she observed the smoke drift across the roof of the building, she understood. These animals, rather than choosing to follow the rest of their pack, decided for some reason to drop down into the dark box below, perhaps to escape the smoke.

Sara watched as two more made the drop and then she ceased her progress toward the door. Why even bother now? She wasn't sure the bird-things could get back out through the skylight—she didn't think so, which meant that they were stuck in there unless she opened the door. But she couldn't be sure they wouldn't attack her if she did that, so she balked at the idea of opening the door and hoping they would all just run out, and she would be able to run in and close the door once again with only her inside. Even with only a couple of days on the job, she knew that things would probably not work out so simply.

Now she could hear the bird-beasts shrieking and warbling in there, excited about something. Maybe realizing they were trapped? She didn't know and she didn't care, since she needed to get herself somewhere safe. Behind her she could actually feel the heat of the fire as it neared, eating up the sawgrass, consuming it on the way to her. She eyed the roof. There might be a way to climb up there from the outside, which might work because she doubted the predators inside could get up through the skylight. But that would still leave her in the path of the smoke, which was probably why the ptero-avians jumped down inside anyway.

She looked down the road, where the rest of the ptero-pack ran toward distant solid ground that wasn't on fire. Behind her, spreading in a vast semi-circle, the swamp-grassy world was flaming. She stood there in the small clearing, wondering what to do. Soon there wouldn't be much choice. She would have to begin the long walk back down the road to the mainland. This clearing was already nearly smoked out, she thought, coughing into her bunched up shirt she held over her mouth. Even if the fire didn't actually jump across the cleared building area, she didn't think she would be able to stand it here.

Deciding she would wait ten more minutes to give the ptero-avians more time to get farther down the road, she coughed again and faced away from the smoke while she moved toward the red supply drop package the helo had dropped earlier. She would go through its contents and take with her whatever she thought might come in handy that she could carry on her way down the road.

CHAPTER 24

Everglades

Sam Gumshoe manned the controls of the airboat. He wore earmuffs to protect his hearing from the loud motor situated just behind him. Sitting next to him on the high seat was Ranger Eric Farley, an eight-year veteran he felt comfortable working with out in the field. He was glad for that as they glided over the wet ground, because he could see the flames in the distance. Behind them and to their right, a second swamp boat with another pair of rangers followed their path. The third boat had taken a more circuitous route in case the direct one proved to be impassable.

Fire teams had been called already, but it would take time for them to mobilize the air units necessary to attempt suppression. Fires this far out, started by lightning, were not all that uncommon and sometimes burned out on their own, although Gumshoe didn't like the looks of the steady breeze that seemed to have cropped up around the same time the boats left the dock at headquarters.

The narrow waterway they threaded through—what some might call a small river or others a large stream—curved up ahead. The water was not clear, but strewn with duckweed, lillypads and other green aquatic plant growth. He throttled down while turning the steering wheel to make the turn, then accelerated again once the waterway straightened out. The banks on either side of the water were dense with drier vegetation, including actual trees. He spotted a ten-foot long alligator dozing on the right-side bank, which remained motionless as they passed. It looked completely normal to him, at least, he couldn't help but think. Then up ahead on the same bank there were dozens of gators basking in a cluster, seemingly oblivious to anything going on in the park except perhaps their napping and when their next meal would come. *As it should be*, Gumshoe thought. He flashed on the briefing he'd attended today prior to getting the boats ready. The strange creatures killing people and wreaking havoc in the park, he'd never heard of anything like it. The Everglades were wild enough as they were without some kind of genetic engineered B.S., that was his thought on the subject.

Up ahead, the river let out on a wide, flat area of shallow water that seemed to have no end. But marring this incredible expanse of wetland was a line of orange and black. Gumshoe tapped Farley on the shoulder and pointed. Fire! His co-pilot nodded before turning around to make sure the second boat was still with them. He watched it fan out to the right as they emerged from the river mouth. The co-pilot of the other boat waved; Farley waved back and they continued out onto the wet grass. The boats had radios to communicate with if necessary, but right now they had a destination—the antenna installation—and they were heading to it. Unless they got separated or encountered a problem with the boats, there was no need to talk.

When the water opened up, they were able to open up the boats' throttles to full speed, zooming along over the inches-deep water almost like a hovercraft, with the giant fan completely above water and providing propulsion; there was no propeller sticking down into the water limiting how shallow they could go. Snatches of green and brown flashed by as they soared over the swamp, all riders keeping a sharp eye out for any possible obstructions such as logs, alligators or patches of bone-dry land. The hull of the boats was such that the bow curved up, so that most obstructions could be ramped up and over rather than smacked into head on, but even so, tearing a hole in the bottom was always an unsavory possibility. As they motored along, the line of fire became brighter and more orange, while the smoke became thicker and blacker. Gumshoe could smell it now, an acrid, tangy sensation in his nostrils.

He checked the GPS unit strapped to his wrist and made a slight course correction. To an observer or passenger in the boat, it would seem like an inconsequential adjustment, but Gumshoe knew that tiny corrections like this were magnified over long distances, meaning that failing to make the adjustment could mean they ended up miles from their intended destination. And in this case, that meant they could lose a ranger. Unacceptable. Satisfied they were heading straight for the antenna building, Gumshoe ramped up the airboat to full throttle once more, feeling the breeze against his face while he watched the swamp burn in the distance. Forks of lightning still arced down to the water in the same vicinity as the fire.

Gumshoe felt a tap on his shoulder and looked off to the left where Farley pointed. He looked in time to see the remnants of what must have been a large splash. "You see what it was?" he mouthed to his co-pilot. Farley shook his head and held his hands up in a *who knows?* gesture. Another mysterious animal out on the 'glades. On a normal day, that kind of thing was a little disconcerting, knowing what natural monsters lurked out here. But today, with the knowledge that a menagerie of altered beasts had somehow been unleashed on the environment, it took on a more foreboding feeling.

The other boat fanned out to the right a couple hundred feet away, since they were on a wide open swamp now, riding atop the wet grass with no channels to negotiate. A pair of blinking lights could be seen in the distance. Farley put a pair of marine binoculars up to his eyes and focused until he pointed nearly straight ahead. He passed the optics to Gumshoe, who steered with one hand while holding them up to his eyes with the other. But the view through the lenses was reassuring. There it was, the antenna building at the base of the tower lights. They were on track, with nothing but open swamp between them and the installation.

Confident in the terrain that lay ahead, Gumshoe eked out every last ounce of speed from the specialty craft. It still rode smoothly over the water, skipping only very rarely when encountering a wind-driven ripple in the water's surface. A flock of birds gliding low over the swamp veered out of their way as the two swamp boats cut across the watery land. It was all going smoothly enough that Gumshoe started thinking ahead to find potential problems.

What if Sara wasn't there when they got to the antenna building? What if she was there, but gravely injured, or even worse, dead? All kinds of bad thought combinations rippled through his head. These served to keep him occupied, though, and before he knew it, Farley was tapping him on the shoulder and pointing to the antenna building, now visible as an actual structure and not a distant blob on the horizon.

He throttled down the air boat, signaling with a hand for the other boat to do the same. As they neared the island of land on the end of the narrow peninsula with the road, the two airboats split up, one going left and the other heading right. They had discussed this tactic back at the staging area, and did so in order to cover the entire area quickly, to see what they were dealing with and learn about any potential problem areas, such as fire lines and where they could safely operate the swamp boats. Both boat men now pulled up the respirator masks that they had brought along as a fire precaution.

Gumshoe neared the edge of the swamp, until he could see the reddish dirt that marked the land on which the antenna building was built. With the engine now on low power, they were able to remove the earmuffs and have a normal conversation. Farley pointed to the roof of the building.

"Are those the creatures the helo pilot was talking about? Bird-things?"

"Looks like them," Gumshoe said, raising the binoculars to his eyes. "That is to say, I've never seen anything like 'em in my life, so I guess it must be them. Look at these things, like some kinda pterodactyl or something!" He handed the binoculars off to Farley, who agreed after taking a look.

"I only see them on the roof," he said, "not on the ground."

"You think Sara's inside the building? I don't see her outside," Gumshoe said.

"She better be in there!" Farley put the glasses down. "I can see how those things got in the way of the chopper extraction. They're huge, and strong looking."

"Don't forget, they also saw some kinda giant bug out here."

"Right, giant millipedes, they said. Just what we need."

"Let's do this," Gumshoe said, as the other boat came back into sight after ducking around the opposite side of the peninsula. Gumshoe picked up his radio transmitter and hailed the other airboat. "Swamp 1 to Swamp 2: What'd you guys see over there, over?"

The reply was immediate, the tone concerned but far from panic. "Fire is close to the island on that side. Those pterodactyl birds they mention are on the roof and a couple of them on the road leading back to the mainland. The wrecked RV is there, too, 'bout a half-mile back. Over."

Gumshoe stared at the bunker with a furrowed brow for a few seconds before answering. "We're going to need to check inside the building. I don't want to use the bullhorn because it might spook those animals. Don't want to rile them up. Let's just walk up to the door and see if it opens, over."

"Roger that, Captain. We all going in or what's the plan, over?"

Gumshoe turned to Farley and spoke off-radio. "What do you think, both boats land, all four of us head up to the door, or one boat hangs back and provides lookout cover while the other boat goes?"

Farley thought about this while eyeballing the narrow peninsula. "Probably one boat should hang back, but close to shore so they can still shoot those things down if need be. No need for all four of us to get ganged up on."

Gumshoe nodded and picked up the transmitter. "Swamp 1 to Swamp 2: you guys land on your side, we'll land on our side. You two stay in the boat and cover us while we go to the door, copy?"

"Swamp 2 to Swamp 1: copy, we both land, you and Farley go up to the door while we cover you, over."

"Bring your long guns and your pistols, over and out."

"Copy on the guns, over and out."

Gumshoe maneuvered the airboat up to the shore about halfway between the building and the end. He didn't want to spook the predators by landing too close, but also wanted to traverse as little ground on foot as possible, where they would be most vulnerable. On the other side of the peninsula, less than fifty feet away across the flat ground, the other airboat glided up onto dry land, coming to rest so that only the rear half of the craft was still over shallow water.

Gumshoe and Farley paused in the boat before stepping out onto land, to make sure the sound of the hull sliding up didn't trigger a response from the creatures. But all seemed to be the same. The tower lights reflected weirdly in the smoky air, casting colored shadows around the area. Gumshoe looked at Farley and nodded while pointing to the bunker door. *Let's go.*

The two rangers stepped out of the boat onto dry land, so as not to make a splash, then began walking toward the building. Gumshoe kept an eye on the roof, where a couple of the ptero-birds' heads were visible facing the opposite direction toward the long road. He glanced over to make sure the second boat team was in position, and was relieved to see one with a rifle pointed at the roof, while the other had eyes on Gumshoe and Farley as they crept toward the door.

Gumshoe and Farley fanned out a little, walking side by side approximately ten feet apart as they approached the door. So far there was no indication that the animals on the roof were paying any attention to them. Gumshoe surmised that perhaps all the fire smoke interfered with their olfactory abilities. He hoped so, anyway. If the fire could be used to their advantage in some small way, he would take it.

They reached the door to the antenna bunker and stood on either side of it; Farley on the right by the handle, Gumshoe on the left. Farley eyeballed the handle, then looked at Gumshoe, who nodded.

Farley opened the door and pushed it inward.

He was greeted by a three-toed foot smashing him square in the face. The impact lifted his body off the ground and knocked him back five feet, where he landed on the ground on his back. Gumshoe fired his shotgun at the towering form, which was silhouetted against the darkness inside the bunker. He saw flesh splatter and the form disappeared back into the bunker, only to be replaced by four more that charged out of the narrow doorway.

Gumshoe wheeled aside while firing off another blast, plastering himself against the wall of the building so at least they couldn't attack him from that side. Also, he wanted to remove himself from the line of his fellow rangers' fire in Boat Two. Sure enough, no sooner had he flattened himself against the building than two, three, four rifle shots rang out, adding their discharge to the increasingly smoke-filled air.

While he stayed out of the line of fire, Gumshoe stared at the downed Farley, searching for signs of life, but the ranger was unmoving. His face was covered in blood. Gumshoe could not see his chest rising and falling. His hand moved reflexively to his belt but swiped an empty space where he thought his radio would be. He was pretty sure Farley would need an airlift to medical facilities rather than a long boat ride back. With a surge of adrenaline, he realized he'd left it in the boat. He was stunned by how quickly everything had gone south on him, the designated Captain of this operation.

Still, he knew there was no point in lamenting that now. The only way out of a bad situation, experience had taught him, was to make it better, one step at a time until it was in the past. Right now that meant preserving the safety of the rest of his crew, then getting medical attention for Farley. And then of course, to find Sara Cliff, who had precipitated this mission.

Where was she, anyway? He hadn't gotten a clear look inside yet, and as more shots rang out around him, driving the ptero-birds away down the road and into the part of the swamp not yet in flames, where the boats were, he had a startling thought. *If she was inside there with those things, she was dead.* Which meant this was now a body recovery mission. But he had to know for sure. He'd get a clear look inside, then he'd know if she, or at least her body, was in there or not. After that, he'd get back to the boat and make his radio report on the situation.

He looked over to the boat crew on watch and pantomimed that he was going inside the building. Shotgun held up at the ready, Gumshoe crept to the edge of the open doorway. Crouching, he poked the gun barrel inside first and then his head.

Empty!

Floors, walls, nothing except for two dead ptero-birds on the floor that could not possibly conceal a body. He glanced up toward the source of light, saw the open skylight, saw the legs of more of the weird creatures stalking about up there. He stepped inside the room with his shotgun pointed up at the skylight. That must be how they got in, he thought, since the door was shut when he got here. He was immeasurably glad not to find the body of the new ranger in here, until another dark thought pervaded his consciousness.

She could be on the roof. Dead.

Damn it. He would have to check the roof in order to declare the area fully searched. He eased quietly back out of the building and waved to the other boat crew, indicating he was coming to them. He would want additional firepower support for what came next. He reached the boat and spoke to the rangers there, both Park Service veterans of at least five years. He quickly summarized the situation, and one of the rangers made the radio call requesting medical support for Farley before taking a first aid kit over to him to see what could be done.

Gumshoe explained that there was no easy access to the roof, and after a brief discussion, the two rangers decided that one would throw handfuls of rocks and mud up there while the other fired a rifle. The combined noise and debris should serve to drive them away. That was the hope at least, but they were bolstered by having driven off the half-dozen that had been inside the building. Hopefully those on the roof wouldn't be more resistant. *And even more hopefully*, Gumshoe thought more darkly to himself, *they would do it without a death toll this time.*

Gumshoe would be the thrower, while the boat ranger would handle shooting duties. After Gumshoe had gathered a decent pile of earthy projectiles, he looked over to the ranger who had gone to render first aid. That man looked back at Gumshoe while kneeling over Farley and slowly shaking his head. No pulse. Farley was gone.

Gumshoe clenched his fists in rage before loading them with rocks and dirt. He waved the ranger back over, wanting him to be prepared in case the predators should come down that way off the roof. Also, he could be another shooter. The third ranger came back to the boat and reported that he had radioed the news of Farley's death to headquarters. A chopper would not be coming out since he had already died, and the fire was a risk for air travel with its reduced visibility, so they would be taking his body back by boat.

With the situation turning more and more dour, they began their assault on the rooftop. Gumshoe flung fistfuls of mud and rock, while the other two rangers fired their rifles just over the roof. About ten seconds into the offensive, two ptero-avians leapt off the roof—toward their boat. One of the rangers switched from rifle to a shotgun and cut off one of the legs of one predator, dropping it, gasping in place, while the other turned and ran toward the road. Meanwhile, two more bird-creatures actually managed to fly a short distance—over the other swamp boat out into the marsh. A couple of rifle shots chased them farther away out into the watery landscape.

Gumshoe held up a hand to cease fire. They watched and listened for a few seconds, but detected no signs of additional creatures still up there. "Okay, I think it's safe to have a look at this point," Gumshoe said.

The three rangers moved to the side of the building. Gumshoe said he would go up himself, so the other two helped to push him up until he could grab the edge of the roof and pull himself up. A sense of relief—but also mystery—flooded him as he took in the scene on top of the building. Blood splatter around the skylight amid shattered plexiglass, a couple of rocks, and one dead ptero-avian. Zero people or corpses.

"She's not up here," he called down, relief plainly evident in his voice. But that begged the question.

Where was Ranger Sara Cliff?

CHAPTER 25

Miami, Florida

Detective Rene Bravia and Officer Francisco Alvarado parked their unmarked police car in the lot of a nondescript office building. On the outskirts of downtown Miami, not far from the International Airport, it was out of sight from the glitz of the beach and entertainment districts, and even from the high-rise office buildings. The semi-industrial area was occupied by companies specializing in manufacturing, shipping, and warehousing.

Owned by BioGen Corporation, the property contained two structures: a no-nonsense office building that they walked up to now, as well as a warehouse-type building behind the office. The expression on both men's faces was grim as they walked up to the entrance, a no-frills single tinted glass door. Bravia had experienced varying levels of cooperation over his career when it came to obtaining search warrants, and with such an unusual case and the paucity of concrete evidence, he hadn't been sure he would be granted one today, or so quickly. But here they were, executing a search warrant issued by a Florida state judge. Probably because the crisis in the Everglades had hit the mainstream media, Bravia suspected. But whatever the reason, it would make gathering information a lot easier than showing up and asking for interviews based on the goodwill and kindness of people's hearts. He knew how that went.

Still, a warrant execution was never free of tension, both officers knew that. Making people do things they don't want to do is never easy, but it was their job and they were ready for it. Knowing that park rangers—fellow law enforcement officers—were being killed in the field gave them additional incentive to shut down whatever was behind the introduction of these dangerous life forms to the Everglades.

Bravia pulled open the door and the two of them stepped into a small but nicely appointed lobby. A single receptionist sat behind a small glass desk. The Cuban woman wore a headset microphone, and currently talked into it while typing into a desktop computer. Bravia heard her tell someone to hold on just one moment, then she pecked at her phone to mute the call and smiled as the two officers walked up to the desk.

"Welcome to BioGen, how may I help you?" she beamed.

Bravia flashed her his police credentials and said, "We're here to speak with Dr. Langston Abernathy." Alvarado also showed the receptionist his credentials while the smile on the woman's face faded to a tight-lipped neutral expression.

"One moment please." She pecked a key on her desk phone and told whoever answered that two policemen were here to see him. Obviously there was some pushback, because the next thing she said was, "They have a search warrant."

She looked at them and said, "He's on his way."

In a couple of minutes, during which they could hear doors opening and closing somewhere back in the main building, not one but four men and two women emerged into the lobby, all with stern faces. Bravia and Alvarado held up their credentials again, which were examined closely by two of the men, one of which introduced himself as Dr. Langston Abernathy. Bravia read from the warrant, which gave them rights to search the premises and interview employees regarding the consulting work done by Dr. Archie Landis of Florida University. One of the other men, who introduced himself as CEO of BioGen, asked to read the warrant in its entirety.

"This is a copy for your records, you can have it." Bravia handed it over and without waiting for a reaction, turned to Dr. Abernathy, who he knew to be a leading genomics researcher, that is, a biotechnology scientist who specialized in working with the entire sets of genes contained within living organisms.

"Dr. Abernathy, I understand it was you who worked most closely with Dr. Landis here at BioGen, is that correct?"

Abernathy nodded. He was younger than Bravia had expected, still in his thirties. Not the stereotypical nerd look, either, this guy wore jeans and a sport coat with no tie, running shoes, sunglasses on retainers around his neck rather than bifocals, and looked to be physically fit. He was by far the youngest person in the room, excepting the receptionist.

"Yeah, he was pretty aggressive about working with me actually, and I liked that. He had some interesting ideas, but a lot of people do in our line of work," he said, casting an acknowledging glance at his colleagues, who nodded subtly. "But the difference is, he knew how to make them actionable. He wasn't all talk, he really kept up an email dialogue until I agreed to meet him in person. We had coffee at this little Cuban café over on Miami Beach. I thought I'd be there maybe twenty minutes. Three hours later I walked out with a new vision and one hell of a caffeine buzz."

Bravia levelled a serious stare at the young PhD. "You know the reason I'm here, Dr. Abernathy. People have been dying in South Florida—including Dr. Landis—and we have reason to believe it's related to the work you were doing with him. Were you working with dinosaurs at all, for example?"

At this, the CEO cleared his throat and put a hand up. "Dr. Abernathy, you do not have to answer that question, and I remind you of the non-disclosure agreements covering your work at BioGen per the terms of your employment."

Bravia barked at the man forcefully, waving the warrant in his face. "Look pal, we can just bulldoze the crap out of your entire facility, turn it upside down, looking for what we think we need to look for, or you can direct us to what we need to know. If we think it makes sense, then everything else will stay untouched. So shut the hell up, people are dying out there! Go read your emails or something while we interview your employees. Don't like it? I can tell the judge and you can adjust your attitude in jail for contempt of court."

Suitably chastened, the CEO narrowed his eyes at Bravia for a micro-second, but then nodded to Abernathy, who appeared mildly amused by the confrontation.

"Let me begin by saying that I wasn't the only scientist here working with Archie. I was probably the one who was most connected with him, but he met with other geneticists and applied bioinformatics experts as well." He paused to see if any of his colleagues would challenge him or possibly add something, but no one did. None of them looked very comfortable. Abernathy continued.

"So—and this is no great secret—" he prefaced, eyeing the CEO, "Dr. Landis was pretty obsessed with the relatively new gene editing tool called CRISPR. Until now, the most radical, headline-grabbing examples this biotechnology has been used for would be things like designing steers that have no horns, changing flower colors, making pig organs compatible with humans, creating custom flavored fruits such as pineapple-cherries....I could go on and on, but I think you get the point?" The entire group of biotechnologists eyed the two cops until they both nodded. Then Abernathy went on.

"Well basically, Archie came to me with concepts for what a layperson might call 'designer gene editing' utilizing CRISPR that were *way* beyond the kind of examples I just gave. But he had a couple of practical holes in his strategies, holes that, technology-wise, I told him I thought I could figure out how to fill in. It turns out that with the equipment and resources available to BioGen we were able to do that and then some."

"What exactly did you do with Dr. Landis?" Bravia asked, holding his hands up. "In layman's terms, if you will."

Abernathy made unflinching eye contact with Bravia. "It's best if I show you." He turned to the CEO and shrugged. "They have a warrant. I like my job, but I ain't going to jail for it." Bravia thought the use of *ain't* from this highly educated professional was slightly disarming, suggesting a toughness to the guy, probably his intended effect in front of his boss.

The CEO shot him a withering stare. "I'll be accompanying him on your little tour, then."

"That's fine," Bravia conceded. "As long as you don't interfere." He turned to the much more cooperative Abernathy. "Shall we begin?"

The young man nodded. "Sure. So to get right to the point, all the 'takeaway' points are best delivered in the lab building—that's the big warehouse building out back. In this building are the offices where we do most of our computer work and then write up the papers that get published in the journals about the cutting edge work that happens in the labs. So I'm going to take you straight there for that reason, it's not that I'm hiding anything in here. I can show you my office if you like, but it won't give you anything. And Landis didn't have an office here, he did all the computer work from his home. Understood?"

Bravia nodded. "Makes sense. Thank you for being so straightforward. Saves us all time."

"That's what I figured," Abernathy said. "So, right this way…." He turned and beckoned toward the door they had just entered from. At this point the CEO conferred briefly with his group, sans Abernathy, and after that, group huddle four of the BioGen bigwigs went their separate ways while the CEO caught up with Abernathy, Bravia and Alvarado as they left the lobby through the door.

They found themselves in a long hallway with doors to the right and left, which Abernathy explained were offices. "We pass through the office building to access the 'lab hangar', as we call it," he said while moving at a brisk pace down the hall. The place was definitely not lavishly appointed, Bravia thought, noting the threadbare carpet, cheap panel fluorescent lighting and lack of artwork. Of course, he had no idea what the offices behind the closed doors looked like, but there was nothing to suggest extravagance that he could see.

They reached the end of the hallway which led straight into a spiral staircase, on which Abernathy led the way down. At the bottom they found themselves in an open social environment, with tables, chairs, music playing softly, vending machines and a few people eating. "Lunchroom," Abernathy explained. "You guys want a coffee, soda, anything?"

Both Bravia and Alvarado declined while the CEO availed himself of a can of Coke from a machine, cracked it open and began chugging it while walking along after the others. Abernathy waved to a female co-worker eating with friends at a table before opening a set of double doors on the far side of the lunchroom. "Through here is the hangar," he promised.

The others followed him through into a covered walkway with Astroturf carpeting, lined on both sides with ficus trees and ferns that transitioned into a non-walkable landscaped area. Bravia peered into the greenery, wondering if there were genetically modified animals living in there, too. The walkway led to the warehouse building, its rollup door currently open. They passed through into an open area with a baffle, a movable wall on wheels set a few feet back from the entrance, to provide privacy and some protection from the elements. Immediately inside that was a storage area of sorts for heavy equipment—Bravia noticed a forklift, stacks of pallets, large bags of soil, and rocks, and a few large boulders strewn about. There were also some metal shelving units supporting computer monitors, CPUs, power supplies and boxes of cabling.

"Seems like a pretty random collection of stuff," Alvarado commented.

Abernathy glanced at the varied items. "Yeah, basically it's because you can think of us as a biotechnology company that makes living animals that we raise ourselves in terrariums or tanks—some big, some small. You'll see what I mean. So we have computer stuff, and pet store stuff, zoo stuff, landscaping stuff, chemistry lab stuff. But I can see how it looks like a random hodge-podge."

"I'll say," Bravia said, taking it all in.

"So if you'll follow me through here," Abernathy said, waving an arm toward a plastic strip door about twenty feet further inside the hangar, "I'll show you the labs."

They walked into the belly of the cavernous hangar. Bravia was surprised to see a veritable hive of activity, with white-coated lab workers hunched over various machines, computers, and animal tanks or enclosures. Abernathy was dead-on about what the seeming hodge-podge of stuff was for, the detective realized. It was slightly warmer in here than outside, and a little more humid, probably from all the water in the various tanks, large and small. There were racks set up with row upon row of fish tanks, like an aquarium fish store, but also numerous larger open round tanks, more like what would be seen in an aquaculture facility. Interestingly, along the sides of the huge space, there were rooms constructed that had closed doors, preventing Bravia from seeing what was in them. In fact, for part of the length of the building, there were actually two levels of these rooms, stacked on top of one another and accessed by a series of catwalks and ladder-like stairways.

It was to one of these rooms that Abernathy led them, pointing out other things along the way. "So I'd like to start our little tour off with a bang, if that's okay with you." Both Bravia and Alvarado nodded, while the CEO frowned. "I'm sure you saw the TV news clips of the giant sailfin lizard?" Abernathy said over his shoulder while he continued to walk.

"You mean that huge dinosaur that killed somebody at an Everglades campground?" Bravia clarified.

"Technically, it's not really a dinosaur, but close enough, and yes, that would be the one." He reached a closed door on the first floor and paused there, arm indicating the space.

"I want you to picture that sailfin lizard that you saw on TV in your mind, and when I open this door, prepare yourself, okay?"

Bravia shrugged and gave a nod. Judging by how close the rooms were together, he didn't see how anything very large could be inside. "Sure."

Abernathy popped a key into the door lock and pushed the door open.

CHAPTER 26

Everglades

The two airboats were underway again, in much grimmer fashion. Gumshoe now rode in his boat with only Ranger Eric Farley's corpse to keep him company, bundled up in a blanket in the bow. *What a clusterfuck this op turned out to be*, Gumshoe thought as he approached the wrecked RV and followed the narrow road toward the mainland. Sara Cliff wasn't out at the bunker anymore, so he decided to look for her along the road. He only hoped she hadn't already been eaten whole, or killed and dragged out into the swamp.

The airboat with his fellow pair of rangers rode on the opposite side of the skinny peninsula, so that they advanced in tandem down the road on either side. The fire continued to blaze nearby and was causing Gumshoe great concern. It roared on relentlessly, very close to the road now on the other side with the other boat, and was starting to wrap around this side as well. It made him nervous to be here. The water they rode on now was very shallow—even for airboats—and had no sawgrass, therefore couldn't burn. But the greater swamp around them that they needed to pass through in order to get back to Headquarters, had taller grass feeding the flames. But he needed to check this stretch of road for Sara, so he kept going, keeping an eye on the raging fire and a handkerchief over his mouth.

#

Ranger Sara Cliff hunkered down in the rear of the trailer, the only portion that was both somewhat intact and dry. Terrified of moving for fear of making enough noise to attract the predators waiting just outside, she tried to silently position herself to get a view outside. With the rain and wind and fire it was hard to hear things, but the gunshots earlier were barely audible, letting her know help was here. Except that "here" was, unfortunately, the antenna building, where they no doubt thought she was, not *here*, in the wrecked trailer half underwater and surrounded by ptero-birds *and* megapedes. And those were just the creatures she had seen with her own eyes. Who knew what else lurked around here?

All she knew was that she heard something different, something that *could* be…Yes! There it was again! The sound of a motor. *Chopper's back!* But how to let them know she was here without getting killed by the mega-predators just outside? Just *inside*, she corrected herself as she saw two long legs stalking through the frontmost part of the partially submerged vehicle. The ptero-bird stalked around a bit, stamping the water with its triple-toed, semi-webbed feet, before stomping back outside of the RV again.

Sara crawled carefully to the window in the bunk, doing her best not to shift her weight such that she would move the structure or make a loud creak. But she had to see what was going on. Were she to not be seen by the rescuers, she would likely die out here. She had no more food, no more drinking water. She *had* to get a ride out of here.

Reaching the window, she lay very still with only as much of her face above the sill as necessary to see out. She was on the side looking toward the bulk of the fire, and the smoke coming her way was black and thick and awful. She started to cough but choked it back, held her head away from the window and waited until it passed, then, with her shirt over her mouth, resumed her surveillance position at the opening.

She could hear the motor again. She looked up into the sky, but saw nothing save for billowing fire smoke. Could be on the other side, she thought, hoping that a chopper was about to land. She was just about to begin the arduous process of turning around and moving to the opposite window without alerting the predators, when she caught movement off to her left, almost beyond her peripheral vision.

What's that? Her brain processed slowly as it came into view. *Metal. Silver metallic structure…boat? Airboat! People—rangers!* As the boat cruised from her left to her right—along the RV—she could see that they were inspecting it carefully, no doubt looking for any signs of her. She noted the rifle held in the hands of one of the men, at the ready. This was it, her chance to be rescued! She could not afford to let them pass her by.

She started yelling, "Hey, hey I'm here!" through the window, but then quickly decided it was better to run out. What if they didn't hear her over the motor and fire noise, but the animals did? So she decided to forego stealth for speed and jumped off the berth, feet splashing into the deeper water on the floor. She tromped through it until reaching the broken down section of siding. Pleased to see no ptero-birds, she was about to step out of the RV when her eyes registered movement in the shallow water immediately outside the wrecked hulk.

Wriggling segments, underwater but now growing larger, more distinct. Suddenly she was staring face to face with one of the giant millipedes. She dodged left, and to her great relief the millipede continued forward into the RV. Perhaps it only sought the shelter of the structure to escape the chaos out here, the boats and the fires, she thought, while waving to the two rangers in the airboat. She hoped the millipede wasn't about to turn around and come back for her.

But now the airboat was pulling up onto the muddy soil, sliding to a stop a few feet away, the ranger not piloting the craft already jumping off to assist her. "Thank you so much! I didn't think—"

But the ranger raised his rifle and fired off two shots in quick succession, to Sara's right, closer than she was comfortable with. But when the six-foot tall ptero-bird teetered to the ground with a *whump*, she was more than glad for the risk he took. He stepped forward and extended a hand. "Sara, can you run?"

"Yes!" She shook his hand quickly, taking comfort in the firm grip.

"In the boat, now! I'll cover you!"

Cover me? What am I, in a war movie now? But she ran all right, she ran faster than she'd ever run in her relatively short life, leaping over the dead ptero-bird and sidestepping a medium-sized millipede that was "only" three feet long. Or was it a chopped-in-half segment that still had nerves, like a chicken running around with its head cut off? Either way, she was around it and flying into that airboat like it was a free luxury cruise around the world. No place she'd rather be.

As soon as she jumped inside, the ranger at the controls offered a hand. She took it and he pulled her up onto the bench seat beside him, giving her a quick but warm smile. She started to explain what happened—why she wasn't at the antenna building, but he waved her down.

"Not now. We'll hear all about it later over some beer and pizza back at the station, sound good?"

She nodded with a big smile. Right about now, that sounded like the best thing ever. The second ranger backpedaled toward the boat, still firing off a shot here and there at a ptero-avian or a marauding megapede.

From her elevated position in the boat, Sara could now see that there was a second swamp boat on the other side of the road, this one manned by only one ranger. She pointed it out to the pilot, who nodded without smiling this time. "Yeah we brought two boats out here. I'm sorry to have to be the one to break it to you that we lost Ranger Farley in a battle with those monsters at the antenna building. We're bringing his body back in Sam's boat."

On closer inspection, Sara could see the bundled human form lying on the bottom-most deck of the airboat. She broke into a quiet sob with the realization that a veteran ranger, and fine man from the little she'd gotten to know him, had been lost attempting to save her life. "I'm so sorry…."

The pilot put his arm around her shoulder. "Don't be. It's not your fault. He came out here knowing all the risks. We had a thorough briefing at Headquarters; no one was required to go. He volunteered. He took down a whole slew of those things before he went down, too. He'll be honored properly and never forgotten." He turned and looked with a furrowed brow at the encroaching conflagration before adding, "If we can get his body back to HQ safely, that is. Not to mention ourselves. We'd better git while the gittin's good."

"No arguments here." Sara managed a weak smile.

The pilot spoke into his radio while also exchanging directional hand signals with Gumshoe in the other boat. The second ranger jumped into the boat, now riding up front, rifle still at the ready. He fired off a shot at one of the ptero-avians that had taken to the air, dropping it square onto the middle of the road.

"Here we go." The pilot backed the airboat up until they had enough water beneath the hull to navigate. Then he turned and faced toward the antenna building again and throttled up. They began to glide over the swamp, picking up speed rapidly as the motor increased in pitch. He handed Sara a pair of earmuffs and she gladly put them on. She'd ridden in airboats before, but it wasn't a big part of her training and she'd forgotten how loud they really were.

When they passed by the antenna installation, Sara stared at the tower lights, still blinking their rapid pattern, now obscured in smoke. She shook her head at the devastation and loss that had occurred there. The other rangers also eyed it, looking for signs of life, but now there were none, human or animal, only dead bodies.

Looking right, the fire was now a wall of flames two-stories high, flush up to the road. Past the end of the antenna building, the flames had spread to the sawgrass on the other side of the road and continued to burn off to Sara's left, where the boats had come from to get here. Both boats slowed as their captains considered a course of action.

Gumshoe pointed straight out from the end of the antenna building peninsula. "That's the only direction that's free of flames. Unfortunately, it also takes us farther away from where we want to go."

"Is there anything over that way?" Sara asked, lowering her earmuffs around her neck.

Gumshoe shrugged. "Not much. There is land, though, and the old missile base."

"Missile base?"

"Yeah, it's an old cold war military facility that was abandoned in the late '70s. The buildings are still there, but not used for anything anymore."

"Beats burning to death!" the other ranger said, swiveling his rifle toward the antenna building.

"Can't argue with that," Gumshoe said as he picked up his radio. "Swamp 1 to Swamp 2: you copy?"

The reply came back from the other boat. "Swamp 2, copy, what's the plan? Doesn't look like we can go back the way we came, over."

Gumshoe nodded as he spoke into the radio. "Copy that, agree. We were thinking that we could head straight out until we reach the old missile base, over."

A pause ensued during which they heard the crackling of flames, then came his reply. "We got enough fuel for that, you think?"

Gumshoe shrugged to himself as he tapped the gas gauge and turned around to look at the gas cans in the back. "I'm pretty sure we do, using all the spare cans. How about you?"

Another pause, and then: "Same here. Pretty sure, but not positive, over."

A crackling ember landed on the deck of the boat, propelled by a strong gust. "I think it's just a chance we're going to have to take, over."

"Copy that. We'd better get going, then. It's a long haul over to that site. Over and out."

"Copy, over and out." Gumshoe put down the radio and put his hand back on the throttle. "Okay, brace yourselves, get situated. Here we go."

Sara pulled herself back more on the seat and put her earmuffs back on, while the ranger down in front stowed his rifle and grabbed a boat rail to steady himself. Gumshoe radioed headquarters to inform them of the fire situation, and that they were headed for the old missile base. Then Gumshoe eased the throttle forward and the airboat picked up speed until it was once again gliding over the swamp water like a hovercraft, motor increasing in pitch the faster it turned. Off to her left, Sara could see the other swamp boat keeping pace with them.

In a couple of minutes, they were at full speed, flying across a swath of swamp that was so far, at least, not on fire. But they also headed even further from any kind of land-based support. Ahead they could see only an endless expanse of waterscape as they glided toward the horizon.

CHAPTER 27

Miami, Florida

Detective Bravia and Officer Alvarez followed Langston Abernathy and the BioGen CEO into the small lab room, which was lit by fluorescent bulbs in the ceiling. A terrarium with heat lamps was set up on a lab bench next to a desktop computer. Printouts of graphs and charts were attached to clipboards hanging from the wall. There was no need for Abernathy to say anything yet, for the two policemen's eyes were drawn right to the tank.

Inside the terrarium was a single lizard, perched on a log that was strategically placed over a water dish. About a foot long, the body of the lizard was a dull green, with bright green swaths on the tall sail on its back.

Bravia was first to break the silence. "It looks like a miniature version of the one that was on TV, that killed a camper in the Everglades yesterday."

Abernathy nodded while displaying a smug grin. "It is a miniature version, all right. But here's the thing: the one you saw on TV?" He waited for an acknowledgement.

Bravia and Alvarado both nodded. "Yeah?" Bravia asked.

"Well, that one was this size too, about a month after it hatched."

"Wha—no!" Alvarado said in disbelief.

But Abernathy only nodded confidently, his grin growing. "Oh yes!"

Bravia pointed at the lizard, which flicked its tongue in and out of its mouth while watching the people. "And how long ago was the one on TV hatched?"

At this, the CEO sucked his breath in slightly and turned away from the conversation. Abernathy answered the question after Gumshoe tapped the warrant paper.

"About six months ago."

Bravia was flabbergasted. "Six…You mean to tell me that huge dinosaur grew that big in only *six months*!"

Abernathy nodded, positively beaming now. "That's exactly what I mean to tell you. But there's more."

Bravia took a deep breath, not sure if he was even ready for more. But at the same time, he had to know, both out of personal curiosity at this point, and because it was his professional duty to know. "I'm afraid to ask. But what?"

Abernathy pointed to the small sailfin lizard. "It's almost surely still growing. We're not sure how big it will get."

At least Alvarado laughed. "Great, so you mean we're going to have Godzilla roaming around South Florida pretty soon?"

Abernathy shrugged. "We don't really know. Most of them, we euthanized when they outgrew our facilities. But it was Dr. Landis himself who released one specimen into the Everglades. He did that on his own, without our blessing. He took it home with him when it was not much bigger than this little guy here. Said he wanted to observe 'the development of its phenotypic expression' or something to that effect. Basically, to see how it looks as it grows as a result of the gene manipulation we did on it via CRISPR."

"And it outgrew his tank at home…" Bravia guessed.

"Yes, and we had predicted that would happen, and urged him to bring it back to us when it did, since we can keep them longer in our big tanks in the warehouse than he would be able to at home. But he didn't listen, I think because he was upset over a misunderstanding regarding his compensation as a contractor for BioGen, and instead he put it in his SUV and drove it to Everglades National, where he let it go."

"And he was aware of the ramifications of this?" Bravia asked.

Abernathy laughed. "Of course he was! Dr. Landis was a professional biologist, not some pet owner who knows next to nothing about an animal they bought on a whim because it was on sale at a store. He wanted to see how it would fare in the wild. He had some pet theory of his that certain genes we introduced into the sailfin's genome would only be expressed when confronted with particular variables present within a natural ecosystem."

"But he died before he could make observations of it?"

"I assume so, yes," Abernathy said. "If he did ever observe it in the Everglades, he never mentioned it to us." The CEO nodded his agreement to this.

"So it's out there, wreaking havoc," Abernathy concluded, "and we have no idea how big it will get. Just thought you should know that."

Bravia jotted a quick notation in his notepad before looking back up at Abernathy. "Thank you. Before I forget, there's something I'd like to ask you about. Dr. Trout at the University of Florida examined some tissue from a lab-engineered specimen—a half-pterodactyl-half bird—and sequenced its DNA using a machine that she says is typical for those in the industry."

"Yes, a DNA sequencer. And?" Abernathy leaned in closer to Bravia, obviously very interested.

"And she says that because of the way the designer DNA was encoded—pardon me, I am a layperson here—"

Abernathy waved his hand and made a face as if to say don't worry about it.

"She said that there was basically the equivalent of malicious code that corrupted her machine when it ran the full sequence."

Abernathy and the CEO exchanged a knowing glance. Abernathy said, "It's true. The thinking was that, look—we have no idea how this gene technology will be used in the future. But it's valuable, we're the ones who did all the early legwork in making it useful, and so—"

The CEO interrupted his employee. "And so we feel it is within our legal rights to enforce what you may think of as digital management rights to our intellectual property."

Bravia made brief notation in his pad and then looked up. "I'm not going to pretend here. This kinda stuff is way over my head and it seems so cutting edge—bleeding edge—that there may not even be a precedent for how to deal with it in court. But as you know, there are people who understand how it works far better than I. Anyhow, I thank you for your cooperation. Is there anything else we should know?"

Abernathy made eye contact with the CEO and shrugged. Abernathy looked back to Bravia and Alvarado and said; "Yes. We did CRISPR work with a lot of animals, large *and* small, not only the big megafauna like dinosaurs and gigantic millipedes, but also small critters."

"Such as?" Bravia prompted.

"Such as the blue-ringed octopus, for example." At the mention of this name, the CEO openly cringed.

"Never heard of it," Bravia stated.

Abernathy explained, "It's a small tropical octopus that happens to be one of the most venomous animals on the planet—one bite will kill an adult human in minutes—and there is no known antidote. The venom is actually produced by bacteria living in the octopus' mouth, and so perhaps you can guess at this point what we—BioGen working with Dr. Landis—did?"

Abernathy's gaze bounced back and forth between the two cops like a teacher giving a pop quiz to students.

Alvarado ventured forth a guess. "Made it gigantic?"

Abernathy shook his head. "Nope. We sequenced the genome of the bacteria that produce the venom. The idea was to incorporate it—to fuse that bacterial genome with the genomes of other creatures---so that a common honeybee or wasp, for example, might have stingers that contain the same bacteria that produce the venom in the blue-ringed octopus."

"Good God!" Bravia exclaimed.

Abernathy shook his head slowly with a wry smile. "Oh believe me, there's no God involved. Just a lot of computer processing power and high-tech lab equipment."

Alvarado also appeared upset. "So some little kid out picking flowers gets stung by a bee, and now, instead of it just being a normal bee sting where it hurts really bad, or maybe if she's allergic she could die, but no. Now if they get stung, it's like being bit by some tropical octopus that'll kill you in a few minutes?"

"That's right," Abernathy confirmed.

Bravia eyed the geneticist and the CEO in turn. "Doesn't it bother you, playing God like that?"

Abernathy fielded the question. "As I was saying, God has nothing to do with it."

"Why not? These artificially created creatures wouldn't exist without you, right?"

"Maybe not right now, but I'm sure that in time they would. Or at least they could. After all, they're just different combinations of naturally existing chemicals that we humans call DNA base pairs. And given enough time, those combinations are bound to come up, to be *selected for*, in evolutionary parlance. Sort of like—you've heard that bit about how a bunch of monkeys with typewriters—given enough time—will independently recreate the works of Shakespeare? It's kind of like that. Yeah, we came along and sped up the process, but then again, maybe people like us *are* the process."

Alvarado couldn't suppress a snicker. "Do they drug test you guys here, man? Because that is some far out stuff; I mean really!"

Abernathy smiled good-naturedly while the CEO read something on his smartphone in the corner of the lab. "Like most jobs I've had since I started internships for my PhD, they don't care what we do as long as we produce results. I can tell you without reservation though, the drug of choice here and everywhere else I've worked is, far and away, caffeine." He nodded to the Coke in the CEO's hand. "But seriously, the other reason I don't have a God complex designing these life forms is because I don't believe in God, at least, not in the traditional sense."

"Atheist, eh?"

Abernathy made a face that suggested he was uncomfortable with that label. "I usually go with the term *secular naturalist*, or maybe *pantheist*. Basically, I don't believe that God made the universe, but that the universe itself *is* God. These creatures we've designed and created using the CRISPR technology—we were only able to do it because we pieced together humans' understanding of nature, and technology—which is an extension of nature—incrementally until it became possible. Nature reveals itself to humanity little by little, and the more we reveal, the more we understand what God really is."

A sharp clacking sound was heard coming from the terrarium, and they all shifted their gaze to the glass tank, where inside the sailfin lizard, that baby dinosaur, had smashed its mouth into the glass. The guts of its prey—a spider—now smeared the clear wall of its temporary prison, a space that would soon be far too small to contain it.

Alvarado summed it up for he, Bravia, and the people of South Florida. "God help us all."

CHAPTER 28

Everglades

The swamp boats sped across the river of grass that was the sawgrass prairie. The antenna building peninsula was far behind them now, even the blinking lights atop the tower no longer visible in the smokey haze. Gumshoe received news via radio shortly after they left the antenna building that the third airboat had gotten word of Sara's rescue and headed back to Headquarters, accessible because of the different route it had taken.

"So it's just us five now," Gumshoe said, indicating the other boat with a nod.

"Six. How could you forget about Eric?" Sara reminded sternly.

Gumshoe nodded solemnly. "Six." They rode on in silence, while the boat pilots sought open patches of water where available to cruise the boats through. Sara looked around as they travelled. They were very far out into the wilderness now, farther than she had ever been. This was one of the most remote parts of the park. They began to see what she knew were called tree islands, little patches of solid ground, like islands in the sawgrass swamp, or slough as it was formally known, that were home to hardwood hammocks. These were dense stands of true trees, as opposed mangroves, which required brackish or saltwater for their root systems. These were actual woody trees such as mahogany or gumbo limbo.

The patches of slightly elevated land were easy enough to spot with their tree cover, but there were enough of them that it made for a kind of obstacle course, with the boats needing to slalom between them to remain in navigable waters. It wouldn't take much, all of them knew, to rip a hole in the thin metal boat bottom. The same hull that was designed to skim like a skipped stone over the water's surface was also not very durable. They were designed to run over marshes and swamps, but getting too near to solid land was risky since there could be protruding tree roots or hidden chunks of coral or limestone.

Once, they had to slow down to navigate between two tree islands, where the water grew very shallow, with exposed tree roots, and Sara got a glimpse of something moving on the land. Something big.

"Hold on, what's that?" She pointed to a cream-colored creature, long and narrow, crawling over the dirt between two mahogany trees. "Doesn't look like a snake," she added.

Gumshoe took his eyes off the controls to check it out. "I'll be goddamned if it doesn't look like a giant flatworm. Hammerhead worm, they're called. I know about 'em because they're seen here, but much smaller, maybe a foot long at most. That thing's gotta be six, maybe seven feet if it's an inch. Thing is, they're poisonous, too. They produce a tetrodotoxin. So a worm that big...." He finished his sentence early as if he didn't even want to think about it.

Sara looked at the worm again. It had a distinctive head, like that of a hammerhead shark. It humped along the ground, parts of it rising and falling as it moved along. Unlike the millipedes, the flatworm was not divided into segments. "What do you think they eat?" she wondered aloud.

"Normally they eat earthworms, other bugs," Gumshoe said. "No idea what that freakish thing eats. Birds, maybe? Bird eggs? Who knows? I'm not sure I even want to know."

Sara shuddered as she looked at the creature. Its back glistened with moisture as it propelled itself in that primitive fashion, seeking sustenance, she supposed, in the only way it knew how.

The ranger in the bow pointed to a nearby tree on the same hammock island. "There's another one, in the lower branches." Indeed, another of the animals was coiled like a python in the tree. "The normal little ones aren't known for climbing," he added.

"Wouldn't surprise me if their genes were combined with a python," Gumshoe speculated. "Word is, that company BioGen's been messing around with the gene pool of different animals."

"CRISPR?" Sara added. She'd been out of the media loop, but was well aware of modern biotechnology advances, and knew that it was likely used to produce such strange creatures as those she'd seen lately.

Gumshoe just shook his head as if to clear his mind of it all. "I'm hoping it gets sorted when we get back. But right now, I just want to get us back."

Sara gawked at the oversized flatworms gliding on trails of mucous all over the isolated hardwood hammock. "Yeah, let's get out of here."

No one gave any arguments, and soon both fan boats had threaded their way out of the maze of hammock islands. Finding themselves on an open swath of slough again, they throttled up. As the boats got up on a plane—the speed at which an air pocket passes under the hull and lifts it over the water's surface-- a heavy downpour commenced, complete with lightning and booming thunderclaps that vibrated the metal boat hulls. But even with the weather, coasting across fire-free water was a blessing.

"Maybe this'll help put out the fires!" Sara yelled, pointing at the rain and then to the fires in the distance, since Gumshoe wore earmuffs. He gave her a smile and a thumbs up, but his muffs stayed on and he kept driving.

#

They had just connected the last full gas can to the motor when Gumshoe pointed to a dim landform in the distance. The visibility had cleared somewhat in the last hour as the rain let up some. "There we go. Missile site is somewhere over there." The second boat sidled up and that captain reported that they only had one-half a fuel tank remaining.

"Should be enough," Gumshoe guessed. "If not, we'll all have to pile in here." He nodded to Farley's corpse, still bundled in the bow of the second boat. "Him too."

"We'll keep to cruising speed, not full speed, to get more mileage," the captain said, and Gumshoe agreed. The pair of airboats set out again toward the distant land, now on their last tanks of fuel. About halfway to the land mass, Sara pointed up in the sky, at the 2 o'clock position from the bow of their boat: A flock of ptero-birds, flying not in a V-pattern, but in a simple straight line, perhaps twenty individuals long.

Not a good sign, she thought. She wondered if they were some of the same ones they had seen back by the antenna building. Could they be following the boats? Then again, that was almost preferable to the alternative, which was that the ptero-birds were in this part of the Everglades, too. How much had they taken over already?

The boats motored into a very shallow bog area at the entrance to a narrow-mouthed bay. The outer edge of the bay was formed by a thin barrier island on each side of the entrance, with a small gap in the middle which they needed to boat through to reach the far end of the bay where the mainland was. Here there were neither tree islands, nor large open marsh areas, but instead a classic swamp environment where single cypress trees here and there grew from the soggy ground. The boats had to be slowed to not much above idle speed in order to safely navigate the maze-like topography.

Gumshoe's boat took the lead, passing under the leaves of a huge cypress before turning sharply to fit between two more. After that he was able to plow across open space toward land before needing to avoid another large tree. The second boat stayed close behind, partly because if Gumshoe's boat had success, then it was safest to follow, but also because they were about to run out of gas. The meandering around obstacles and threading their way consumed more fuel than the open beeline routes they'd been able to use for much of the trip. So it was no surprise when, about halfway to the bay shoreline, the motor of the second fan boat sputtered to a stop.

"We're out," the captain called.

Gumshoe eased his swamp boat up to theirs. "Come aboard. Tell you what though," he said, eyeballing Farley's body. "Why don't you anchor here, I'll mark the position on my GPS, so we can leave him here and pick him up later."

The captain agreed. "Gonna be crowded with four of us on board. If we weren't this close to land, I wouldn't want to but...."

"Right, this'll be an easy pickup. Come on, let's get going."

They anchored the out-of-fuel swamp boat and, after its captain transferred to Gumshoe's boat, the four of them continued on towards the shore. A tear traced down Sara's cheek as she watched Farley's body disappear from view in its anchored boat. *It's because of me, he died trying to help me....*

There was no telling how long she might have wallowed in such melancholy thoughts if not for Gumshoe's co-pilot informing them he saw a clear path to shore. One of the rangers picked up a long pole, and Gumshoe killed the engine, still very loud even at idle speeds. He ditched his earmuffs and looked around.

"Let's listen for a minute." All was quiet but for the ripples of water as they poled along between cypress trees. The ranger not poling parted curtains of hanging moss that they passed under, and then they were staring at a solid shoreline they could walk out on. The sound of the airboat's hull gliding up onto the dirt brought home the fact that they were nearing the end of their journey, whatever that may entail.

The four rangers exited the boat, Gumshoe taking a flashlight from the boat as well as a coil of rope. On the edge of solid land, they took stock of their surroundings. The grove of cypress trees gave way to an open area about a hundred yards in.

"Missile site should be over that way," Gumshoe said, already starting to walk in that direction. "From there we can arrange for pickup."

They trooped off into the forest as a group, spread out in a horizontal line with Gumshoe and Sara in the middle. "Eyes up, too," Gumshoe warned. "Who knows what kind of animals could be loose around here."

Sara's gaze was already roving up, down and all around as they trekked through the mossy forest. She expected to be attacked by something, but by the time they reached the edge of the forest, no animal presence had made itself known. She hoped it meant they had travelled far enough that the genetically modified animals would no longer be a threat.

They emerged from the cypress forest onto an open, flat grassy area. Sara pulled on her sunglasses against the brightness after being in the dim cypress grove.

"Which way?" she asked the group.

"Think we should hit a road if we go straight long enough," Gumshoe said. No one had any better ideas. So the four rangers began walking straight ahead across the grassy field. The rain was still present but had thinned to a drizzle, and the sun was hidden behind gray clouds. The ground was wet but firm and they made good progress across the grass. It was strangely quiet though, with zero sounds of humanity or animal alike.

Gumshoe was right about the road, for they came across it after a short hike. An empty cracked and faded blacktop with no markings bisected the grassy plain. To the right, it headed off to seemingly nowhere. To the left, however, was a long boxy object.

"Anybody think to bring binoculars?" Gumshoe asked. "Left mine on the boat."

"Mine too," the pilot of the other boat said.

"Guess we should head that way then, see what that is." No one objected and so they all moved off in the direction of the unknown thing. As they moved toward it, Sara caught movement off to their right, where the grass gave way to a stand of palmetto and cedar trees. Flock of birds? Much too small to be ptero-birds, so she wasn't worried. Normal animals still existed out here, after all. Not everything alive out here was some kind of genetically engineered monster. *Right*? The congregation of small black birds lit from the trees and took flight in a startled murmuration.

"Just a flock of starlings," Gumshoe said, sensing Sara's concern.

She nodded as they continued to walk toward the man-made object. She was trying to discern what it could be again when she heard the trees rustle behind them and to the right, and felt the earth beneath her feet shake.

"What is that?" one of the other rangers asked, stopping in his tracks.

He held a Nalgene bottle in his hand, and the water inside sloshed slightly with the next tremble of earth.

CHAPTER 29

Sara was the first to see it. At first it blended in with the treetops, but when it emerged from the trees, its coloration changed somewhat to match the surrounding grass, and she discerned its form. For a couple of seconds, she had to tell herself that she was okay, that she wasn't suffering hallucinogenic visions brought on by stress, that this was a real thing in front of her eyes. A real animal.

Its sheer size was what threw her. And the weird, snake-like head and neck.

Dinosaur. That's the word her brain tossed around. Nothing else could come close to explaining it. Just this lumbering, gargantuan, color-shifting beast literally shaking the ground as it walked. She had trouble snapping out of it, so compelling a vision did it make. But she had to. She knew she had to or the consequences would be insurmountable.

"Giant dinosaur!" she called out dumbly, too shocked to be more coherent. But it was sufficient to get the attention of her fellow rangers. All of them stood agog in the presence of the beast that should not be.

"It's the sailfin lizard they were talking about today!" Gumshoe said. "It's even bigger than I thought."

"Ben Offstead said it was huge," the co-pilot ranger said, "but I had no idea…"

"This is the one that killed that camper," the other ranger said.

And then the sailfin dino brayed loudly, its neck rising high to hold its head up while it produced the vocalization. When it completed its performance, the massive beast began to lumber toward them. The water bottle was dropped on the ground as all four rangers turned to run.

"Don't stop!" Gumshoe warned as they pumped their legs to sprinting speed. None of the others looked like they needed that advice as the four of them ran like proverbial bats out of hell. Although they ran simply to escape the marauding creature, caring not where they went as long as it was away from the beastly danger, Sara fixated on the long boxy object that now grew more distinct. It was hard to make out much detail as she bounced along, but it now looked like a series of squares rather than one long rectangle.

They continued to run toward it even as they felt the ground quaking beneath their feet. The dino-lizard galloped after them, moving terrifyingly fast for something so large.

"Keep...going!" Gumshoe reminded them unnecessarily. It was actually he who was slightly behind the others. The dinosaur, on the other hand, was rapidly gaining ground. Sara took a terrified look behind her, craning her neck around without slowing down, despite the pain it caused. It quickly became apparent that the sailfin-dino would be upon them very soon, and that were they to avoid contact with it, their best bet was to put the rectangular thing between them and it. That's still how she thought of it—just this rectangular thing, but as she ran past it, she realized what it was.

A train of little cars chained together.

"Tram!" Gumshoe called out, crystallizing the concept for her.

Instantly, Sara thought of the tourist attraction near the missile site, a "historic tram tour" of the abandoned cold war facility that sprung up on the eve of the Cuban Missile Crisis. And here it was, just sitting there, the only thing between her and a certain messy, untimely death.

Reaching the tram, the group split without slowing their run, with Sara and the co-pilot taking the right side of the tram, and Gumshoe and the other ranger on the left.

"It's almost on us!" the ranger with Gumshoe yelled. No one even responded 'keep going' or anything like that. All of their minds began to cloud with the fog of panic. The sailfin beast ran even faster, within seconds now of overtaking its prey. The group ran the length of the tram cars, maybe ten of them linked together, with a longer engine cart in front. They got to this and then all four of them huddled around the front while the sailfin reached the end of the tram train.

The mega-dino's head changed to a beige color as it loomed over the rear of the tram, matching the vehicular shade. The three male rangers each drew their pistols, knowing they were comically pitiful weapons against such a mighty force, but at the same time aware that it was all they had.

Sara, seeing the pistols drawn, tried something different and jumped into the tram cab. She saw a silver up-down lever switch, flipped it up and saw a couple of lights wink on. She stepped on the pedal, expecting nothing to happen since this thing had been sitting out here in the middle of nowhere for who knows how long. She knew the tram tour existed, but figured this was the off-season for it, and so had been sitting for some time. To her great surprise, the tram car lurched forward, scattering the men out of the way. They put their hands and arms on the front of the tram car as they peeled off, with Gumshoe and the other boat captain spinning off to the left side, and the other ranger to the right.

"Hold on!" Sara cautioned, as she squashed the accelerator pedal with her right boot.

Gunshots rang out as someone opened fire on the sailfin dino. The tram picked up speed as Sara gripped the steering wheel, fighting it for a few seconds as she got used to the handling, but then straightening out the line of cars as she accelerated forward. Because they were shooting, Sam and the two rangers all latched on to the tram at different cars. Gumshoe ended up closest to Sara's lead car, two cars back, while the other airboat captain was one car behind him. By the time the third ranger could hop aboard, he was three cars from the end, which put his closest to the thrashing sailfin lizard.

The mega-beast towered over the tram. Even though its two front legs were positioned right behind the caboose car, its snake head, held up high on that snake-like body, hovered over the middle car. Saliva rained down from its open maw as its black, forked tongue flicked in and out. More gunfire rang out but no one could tell if they were even hitting the beast; if they were, it was having no effect.

Then the sailfin dino pushed off its hind legs into a jump, and placed its front two legs on the back of the second-to-last rail car. The ranger in the third car back found himself face to tiny snake-face with the weird beastie, and as he pumped his last loaded shot into the chest of the scaly behemoth, the slender but powerful neck slammed its own tiny head into the ranger's face, knocking him senseless. He went limp and slipped off the tram car, coming to only when falling out of the car's open side. He swiped a hand up toward the handrail on top of the seat back, but missed it and hit the ground, landing forcefully on his back.

The sailfin lizard abandoned the tram and stood over its fallen victim, its skin flashing a dull red color. Then, as with the camper earlier, it simply lowered its body onto the man, smothering and crushing him as the tram rolled off up ahead.

In the lead tram car, Sara felt the tram wobble back as the sailfin jumped off of it, and then gasped as she watched the last two cars separate from the tram and roll off on their own. One of them bashed into the mega-lizard, which caused the animal to stand and whirl around. It nudged the car with its head until it tipped over, then turned back to its human victim. Sensing it to be dead or at least suitably helpless, it lowered its tiny head to the man's stomach.

"Keep driving, he's gone!" Gumshoe advised from his position in the now shorter tram. The other ranger pumped two more rounds into the side of the mega-creature. The skin flashed orange for a second where the projectiles struck. Then he holstered his pistol and turned around, shocked to now be in the last car on the tram. Luckily the sailfin was busy gorging on the fallen ranger. Its tiny head lifted up once and stared at the ranger on the caboose car as he rolled away, and then bent back down to its bowl of innards.

In the front, Sara continued driving while behind her, Gumshoe jumped the gap from his car to the one right behind Sara's. He leaned forward and pointed off to the right. "You see that tower?"

Sara glanced in that direction and nodded. A concrete platform of some type jutted out from a tree canopy. "Is that the missile base?"

Gumshoe shook his head. "No, it's a tourist observation platform. Fifty feet high, offers a view of the surrounding canopy and waterways. If we climb it, we'll be able to see where the missile base is for sure. I don't think it's far from there."

"Okay, I'll head for it." Sara turned right, angling the tram in that direction. As soon as she straightened out the train, a red light started to blink on the dashboard. "Low battery," she said.

"No surprise there," Gumshoe said. "We're lucky it worked at all."

"Wasn't lucky for—" Sara started, but Gumshoe cut her off.

"Not now, Sara, please. I know this is tragic, but we're not out of the woods yet ourselves. Let's get to the tower. We should be able to make a radio call from up there."

She adjusted her grip on the steering wheel and lightened her foot on the accelerator, hoping to keep going the remaining distance to the tower before the battery drained completely. Gumshoe craned his neck to look back at the sailfin while the other ranger monkey-barred his way forward by climbing from one car to the next.

"That thing is still busy with—well you know," Gumshoe finished, not wanting to mention it was eating their dead friend's corpse and that was what was saving them right now.

"We're losing power now, nothing I can do, I'm light on the accelerator but it's still dying."

Up ahead, the tower sprung from the treetops maybe a football field away. Gumshoe turned around and spoke to the other ranger. "Battery's dying. Get ready to bail out and we're gonna make a run for it to the tower."

"Okay." He made his way to the car behind Gumshoe's and stayed there, looking back at the sailfin, still gorging in place. The tram rolled on toward the edge of the woods, where an opening led to a path leading to the tower.

"I see the way," Sara said, steering the lead cart in that direction. As soon as she made the adjustment, the forward momentum of the whole tram slowed noticeably. She pressed on the accelerator but no additional speed resulted. The blinking red light on the dash changed to steady red.

"This is it. Can't go any faster. It's slowing down. Battery's done; we're just coasting."

Gumshoe turned around to check on the sailfin lizard, looming big as a house behind them.

"Still feeding. We can run faster than this tram now, but the motion of the tram is quieter than the pounding of our feet, so we should ride it while we can. But as soon as we coast to a stop, we ditch and run for the path. Clear?"

Sara and the other surviving ranger said they were. They positioned themselves to bail out, with Sara remaining behind the wheel to steer for the path, now about fifty yards away.

"It's on the move!" the ranger in the third tram car said.

Sara checked the rearview mirror and saw the loping mega-beast, its neck too long to be seen in the mirror. She worked the tram controls, trying the pedal again to no avail, pressing a couple of buttons and flipping switches she wasn't sure what they did. One of those turned out to be a horn, and although it only sounded for a fraction of a second before she flipped it back off, it was enough to catch the lizard's attention. It began to charge, moving even faster than before, its body slightly wobbling and swaying side to side while its neck and head leaned forward straight out in front of it.

"Go, go, let's go!" Gumshoe yelled, eschewing silence and stealth for maximum speed. The trio of park rangers fled from the tram, which continued to roll sedately without them down a gentle slope. Behind them, the lizard brayed, loud and hissing, sort of like a fire extinguisher being sprayed. Up ahead the opening into the trees was about fifty feet away. They sprinted for it, Gumshoe slightly in the lead, while Sara and the other ranger ran side by side just behind him.

As they neared the path entrance, Sara could feel the ground shaking again as the great lizard caught up to them. She turned around once without stopping, petrified to see the massive chest wall of the lizard towering above her, its tiny head dangling below it out in front, even closer to them.

They tromped onto the path, about ten feet wide and consisting of dirt and some crushed limestone. It wound off to the right, although the tower loomed out of the forest canopy straight ahead, so it must take a meandering path to get to it, Sara thought. She wasn't sure if that was good or bad. Good, because on a straightaway, that mega-beast sure was fast. But bad, because it meant they had farther to go to reach the tower. The tree cover was too thick to penetrate with any confidence, a dense tangle of mangrove roots, transitioning to hardwood trees, festooned with lush hanging curtains of moss and spiderwebs.

They followed the path around the first turn as the sailfin dino reached the gap in the trees and followed after them.

CHAPTER 30

Sara saw the long dirt straightaway and cringed, knowing she would have to coax even more speed out of her already overworked legs, lungs and heart. She redoubled her efforts, now hearing one of the rangers scream behind her; she couldn't tell who by the guttural utterance. Not one of pain, as if the lizard reached them and was stomping them into the ground, but one of pure fright at the realization they were being pursued like mindless prey items destined to end up literally in the belly of the beast, that not to run fast enough for the next few seconds meant death, pure, swift and certain.

The trio of rangers hit the dirt straightaway with Sara still out front and the two men side by side a few feet back. On either side of the trail, the jungle-like woods threatened to close completely over the road overhead, filtering the sunlight to the point it was almost dark. But this small handicap that made it hard to see where they were going and forced them to remove sunglasses while at a full run without slowing down also turned out to be an advantage. The oversized sailfin lizard was tall enough—especially with its head sticking straight up—that its upper body cleaved the canopy leaves, slowing it down some as it parted the canopy to move forward.

Ahead, the trail curved back to the left. Sara dared take a second to look up, trying to spot the tower. There it was, straight ahead through the jungle now, which was still impenetrable on all sides of the path. The curvature forced her to slow down, and then she saw another curve—also left—coming up after only a very short straight shot. They followed the road, but soon found that the short curves had become the norm. The path wound tightly this way and that through the dense woodland, and somewhere close behind, the dinosaur followed them.

It all became such a blur to Sara that her mind closed in on itself, like an intense tunnel vision that allowed her only to follow the path, to shut out all other stimuli such that 100% of her energy was funneled into following the path as fast as humanly possible. It worked, because before long the other two rangers were out of sight behind her, and up ahead, the terrain was finally changing.

"I see it!" she blurted, lungs on fire to the point that she wasn't sure she'd be able to belt the words out. But she knew she had managed it, that it wasn't just a figment of her consciousness, when Gumshoe's voice came from behind: "Stairs in the middle of the tower. Go up."

Sara wasn't exactly sure what that meant, but she filed it away for near-future reference while she fled out of the path into an open meadow area that was still surrounded on all sides by lush greenery, with no other outlets she could see.

But there it was.

The tower, centered in the open space, unmissable in its man-made interruption of the natural beauty, the reason it was here. Sara did her best to drink in its details as she ran toward it. What was it Gumshoe had said only seconds earlier? Stairs? Middle? Because "tower" was a little deceptive. This wasn't some utility pole with a flat board on top, or a lookout structure like the crow's nest atop a ship's mast. A hollow square structure in the center rose five stories into the air—at least twenty feet higher than the surrounding canopy. Situated on top of that was a large rectangular platform, complete with a waist-high railing around its edges. Sara ran to the middle of the center support and saw that it did indeed contain a stairwell, one that switch-backed inside the support structure up to the platform.

She bolted for that, knowing it was the way up. Behind her, Gumshoe was shouting urgencies like "Go!" as if she needed any prompting. She turned around to check on the sailfin's progress and was shocked to see only its skinny neck and head wavering above the canopy, very close to the edge of the clearing by the path exit. It was definitely still pursuing them. She willed herself to run even faster across the open space toward the platform. It seemed like the longest forty feet or so she'd ever had to traverse, but she got there, feeling a sliver of comfort in the shade of the big structure as she passed beneath it.

But her minor victory was marred by a throaty grunt coming from one of the two men behind her. She identified the opening of the stairwell and then turned around to see what was happening. Gumshoe still dashed toward the structure, but the other ranger had tripped and fallen hard, face mashed into the scrubby grass, one leg still in motion as he flopped over. At the same time, the sailfin dino burst out of the path exit into the clearing.

Sara's heart seemed to stop as she watched the scene unfold from the base of the stairs. "Get him, Sam! Pull him up!" But Gumshoe hesitated way too long, and the sailfin was nothing but purposeful motion as it barreled toward its downed prey. "Sam!" she pressed. It was enough to get him to draw his gun as he backpedaled, but clearly it was too late. The fallen ranger started to get up, but he had turned an ankle on the way down and as soon as he put weight on it, he went down again. Gumshoe blasted three rounds into the onrushing dino, but with the head making for an impossibly slim moving target, he had to settle for chest shots. Four slugs ripped into the reptilian chest wall, but if they had any effect other than the orange colorbursts on impact, it wasn't yet apparent, for the mega-predator charged on.

Nearly tripping backwards himself, Gumshoe shot off one more round and then turned to sprint for the tower. The sailfin's gargantuan bulk descended on the fallen man, and this time, Sara was more analytical about observing the kill. Same method, she noticed—stomp and stun, then lower that snake-like head to the belly to open the guts. She had to wonder how even a whole human could be much more than a snack for the titanic organism; it must need many more calories than that to sustain itself. Maybe it was omnivorous and also ate plants?

But she had no time for serious contemplation on the matter. She needed to ascend the steps and get to the safety of the tower platform, five stories up.

"Going up!" she called back to Gumshoe, deciding she could not afford to let the grief of losing yet another co-worker overtake her now. Later she would process it all, but today she needed to be fully present in the moment if she were to get out of this alive.

"Right behind you!" Gumshoe returned, feet still pounding the dirt.

Sara was already climbing stairs, ascending the switch-backing half-flights three steps at a time while using the handrail to pull herself up as an assist. The steps were mesh grating, and so she could partially see below when Gumshoe reached the bottom and started his own climb. As Sara vaulted up the metal flights, she would get a glimpse of the sailfin feasting on the fallen ranger when she made a turn, and then be blind to it as she went up the other half-flight. Below her she could hear the echoing of Gumshoe's footfalls as he ascended the metal stairs.

Sometime between when she entered the stairwell and when she emerged on top of the observation platform, it began to rain hard again. Sara emerged into open air on the observation deck with the sound of raindrops pelting the wooden deck. She glanced down one more time to make sure Gumshoe was still coming and saw him working on it about halfway up. Then she moved to the rail facing the trail where they had exited from, and saw the sailfin dinosaur approaching that side of the tower.

Her heart stopped.

She was looking down on the head of the thing, but not by all that much, perhaps ten, fifteen feet. Hard to tell with it swaying back and forth in the rain. She took a deep breath and put her hand on her chest, feeling her heart start to beat again. The beast appeared to be confused, for it had stopped next to the tower and was investigating how to get in, sniffing out where its prey had gone with its forked tongue grooving in and out of its slender head.

Sara froze in place, not wanting to give away her position with obvious movement. She began backing away ever so slowly, sliding her feet along the deck rather than stepping, hoping to make her movements as smooth and silent as possible. But then she heard Gumshoe nearing the top of the stairs, tromping away as he sought to reach the deck as quickly as he could.

Sara turned and bolted for the centermost portion of the deck, figuring she could get far enough away from the beast at this point if it did jump or lunge all the way up to the edge of the platform. It didn't make an aggressive move though, but rather began walking slowly around the base of the tower, no doubt looking for a way up or to see if it could reach its prey some other way.

Gumshoe stepped up onto the platform, pulling his ranger's wide-brimmed hat down tighter on his head against the driving rainfall. He looked at Sara, who had backed all the way up to the railing guarding the stairway entrance, and asked, "Where is it?"

"It's walking around now ..." she turned her head to see if she could find it. "There!" She pointed off to their left, behind Gumshoe. She turned and saw the great sail of the beast rise and fall almost as high as the platform while the beast walked along the tower's perimeter. Satisfied they weren't in imminent danger, Gumshoe unclipped his portable radio from his belt.

"This height means we'll have good signal transmission. I'll request a chopper." While he made the radio call to ranger headquarters, Sara turned her attention to their greater surroundings. She walked out from the stairwell entrance, though was careful not to get too close to any edge of the platform. But they had come up here, after all, to locate the missile site buildings. So where were they? They were still surrounded by jungle, but it was thicker in the direction from which they had come. In fact, another path snaked into the treed sector opposite the larger one from which they had come, and at the end of that path was an open area featuring a complex of old, white buildings.

She heard Sam holding a terse yet information-laden radio exchange as he conveyed their general location and tried to work out a pickup point. Apparently satisfied, he signed off and turned back to Sara, who pointed out the old buildings.

"That's the missile site," Gumshoe confirmed.

"Doesn't look like too much is there, really. Maybe we should just wait here?"

But then, as the rain began to let up, Gumshoe pointed again, this time about ninety degrees to the right from the missile site. "Not sure about that. Big problem incoming."

As Sara looked in that direction, her heart sank. Coming in low over the treetops was a flock of ptero-birds, organized in the same weird straight line formation the others had adopted. She didn't know if they were the same individuals or another flock (how many creatures had been loosed out here?), but regardless, they were a threat and they were flying their way, fast. Sara took one more look at the buildings and the new path that led to them. There was only one option she could think of, and that was to head back down—but not all the way down.

"To the stairs, let's go," she said to Gumshoe as she hopped down the first flight.

"Where you going?" He started down after her.

"Not all the way down, but we'll be safe in here from the flying things and the sailfin. For a little while anyway. Until we can figure something out."

Gumshoe had no rebuttal and skipped down the stairs after her. About halfway down, they paused on a landing and rested, with Sara looking up and Sam looking down. They were indeed safe from all predators for the moment. Gumshoe reloaded his pistol and looked at Sara with a frown. "Ten rounds left. Good news is they do more damage to those bird-things than to the giant dinosaur."

Sara patted her own weapon, still holstered on her hip. "I haven't used mine yet, still have a full magazine."

Gumshoe nodded, surprised. "Well that's good news. Think you can hit one of those things?" He nodded up to one of the ptero-avians, only partially visible for a second as it flew across the sliver of sky above the stairwell opening. Sara shrugged as she looked up at them. Funny how she didn't feel nervous about it, whereas only a few days ago she'd have been super-uncomfortable if asked to shoot a large animal where human life— including her own—depended on her accuracy. But now she realized it was that or nothing. Live or die, she'd already seen how that could play out. She nodded and said, "Sure."

Gumshoe returned the nod and then pointed downstairs. "It's that thing I'm most worried about, but of course we've seen what the flying ones can do."

Sara nodded grimly in reply. "There is one good thing about the ptero-birds being here."

"What's that?"

"They might distract the dinosaur."

"Let's hope so. You think we can make a dash for that path that leads through the woods to the missile site?"

Sara shrugged. "I think we have no choice. But I also think I can provide that distraction first."

Gumshoe looked surprised. "How so?"

"If we can shoot one of the pteros down, the sailfin might stop long enough to eat it. While it does that, we make our break for it."

"You think we try from up there or down on the ground?"

"Maybe split up? One of us goes high, the other low. When we drop one, then we both split for the missile site."

Gumshoe nodded. "You want high or low? High's probably an easier shot but then you have longer to run."

Sara nodded. "You're the better shot, and no offense but I think I'm a shade faster, so how about you take low. Remember, we only need one or two of them down at most. We don't want to start a war. The noise could even attract more of them."

"I'm ready."

They split up, Sara walking back up the stairs to the observation deck, while Gumshoe descended to the ground. Up top, Sara was pleased to see that no ptero-birds occupied the platform. She counted four of them in the air nearby the deck, which meant there had to be more on the ground. She exited out onto the deck, which offered no cover other than the stairwell itself, which had a railing around the opening on three sides.

Glancing down at the ground, she saw two ptero-avians picking and pecking what little remains of the ranger's body were left behind by the sailfin monster. No sooner did the thought pass through her brain—*those are your targets*—than a shot rang out below and she saw the head of one of the bird-creatures explode in a splash of red like a squeezed ketchup packet.

Taking her cue, Sara assumed a firing stance and sighted on the remaining ptero-bird, which still stood over its carrion, but looked around on high alert status. She held her breath and pulled the trigger slowly. *Bang*. The shot tore through the creature's mid-body, knocking it off its scrappy meal. Then, without re-sighting, she raised the barrel ever so slightly and fired again. This second round also found its way into the primitive body and down the bird-beast went, toppling nearby its fellow diner.

The sailfin, which had been circling the tower about halfway out to the tree line, now stopped walking, its long neck and head pointing to the fallen pteros. Then it started to amble toward them. Sara crouched on the platform, remaining still so as not to distract it. She wanted it to go to the fallen creatures. It walked toward them, stopping once or twice to sniff the ground, and once or twice to sniff the air while looking vaguely toward the tower. But then it changed course and walked at ever-increasing pace until it worked up to a slow trot, to the site of its last meal. It bent its long-necked head down to one of the ptero-birds and went to work satisfying its primal need.

Sara slipped back into the stairwell, trying to make as little noise as possible. When she emerged at the bottom, she could see Gumshoe already trotting across the field toward the far path. She eyed the still flying pteros in the sky, all of which now converged in the air over the sailfin. This was the most terrifying part of the journey, traversing the open field, where she could be simple prey for either the pteros or the sailfin, should they decide to attack her.

She took off after Gumshoe.

CHAPTER 31

Sara felt the comforting embrace of the tree canopy shadows as she dashed onto the path that led to the abandoned missile base. She couldn't see Sam Gumshoe, who was somewhere up ahead, but the path curved left after only twenty feet or so. She followed the course, which was curvier than the last one, not allowing her to maintain a full-on run for very long before she had to slow and make a turn. Even so, it wasn't long before she rounded a corner and then saw her fellow ranger's boot heels kicking up as he followed the next curve around.

"Right behind you, Sam!" she called out.

"Quiet! Don't give away our position!" came his stressed-out response.

She imagined herself yelling back at the top of her lungs, *Okay then, I won't talk anymore!* And actually had to suppress a laugh. It reminded her of something her old college roommate would have said, and for just one second, she was free of the stress and worry of her predicament. But only for just a second, because after that, she heard a rustling of trees somewhere behind her, and she knew what it meant. She hoped she was wrong, but she knew she was not, so she forced herself to find a way to make better time through the winding jungle path. She hugged the inside of the turns as soon as she could see which way it was going next, and ignored the burning of her muscle fibers as they protested the prolonged exertion.

Bright light up ahead, the open air and end of the tree cover! She came out of a turn and sprinted down the last of the path, a blessed straightaway that allowed her to build up to maximum speed. She could see Gumshoe out there too, who didn't stop but continued to run toward the compound. As Sara exited the path, she did her best to take in the layout of the old missile site.

A large white building lay straight ahead, a couple of hundred feet away, the size of either a large garage or small warehouse. Numerous smaller outbuildings were spread out behind that, connected by narrow roads that were paved but looked as though they had seen much better days. Gumshoe stopped about halfway to the main building and turned around, panting heavily with his hands on his knees while waiting for Sara to reach him.

She was almost to him when she called out, "Sam, where are—" but he was clearly not listening. His eyes widened and he pointed over her shoulder. Sara turned around to look in time to see the sailfin dino crashing through the trees near the path exit. It burst out into the clearing and then launched into a full run, its weird snake body-head wavering around as its house-sized body shuffled at them like a tank.

"To the big building!" Gumshoe shouted as he spun around and ran. Sara also put herself into fast motion, pumping her legs rapidly until she reached her top sprinting speed. As she neared the building complex, the grass transitioned to a paved apron surrounding the main structure. She saw Gumshoe slow as he reached the building, while she continued to sprint. Then she could hear the rasping noise of the lizard's foot and toe-pads sliding across the pavement. It was catching up.

"Open it!" she screamed, worried now she was about to be overtaken by the terrible beast and stamped into the pavement before the little snake head wormed into her belly. "Get it open!"

She heard the soul-shaking rattle of a locked doorknob being tried, then a louder thumping as the door was forcefully pressed into its frame. She saw Gumshoe leave the small door and run to the larger garage-style door that took up most of that side of the building. *That's not going to work*, she told herself, her mind approaching panic state even faster than her legs were running. *If the regular door is locked, why would that be open?*

But Gumshoe turned his body sideways, gripped a latch and pulled. She heard the rumbling of a metal door sliding on wheels over concrete. He slid the door open enough for a person to fit through and then turned and beckoned her with a wave. *As if I need an invitation*, she thought, slowing a little as she neared the building. The great lizard was right behind her.

Sara had no idea what was inside the structure and didn't care. She reached the door and flung herself through the open space after Gumshoe, who immediately slid it shut after them as the dinosaur rushed the building. She kept running even after being inside because she had seen how fast that bulky animal was moving and didn't think it would be able to fully stop itself before crashing into the building, even if it wanted to. And it probably didn't want to, she thought, scanning her new surroundings, looking for room to run.

The inside of the space was big, but short of what most people would call cavernous. Inside was a giant disarmed missile, part of the exhibit open to tourists, along with its 1960's firing and control mechanisms and accompanying interpretative signage. All of these exhibit items had been moved to the far left side of the space. Right now, though, Sara didn't care what was in here, she only wanted to escape the marauding predator. Still, it was the rest of the big room's contents that held her attention.

Extensive rows of aquaria, tanks and terrariums were stacked on high shelving units taking up the rest of the room's available space. She caught glimpses of strange animals, small and medium-sized, including the hammerhead flatworms, other creatures swimming and crawling, and even flying, she noted, eyeing a caged-in aviary on the right side of the space. Gumshoe passed one terrarium and pointed dramatically. "Sailfin dino—it says, '*Dimetrodon*-python hybrids!"

"Great, now we know what we're dealing with," Sara said, continuing to run toward the far wall, even past Gumshoe, who had stopped about halfway into the building after shutting the door. "The sign on them also reads, "MIA to PVG—I happen to know that's Shanghai International Airport. Date is this Monday. And this other one here," she said, moving to another tank with strange salamander-looking creatures, "MIA to Hong Kong International. BioGen must be using this as a staging facility to both release animals into the wilderness at the same time they're shipping some of them out to paying clients around the world!"

"I have a feeling they won't actually be shipping any of these," Gumshoe said with a deadpan finality.

"Why's that?"

"Because I don't think that *Dimetrodon* out there is going to stop. I hear it coming."

"Do you really think it's not going to stop, because—"

He never got to finish his sentence because at that moment a thunderous metallic crash was heard as the entire rollup door buckled sharply inward. Gumshoe turned and ran with Sara to the far side of the building, moving around one of the long missiles on the way. When they reached the other side of the missile, they paused in front of a long stack of aquaria filled with black and white striped swimming snakes. A red skull-and-crossbones sign in front of the tanks cautioned, BANDED KRAITS, DEADLY VENOM, APPROVED HANDLERS ONLY.

"Wow, banded kraits are the world's most deadly poisonous snakes. They're actually—" Sara began, but she broke off as the middle section of the rollup door came flying inside. The leg and shoulder of the rampaging behemoth was soon to follow. The scraping of metal on the concrete floor tore at their ears. "Sam, it's in here. It's in here!" Her voice broke into a scream. "Is there another way out?"

Gumshoe eyeballed the length of the back wall, hoping for a regular exit door, but there was only solid wall, no rollup door or anything. The sailfin dino shook off a barrage of scrap metal and bulled its way full inside the building.

"No other way out except past that thing. But I have an idea. Help me tip these tanks over."

"What? Why?"

But there would be no time for explanations. The rollup door was ripped off completely and crashed to the floor as the sailfin beast came rampaging through, barely big enough to fit inside through the open wall.

The pair of rangers positioned themselves so that they stood behind the rows of aquaria containing the deadly sea snakes. Gumshoe put his hands on the shelving unit, which was a standalone, not fixed to the wall or floor. "Let's knock it over."

Getting the idea, Sara moved five feet away from Gumshoe and gripped the shelves. The sailfin started to walk in their direction, moving slowly because the top of its fin scraped on the ceiling, which confused it and caused it to swivel its snake head around. But it continued plodding toward them.

"On three," Gumshoe said, bracing himself against the heavy rack of water-filled tanks. He did the countdown and the two of them pushed with all their might, but the shelving unit barely wobbled. The water-filled aquaria were far too heavy. The sailfin dino continued walking further into the building, head swaying about crazily this way and that.

Then Gumshoe's hand brushed against the coil of rope he'd clipped to his belt after taking it from the airboat. "I knew this would come in handy," he said, unclipping it. Working fast, he threaded the rope through the top-most shelf bars, running it from one side to the other. There was still enough slack left over to bring both ends a few feet out in front of the aquaria racks. "I need you to help me pull," he said. Sara, wary of the approaching sailfin, ran around to the front of the shelving unit with Gumshoe.

The two rangers each grabbed one end of the rope that was now threaded through the rack of aquaria. Gumshoe made eye contact with Sara. "On three, we pull, okay? Hard! It's going to tip, and make sure you get *behind* it as soon as possible, or you'll be dead by snakebite before that dinosaur can reach you."

Sara eyeballed the sailfin and didn't see how that could be true, even knowing how venomous banded kraits were, but she got the point. Besides, there was no time to think about it. "Let's do it!" The pair of rangers, backs to the onrushing dino for a few terrifying seconds, counted down from three and then pulled on the rope with all their strength. Sara's hands burned from the cuts she had sustained breaking the skylight on top of the antenna building roof, the rope slicing into them. But with no other choice, she endured the pain and pulled...

The shelving tipped this time, teetering on the front legs and hanging there for a second before beginning the fall forward. Gumshoe let go of the rope first, started to run and yelled for Sara to do the same.

"It's going, it's going—run back or the snakes could bite you!" Gumshoe yelled. He and Sara sprung backward from the falling shelf unit as it began its fall to the concrete floor. The thought of landing on top of dozens of highly venomous sea snakes was almost worse than being stomped into submission by the sailfin dino, and so Sara didn't worry about whatever might happen to her as a result of running backwards. As it happened, she landed painfully on her butt, with her back slamming into the rear wall. Gumshoe fell sideways onto the floor a little in front of her. She sat there stunned for a second, but the sight of the sailfin-dino plowing toward them spurred her to get up.

The wall of aquaria impacted with the floor a moment before she gained her feet. The sound of the water-filled tanks shattering was like a bomb going off, deafening in the echo-conducive concrete and metal building. Even the sailfin-dino paused its forward charge, the head still atop its stalk of a neck while it attempted to process the event.

It didn't take long. Before all the water had drained from the shattered tanks, as well as those couple that had not broken, the sailfin resumed its predation-driven march toward the back of the room. Sara slinked back against the wall in abject fear. Gumshoe feinted left and right on light feet, like a boxer. The sailfin picked up its pace, resuming charge mode. It plodded right through the spilled water of the tanks, paying no mind to the wriggling black-and-white snakes that had been let loose.

Sara eyeballed the dino's feet. She watched it stamp on top of a couple of kraits, but still it kept coming toward her. She ran sideways, to the right, while Gumshoe took off to the left. She glanced over as she ran and saw only a writhing mass of sea snakes and seawater sluicing across the floor beneath the massive dino's feet. When she reached the corner of the room, she stopped and watched, anticipating whether she'd have to make a break for the entrance, or go some other way. Gumshoe was doing the same from his opposite corner.

The sailfin trounced its way over the fallen tank shelf, then made a sudden turn in Sara's direction. It waddled toward her, its right side brushing the far wall as it walked. Sara shrieked, now doubting completely that she'd be able to escape the corner in time. What had she been thinking? And then, when the sailfin dino's chest was no more than ten feet from her, it suddenly stopped moving forward and collapsed in a heap on the floor.

Sara held her breath while she eyed the fallen mega-predator carefully. She saw a couple of snakes still attached to one of its legs. Others skidded across the floor nearby, trying to swim on wet cement.

But they had done their job! The sailfin-dino had succumbed to multiple simultaneous doses of their fast-acting venom.

"Let's get out of here, Sara, c'mon, in case it wakes back up!" Gumshoe's voice brought Sara back to reality.

"And watch for snakes!" Gumshoe added. "Stick to the perimeter!"

Sara kept her eyes on the floor as she followed the wall around the room, while Gumshoe did the same on the other side of the structure. One time she had to jump over a banded krait that was unmoving on the floor near the side wall, but it made no move for her as she bypassed it.

They reached the open wall at the same time, walking over the fallen rollup door to reach the outside. It was raining again, and rain had never felt so good to Sara as she tilted her face toward the sky and opened her mouth. Gumshoe walked up to her and looked her up and down.

"Are you okay? You weren't bit, were you?"

She shook her head. "I'm okay. You?"

"Me too. We should have help arriving soon. But listen, those animals in there, they're not natural...." He cocked his head toward the open building, where tank upon tank of unauthorized genetically modified organisms and naturally occurring exotic species co-mingled in captivity or escaped from their upturned tanks.

"We need to report them right away," Sara said. He shot her a smile that suggested her naivety was endearing to him, but not the course of action he wanted. He nodded to a small gas pump to one side of the building, used to service park ranger vehicles that maintained the remote facility. "We could destroy it all, including the sailfin, in case the venom wears off and it wakes up. Say it was a fuel leak, that the dinosaur knocked the pump loose and the metal door created a spark...."

She looked at him and nodded. The faint sound of beating helicopter rotors made itself heard in the distance.

"C'mon." Gumshoe turned and ran for the gas pump. When he and Sara reached it, he used a ranger-issued key and unlocked the pump. Then he extended the pump as far as it would go, which reached to the entrance of the building. "Stand clear."

Sara backed away while Gumshoe pressed the nozzle lever and gasoline began pouring out onto the floor just inside the building. He walked back and forth, spraying the nozzle inside the room as far as he could. Then he dropped the nozzle and let it spool back into the pump. In a trash can he found a couple of two-liter soda bottles and filled those with gas from the pump. He left the caps off and threw them deep inside the building, one of them landing next to the fallen sailfin.

He turned to Sara. "Got a light?"

"Sorry, don't smoke."

"Good for you. I quit a decade ago. We'll have to light this candle some other way then. Let's find some rocks." He walked around until he had picked up a handful of smallish rocks. Sara found a few also. Then Gumshoe started skipping them like stones into the building's entrance. The first couple hit but didn't spark, bouncing harmlessly into the open structure.

Then Sara tried it with a larger stone. She side armed it, again recalling her youth on the softball field. This time they saw a spark as the rock hit the dry pavement right next to where the gas had spilled. The spark landed in the gas and the fire was instantaneous.

"Get back!" Gumshoe warned, and the two rangers ran away from the building. Inside the structure, the fire took hold, filling the building with black smoke.

Overhead, a helicopter became visible in the distance. Gumshoe's radio crackled and he picked it up. He turned to Sara and said, "It's Dispatch!" Then he told Kevin they were at the old missile site, it was burning, and the chopper was in sight. Once the pickup was confirmed, he handed the radio to Sara. "Kevin wants to say hi."

Sara blushed a bit as she took the radio. How nice it would be to hear his voice. "Hi, Kevin."

"Hi, Sara! Heck of a start to your new job. Maybe you want to get some real food when you get back to the station?"

"That'd be great."

"I'll have something ready for you. See you then. Don't miss your helicopter." Kevin signed off, and Sara gave Gumshoe back his radio.

"Here they come," he said, pointing to the low-flying chopper.

He and Sara moved to a spot on the edge of the concrete apron, sufficiently far from the flaming building while leaving room for the 'copter to land. As they waited, Sara stared inside to the inferno that was like a scene from hell itself, with genetically engineered monsters perishing in flames born of human desperation.

Also overhead, as the helicopter approached for its landing, four ptero-birds glided over the wetlands.

EPILOGUE

Miami, Florida
Three days later

Dr. Rebecca Trout shook her head yet again as her gaze bored into her laptop screen. The headline-grabbing action that had unfolded in the Everglades may be over, but her work here was just beginning. In the wake of the devastation were dozens of different creatures to characterize, mostly through DNA sequencing and analysis. It would probably take years to get to them all, and so she had decided to start with the most spectacular and work her way down the list.

She was currently looking at the sequencing results for the giant sailfin lizard, the animal that was most puzzling because of its sheer size and rapid growth. In attempting to isolate the genes responsible for the gigantism, as well as the rapidity of growth, she had discovered something interesting. A very large stretch of DNA—enough to code for an entire higher mammal, she guessed—had been inserted into the lizard's more natural DNA (although it, too, was a genetic combination from several lizards). She knew the mammalian DNA had been artificially inserted, rather than being inherited from mating parents, since it followed a string of junk DNA that served as an indicator something had been incorporated that was not intended to function, like a comment line in computer programming code—it can be seen, but it doesn't execute.

Rebecca had studied enough DNA sets for her to be able to recognize certain genes without having to look them up. She knew, for example, that most higher organisms had almost the same genome, for example, humans and chimpanzees shared ninety-eight percent of their genes. Chickens, on the other hand, share approximately sixty-seven percent of their DNA with humans. Even bananas have about sixty percent of identical genes with *Homo sapiens*, due to the basic cellular maintenance functions being much the same for all living beings. And what she was looking at now on screen was definitely characteristic of a human genome, of that she was sure.

Whatever it was, it had been inserted into the dinosaur-like DNA in such a way as not to be expressed, but still be there. Essentially non-executable "junk" DNA residing in the genome of a resurrected living dinosaur. It would actually be passed on to the next generation if this animal were to reproduce. And it probably already had, Rebecca noted, thinking of the small lab specimens at BioGen—whose headquarters had been seized by federal officials--and the fact that more than one large sailfin was seen free-roaming in the Everglades.

So, the DNA was human, she knew that by simply comparing it to known sequences such as those available from commercial services similar to 23 & Me. But whose was it? It could be a proof of concept by BioGen, using one of those known sequences from an anonymous human donor. Or it could be one of the BioGen employees. Or, she thought further, looking around the room now, it could be...

Rebecca got up from her lab stool and walked to her inner office. *I wonder if it's still there*...She flashed on her Departmental Christmas party, what was it—two years ago now? She and Dr. Landis had gotten a little tipsy on champagne and got to talking about gene sequencing of humans, typically a hot-button debate, depending on what it would be used for. Would insurance companies deny coverage based on certain genes that have not yet been expressed, for example? Working with human genes was not allowed without jumping through strict regulatory hoops, but Archie Landis had offered a workaround. "Let's go to your office, I'll show you," he'd said.

She went there with him, slightly concerned that he might be tipsy enough to make a pass at her, but he'd never done it before so she felt comfortable enough being alone with him. When they reached her lab, he followed her back to the office and told her he needed some scissors. He put them up to his head and lined them up with a lock of his silver hair.

"You sure you want to do that, you don't have a lot of that left," Rebecca kidded. Landis smiled but his answer was the *snick* of the blades as he snipped his hair. He held up the separated lock between his thumb and forefinger, then set the hair down on a spot on Rebecca's desk free of books or papers.

"There you have it. My DNA. Feel free to do with it as you will, maintaining my anonymity, of course. And also, of course," he added with a tilt of the head, "that you return the favor." He then handed her the scissors. "And now you have something for me?"

Rebecca reached a hand back to sweep her long, brown ponytail over her shoulder. She cut off a piece about the same length as Landis had given her, and then placed it between his outstretched fingers. "Anonymity for me too, please, if you do anything with it."

He smiled at her. "Of course. I guess we'd better get back to the party before they start asking the wrong kinds of questions."

Rebecca gave a short exhalation that stood for a laugh. She highly doubted anyone would suspect them of a romantic relationship, which seemed to be what he was insinuating. "Well I mean, we were exchanging DNA, after all," Landis tried, still awkwardly continuing the joke.

Rebecca let it slide, choosing to ignore it while placing Landis' hair in a plastic specimen bag. She handed him one for the sample she gave him and he dropped her hair into the bag while walking to the exit, sensing it was time to end the private liaison...

Now, Rebecca tried to recall exactly where she had left the sample of Landis' hair as she walked behind her desk. *Taped it to the inside of one of the drawers.... Here it is.* She pulled the plastic bag off and held it up to the light. Landis' hair, just like it was the day he clipped it off. She took the sample...*weird to think of it like that, but I guess that's what it's become, a biological sample....*out to her main lab and stopped at the DNA sequencer.

She tried not to think about the circumstances too much and just went into autopilot mode, loading the hair sample into the machine in that practiced way that had become almost robotic to her. While the machine processed the sample, she couldn't help but think back on her relationship with Dr. Landis. He had sort of a crush on her, didn't he? She realized now that she had tried to pretend that no, it was just her overthinking things, trying to read too much into the relationship that was purely professional at its core. But then, they were both single, weren't they? He by divorce, she by choice, choosing to devote her life to her career, at least for now. The age difference was to her, insurmountable, but perhaps to him it was not. He had to be at least twenty years her senior—did he really think that anything could, or should work between them? She hoped not. She had liked him and enjoyed his company but not in a romantic way.

Her thoughts were interrupted by the chime of the sequencer announcing it had completed its work. She smiled to herself at how much her life was directed by machines. At home, the washing machine chimed when a load was done; at work, the sequencer chimed when it had completed a DNA sequence....

She eyed the screen on the sequencer and its gigabytes-long string of As, Cs, Gs and Ts, the genes that made up her former colleague. There it was, the complete set of genetic instructions responsible for the production of one Dr. Archie Landis. The nature part, anyway, Dr. Trout knew, as she pressed buttons on the machine that would send the output file to her laptop. Nurture no doubt also played a significant role. Had Archie not gone to college, for example, he would have turned out completely different, right?

At her laptop, Rebecca set up the text compare program again, this time with the human DNA found in the sailfin dino genes that she was sure was Dr. Landis', and then the DNA from Landis' hair that she knew to be his. She executed the compare program, sure she would see the green "100% match" graphic pop up when the analysis was complete. To her dismay, however, a different result was displayed. She gawked at the screen with narrowing eyes as she read the result of the comparison:

99.9% match

Rebecca's mouth dropped open in utter surprise. A less than perfect match? Impossible! A layperson might consider such a minor difference from 100% to be insignificant, perhaps nothing more than a rounding error. But as a biologist, Rebecca knew that was not the case. A human and a *banana* shared 60% of their DNA, for crying out loud. She knew the genetic difference between two humans was not more than 0.01%, making them about....99.9% the same, genetically. She stared, transfixed at that number on the screen, for it could mean only one thing.

The DNA contained in the sailfin dino animal was human, all right, but it wasn't that of Dr. Archie Landis. So then whose was it? She thought back to her earlier guesses, revisiting them with this new insight. BioGen employees...random anonymous donors from commercial DNA services.... She ran her fingers through her long hair as she considered the options. There was no practical way for her to check into those possibilities. It wasn't Archie himself, that was the main thing, she supposed. She let go of her long ponytail, allowing it to fall back against her lab coat, staring at her brown hair as it contrasted with the white fabric.

Her hair...she flashed back to that night years ago when he had given her his hair...*and she had given him hers. Oh no...he wouldn't have, would he?* But the thought was loose now, the cat was out of the bag and she had to know for certain, one way or the other. She found a pair of scissors and snipped off a lock of her own hair. She took it straight to the DNA sequencer and prepped the equipment for another round of sequencing. She loaded her own hair sample into the machine, started the sequencing process and waited.

While she did, she picked up the remote for a small TV mounted on the wall she sometimes used to watch the weather channel, usually during hurricane season, so she could work without feeling disconnected from what was happening in the outside world. Now she had it tuned to a local news channel, still humming with follow-up reports on the devastation caused in the Everglades.

Rebecca watched as a female Hispanic reporter in a tight-fitting dress and high heels smiled at the end of a live broadcast, thanking Ranger Ben Offstead for his time to be interviewed, and expressing how grateful she—and everyone—was that the genetically modified animal threat in the Everglades had been contained.

As Offstead departed the scene, the camera zoomed in closer on the reporter, who stood in front of a colorful flowerbed. Behind her, honeybees flitted from one blossom to the next, going about their pollination as they had for untold millennia. As she wrapped up her live report, a small girl could be seen walking behind the reporter to pick a flower. Just as the child reached out a hand to pick a colorful bloom in the midst of a dozen buzzing bees, her mother, concerned she was interfering with the live TV broadcast, grabbed her by the hand and pulled her off camera.

The DNA sequencer chimed and Rebecca turned to look at it as if it was an intruder. *Time to find out.* She got up and walked to the machine. The sequencing had been successfully completed. She repeated the process to send the results to her laptop, and once again set up the text compare program with the DNA that had been inserted into the sailfin dinosaur. Again, she executed the program and again, she read the result of the comparison:

100% match

She slowly brought her hand to her mouth in disbelief. *It's me.* Landis had inserted her DNA, not his, into that monstrous creature. *As non-executable junk DNA, but still...* The large and small sailfin dinosaurs had been killed, but how many smaller ones were still out there? When they reproduced, that would pass her own complete set of genetic instructions on to their progeny. What if someday, the creatures mutated so that the segment of DNA they contained that was *her*.... was expressed? She shivered in spite of the normal room temperature. And then something else tugged at her subconscious, something even more worrying....

Everyone was saying that the threat of Landis and BioGen's rogue monsters was under control for now, but she didn't buy it. Not for a second. Look at what they had done, inserting entire human genomes into resurrected dinosaurs that could reproduce. There was no telling what else they had accomplished that hadn't even been discovered yet, that wouldn't be discovered or perhaps even understood for years or decades later. She glanced up at the TV where the live report had just switched back to the studio.

Contained, huh? Rebecca thought, shaking her head. For now, she supposed, unless Landis and BioGen's work with human DNA was even more extensive than anyone knew.

For now.

THE END

 SEVEREDPRESS

CHECK OUT OTHER GREAT DINOSAUR BOOKS

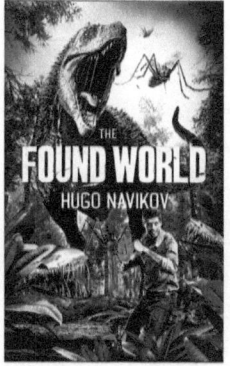

THE FOUND WORLD
by Hugo Navikov

A powerful global cabal wants adventurer Brett Russell to retrieve a superweapon stolen by the scientist who built it. To entice him to travel underneath one of the most dangerous volcanoes on Earth to find the scientist, this shadowy organization will pay him the only thing he cares about: information that will allow him to avenge his family's murder.

But before he can get paid, he and his team must enter an underground hellscape of killer plants, giant insects, terrifying dinosaurs, and an army of other predators never previously seen by man.

At the end of this journey awaits a revelation that could alter the fate of mankind ... if they can make it back from this horrifying found world.

HOUSE OF THE GODS
by Davide Mana

High above the steamy jungle of the Amazon basin, rise the flat plateaus known as the Tepui, the House of the Gods. Lost worlds of unknown beauty, a naturalistic wonder, each an ecology onto itself, shunned by the local tribes for centuries. The House of the Gods was not made for men.

But now, the crew and passengers of a small charter plane are about to find what was hidden for sixty million years.

Lost on an island in the clouds 10.000 feet above the jungle, surrounded by dinosaurs, hunted by mysterious mercenaries, the survivors of Sligo Air flight 001 will quickly learn the only rule of life on Earth: Extinction.

CHECK OUT OTHER GREAT DINOSAUR BOOKS

PRIMORDIA
by **Greig Beck**

Ben Cartwright, former soldier, home to mourn the loss of his father stumbles upon cryptic letters from the past between the author, Arthur Conan Doyle and his great, great grandfather who vanished while exploring the Amazon jungle in 1908.

Amazingly, these letters lead Ben to believe that his ancestor's expedition was the basis for Doyle's fantastical tale of a lost world inhabited by long extinct creatures. As Ben digs some more he finds clues to the whereabouts of a lost notebook that might contain a map to a place that is home to creatures that would rewrite everything known about history, biology and evolution.

But other parties now know about the notebook, and will do anything to obtain it. For Ben and his friends, it becomes a race against time and against ruthless rivals.

In the remotest corners of Venezuela, along winding river trails known only to lost tribes, and through near impenetrable jungle, Ben and his novice team find a forbidden place more terrifying and dangerous than anything they could ever have imagined.

PANGAEA EXILES
by **Jeff Brackett**

Tried and convicted for his crimes, Sean Barrow is sent into temporal exile—banished to a time so far before recorded history that there is no chance that he, or any other criminal sent back, has any chance of altering history.

Now Sean must find a way to survive more than 200 million years in the past, in a world populated by monstrous creatures that would rend him limb from limb if they got the chance. And that's just his fellow prisoners.

The dinosaurs are almost as bad.

 SEVERED**PRESS**

CHECK OUT OTHER GREAT DINOSAUR BOOKS

FLIPSIDE
by JAKE BIBLE

The year is 2046 and dinosaurs are real.

Time bubbles across the world, many as large as one hundred square miles, turn like clockwork, revealing prehistoric landscapes from the Cretaceous Period.

They reveal the Flipside.

Now, thirty years after the first Turn, the clockwork is breaking down as one of the world's powers has decided to exploit the phenomenon for their own gain, possibly destroying everything then and now in the process.

A MAN OUT OF TIME
by Christopher Laflan

Five years after the Chinese Axis detonated an unknown weapon of mass destruction off the southern coast of the United States, Special Ops Sergeant John Crider and the members of Shadow Company have finally captured what they all hope will lead to the end of the war. Unfortunately, the population within the United States is no longer sustainable. In an effort to stabilize the economy, the government enacts the Cryonics Act. One hundred years in suspended animation, all debt forgiven, and a chance at a less crowded future are too good to pass up for John and his young daughter.

Except not everything always goes as planned as Sergeant John Crider finds himself pitted against a land of prehistoric monsters genetically resurrected from the fossil record, murderous inhabitants, and a future he never wanted.

www.ingramcontent.com/pod-product-compliance
Lightning Source LLC
Chambersburg PA
CBHW032005170626
46807CB00006B/2654